—〰—

Beth propped herself up a bit and looked more closely at her new prison. It seemed vaguely familiar, she thought. Then she remembered. She had come here many times with Shannon. This was Shannon's old room and her old bed. It hadn't been used in years.

She lay back and set her eyes on the object hanging above the bed. For a moment, she thought it was an old pest strip of some kind. Upon closer inspection, she saw movement and behld the most ghastly tarantula staring back at her. The sound that tore from her throat was little more than a gravelly moan. When Leonard reentered the room, Beth lay cuyrled in

"I see yo

Beth's ey

she wasn't at

horror and t

laugh mania

phobic."

He laug

worked out

you'd better

SECRET THUNDER

ANNETTA P. LEE

Genesis Press, Inc.

Mount Blue

An imprint of Genesis Press, Inc.
Publishing Company

Genesis Press, Inc.
P.O. Box 101
Columbus, MS 39703

Copyright © 2007 by Annetta P. Lee

ISBN 13: 978-1-58571-204-5
ISBN 10: 1-58571-204-3
Manufactured in the United States of America

First Edition

Visit us at www.genesis-press.com
or call at 1-888-Indigo-1

DEDICATION

I dedicate this book to my Lord and Savior, Jesus Christ, who placed a desire in me to proclaim through fiction.

To Marsha, who saw this book several years before it was penned.

To Kenneth, whose patience and support keeps me going strong.

PROLOGUE

Austin, Texas
February 14, 1995

Beth McDade stared out the car window, an intense sense of fore-boding wrapping itself around her like a wet shirt. Tension hung in the air between her and her fiancé like a thick fog.

"Thanks for dinner," she murmured, attempting to break the tense silence. "It was a lovely valentine."

No response.

Michael Baker continued barreling down the Texas highway as if he was late for an appointment. He kept his eyes glued to the road. Apprehension permeated her very core. The dread she had felt all evening had her nerves on edge. She didn't know how to confront it, how to make it go away.

Beth tried to dismiss the unsettling feeling, blaming it on the headache she'd been nursing much of the day. She forced a smile as she thought of the warmth that had enfolded her when she and Michael had stepped into the atrium of the most elegant restaurant in Austin. Considering their argument of the previous weekend, she thought this date had gone wonderfully. Dinner had been perfect. Even the drinks Michael had downed so quickly hadn't troubled her much. But the quiet drive back to the university dorm was different—unnerving—scary.

She nervously twisted the ring around on her finger. Michael had asked her to marry him right out of high school. She had been elated. Her father, however, was against it and convinced them to wait until she finished college, clearly hoping the attraction would fade once she was away. But his hopes were crushed when he learned that Michael had also enrolled at the University of Texas.

Lost in a tumble of thoughts, Beth cringed when Michael turned the car toward the back side of the university grounds. Pulling off the regular path, he drove deeper into the woods, far beyond the dormitories.

"There's a bluff out here I want you to see," he said, grinning at her. "It reminds me of your favorite spot on the creek back home."

"Oh," she said, nodding cautiously. The tension in her chest began to tighten, but she refused to let her anxiety show. She was being silly, she thought. Surely, Michael wouldn't spoil such a wonderful evening with another wrestling match.

Once he had brought the car to a full stop, he sat a long while wordlessly staring out the window. Though his back was turned toward her, his head was tilted at an angle suggesting dominant defiance. Beth looked away, clueless as to how to ease the strange awkwardness.

She distractedly began turning her hand this way and that, watching the way the diamond sparkled in the soft glow of moonlight. She had worn it now for almost two years, but she wasn't quite as ecstatic as she had been when he first slipped it onto her finger.

Beth was yanked from her reverie when Michael abruptly began caressing her arm. His hand felt alien, his touch unwelcome. She drew back, but the inside of the car seemed to close in around her. Ignoring her resistance, he impatiently pulled her into his arms and kissed her roughly on the mouth.

"Too rough," she scolded, placing her fingers between their lips. "Why are you being this way?"

"I really need you," he said pulling her back toward him. "Can't we—"

"You know how I feel about that! We need to wait, Michael. Just a little while longer." Heart pounding and throat constricting, Beth cast fear-filled eyes around the car. Her heart stood still when she spied the blanket on the back seat. He had planned this all along, she thought. Suffused with an unbearable feeling of betrayal, Beth stared at Michael incredulously.

"For crying out loud, you're still acting like a bound-up little girl. We're adults now, Beth. You've been out from under the thumbs of your preaching daddy and brother for two whole years. It's ridiculous to wait any longer."

She glared at him. "Take me back to the dorm this instant."

"I don't think so," he said, grabbing her left wrist. "I'm a man. And I have needs."

Already poised for flight, Beth pushed open the door and rushed out into the chilly night. But Michael caught her before she could get away and shoved her so hard the pumps she was wearing went flying.

"Stop it, Michael," she screamed, struggling to free herself from his grip.

"Maybe I'm just not enough like David Spencer," he sneered, backing her deeper into the brush. "Is that it? Do you dream of *him* when you let me kiss you?"

Before she could protest any further, he had thrust her against an evergreen, savagely bringing his mouth down hard on hers. Despite the thickness of her jacket, she could feel the rough bark of the tree digging into her back. Her entire body shook violently as she tried with all her strength to push him away. She had never in her life experienced such bottomless terror.

Playing for time and hoping he would loosen his hold long enough for her to get away, Beth tried distracting him with a question. "What does David have to do with anything?"

But nothing was going to deter him. He uttered a guttural sound and pushed her down beneath the trees and began tearing at her clothes. Her fierce hitting and kicking at him had no effect. Michael was like a madman. She had never seen him so possessed. His face was cold and cruel. His eyes had an unnatural glow, and he looked at her as if she were a stranger.

She screamed, hoping someone, anyone, would hear her. Then he backhanded her.

"Shut up! You've always measured me by David. All those years, trotting behind him in the woods and he never laid a hand on you. I've

3

never measured up, have I? Well, you can dream of him all you want. After tonight it won't matter."

Somehow Beth managed to break free, scrambled to her feet and started running. Tears stained her cheeks and blurred her vision. How could Michael be jealous over a childhood crush?

"What's wrong with you?" she shouted, still running. "David is Carl's best friend. I was only a little girl then, and he's nine years older than me. He's like…like family. You know that."

Her bare feet caught on something hard, causing her to stumble. Michael was on her in an instant. She dug her nails deep into his face and shoved him away, screaming all the while.

He clamped a sweaty hand over her mouth and pulled her toward the car. "I'll tell you what I know, Miss Good Girl," he said through clenched teeth. "I know you still have a crush on David Spencer. Anyone can tell by the way you still talk about him."

Beth's breathing was so constricted she felt lightheaded. Her heart pounded against her chest as she continued to struggle. Terrified that she might lose consciousness, she took a deep breath, resolving to hang on despite the pain.

"Forgive me, Lord."

ONE

Plover Creek, Texas
May 1999

"Murderer!"

The accusation, driven by shock, was out before Beth could stifle it. She looked around her office, her moist palms tightening on the phone.

"Sis, settle down," her brother, Carl, pleaded over the phone. "As always, you're being irrational. Now, do you need me to send someone to pick you up?"

She leapt up, causing her chair to crash against the credenza. Her voice was high-pitched, her face flushed. The sadness in her brother's tone did little to placate her inner fury. In a pointless effort to forestall grief, she let her thoughts run wild.

"I'm not coming to the hospital, big brother. And I'm not being irrational. I'm being observant. Our family has been beguiled into his trap for years. And now that Daddy is dead, he has us right where he wants us."

Beth became vaguely aware that her boss was standing in the doorway to his office. He cautiously moved toward her, but his presence barely registered, as she was focusing on the voice on the other end of the line.

"Get a grip, Beth. You're being way too reckless with your words. For God's sake, you work for an attorney! You just can't toss out accusations like that."

Before Carl could get another word in, Beth hung up the phone and turned to face her boss. Taylor had heard most of the conversation, and he instinctively pulled her into a comforting embrace. "Your father has passed away?"

"Y-y-yes," she stammered, still fuming.

"I'm so sorry. You go on home. I can get the letter out to the Walters Foundation."

"I finished the letter an hour ago," she said, pulling away from him. "All I need is your signature."

"I thought Reverend McDade was doing well and scheduled to go home tomorrow."

She wouldn't look at him, fumbling instead with papers scattered over her desk. "Me, too."

Her throat felt tight, reflecting her mounting frustration and suspicion. Remembering suddenly that the letter she was hunting was still on the printer, Beth retrieved it and placed it on her desk in front of Taylor. "I used the letter from the Miller file to shape this one," she said. "You have two minutes to look it over and sign."

Taylor raised a questioning eyebrow. "Beth, don't you need to take some time to grieve? It's too much—"

"You'd better get on down to the courthouse before Judge Harden sends someone after you," she interrupted. "He's already warned you about coming late to his courtroom."

Taylor hurriedly scribbled his signature. "You're right. I'll drop this by the post office. You get out of here."

Looking calmer than she felt, Beth pulled the document from her boss's hand. "You'd better go now. I'll take care of this."

She was still typing the address when she heard the outer door close. The moment she heard his sports car pull away, the tears she had held back rushed forth like a sudden downpour.

It pained her that her father had died less than an hour ago. But it bothered her greatly that George Tubbs, the town pharmacist and presumably a family friend, was with him just before he died. And it bothered her even more that she couldn't even grieve properly because of the rage gnawing away at her innards.

For the last four years, she had set high standards for herself, including being a responsible businesswoman who carried her own weight on the family horse ranch. It also meant that she would do everything she could to keep the ranch going. That's why she had taken the job with Taylor after she had quit school and come home.

But now she faced another personal tragedy, and the reality of it made her ache. Fear sat in the pit of her stomach like a giant stone nothing could dislodge. Maybe Carl was right and she *was* being irrational. But something didn't feel right. Even so, she refused to fall apart, especially for something she could do nothing about.

Beth wiped away the last traces of her tears. She would handle the loss of her father just fine. Or as well as she could. Without a clue as to what George Tubbs might have said to her father to upset him, she was certain he had done something. What could it have been? Why was he even there?

Though she tried to suppress her growing suspicion, it refused to be stilled. In the wake of dropping out of school, she had turned into a suspicious, pessimistic woman. She knew her allegation against Mr. Tubbs was, on its face, absurd. But no matter how much she tried, she neither liked nor trusted the man. She felt a sudden rush of guilt. She should pray, she thought, but she had felt spiritually alienated for so long it no longer worked for her.

Beth shrugged off the regret and let her mind revisit the current state of the family's affairs. First, their clients all abandoned them in a very short span. None of the banks would give them a loan. Then, out of the blue, Mr. Tubbs comes to her place of employment in Dallas and makes a bid for the ranch.

The McDade Horse Ranch had been an interim home for hundreds of quarter horses for longer than she had been alive. It had provided boarding, recreation and stud services for clients from as far away as Kansas, Oklahoma and Arkansas. The ranch had an abundance of trees—maple, oak, cedar, pine and sycamore. It had two ponds, a creek and a three-story brick house that she still called home.

She closed her eyes, recalling her father's account of how he acquired the ranch. "It was a miracle of God," he would say. "It was impossible for a black man to get his hands on such prime real estate back then. But God fixed it."

Beth winced as she thought of how his eyes would beam when he talked about God's way of answering prayer. He had taught *her* to pray, seemingly before she could even walk.

Until four years ago, Rev. Ray McDade had been a strong civil rights advocate in the district, as well as pastor of the Plover Creek Community Church. But his stroke had changed all that. After she had come home from college, she and Carl had taken over the running of the ranch. She had done everything in her power to protect her dad from the reality of steadily losing what he had worked so hard to build.

The bunkhouse, built out near the stables past the barn was empty now, as they had recently laid off all hands—all except her best friend, Manny Jefferson. And she wasn't at all sure how long they could guarantee *him* a salary. Her job as legal secretary didn't pay enough to keep an entire ranch operating smoothly. Carl had quit his job as a truck driver and assumed the duties of pastor at the church, but his salary wasn't much help, either.

She closed her eyes for a moment. The face of George Tubbs appeared in her mind and she quickly opened them again. Loathing was her dominant emotion whenever she thought of him. He had always been too eager to please—too obliging, too happy. His presence always seemed to arouse her vague memory of, at age eight, getting separated from her mother in his drugstore.

She recalled overhearing him tell another customer that the little McDade girl was strange and could cast a curse if of a mind. Despite not understanding what a curse was, she had been hurt by his words at the time.

Beth rubbed her temples, trying to relieve the low-grade headache beginning just behind her eyes. She had taken a couple of days off when her dad was first admitted to the hospital. His doctor had assured her and Carl that he would come home on Saturday. So she had returned to work.

Beth picked up the phone to call David in Seattle. She warmed at the thought of his comforting voice, but quickly returned the phone to its base. She wasn't ready to talk with anyone. Not even David Spencer.

People probably thought her cold and uncaring for not rushing to join Carl at the hospital. She had heard it in Carl's voice. She had seen it in Taylor's eyes. But whether they liked it or not, this was how she was going to handle her pain.

She would *deal* with it, the same way she had dealt with everything else. Death wasn't new to her. It had been around her since the death of her mother when she was a teenager. Dealing with it was what had made her strong. She glanced at the picture of Carl and Ray McDade on her desk. She and her brother had suffered a great loss, but it wasn't the first and it certainly won't be the last. Tears once again burned the back of her eyes, but she fought to hold them back.

Had she been superstitious, she would be tempted to think that providence was against her. It seemed everything she had tried to save her family's ranch had failed miserably. And now with her dad gone, there was no real need.

It was mid-afternoon by the time Beth had driven from Dallas to Plover Creek. She pulled her car around to the back of the house, near the barn, and whistled for her personal mount. Within moments, Midnight, her beautiful black and white gelding, trotted to the fence to greet her.

"Hello, pretty boy," she whispered, pressing her face against his neck and making soft kissing noises. Snorting, Midnight moved closer, giving Beth a friendly shove. She reached into the can she kept by the fence for an apple treat, which he eagerly plucked from her hand.

After a moment, she kicked off her pumps, raised her skirt and, using the fence for support, climbed onto Midnight's bare back.

"Beth."

She turned reluctantly in response to her friend's voice and watched as he reined Aster, the ornery gray stallion, beneath the trees on the southern ridge.

"Hey, Manny."

He jumped to the ground and strode toward her. Manny had walked with a deep limp since childhood, but could move with the speed and grace of a colt. She didn't move to be comforted and he didn't reach for her. He knew her well enough to understand that she didn't want that right now. His shoulder brushed against her as he sat down beside her on the smooth sycamore that now grew almost horizontal to the ground.

His eyes were red and puffy, but his coffee-brown face offered her a warm smile. "You being bullheaded again," he said. "You need to let yourself grieve."

"Not now," she said, looking away. "I didn't see many of the horses. Did the owners come get the rest of them today?"

"Beth."

"Not now, Manny," she whispered, jumping to her feet. "Please."

Manny remained seated, and as if she had said nothing, continued. "Miss Virgie is having a hard time of it. We had to put her to bed."

A spasm of emotion threatened to break through, but she managed to suppress it. She was extremely fond of Miss Virgie Patterson. Beth took great pleasure in the protective attitude the old woman had toward her. Miss Virgie had sat with her dad during the week while she and Carl worked.

As long as Beth could remember, the woman had been a sort of matriarch to the entire community and could be quite imposing when of the mind. It seemed everybody was intimidated by her blunt vim. She had been the mother of one child. Beth never knew him, as he died at thirty, just months before she was born. The old woman had since semi-adopted Ray McDade, Beth's dad. For her, losing him must be like losing another son.

Beth turned back toward Manny. "I'll go by and see her. Maybe later tonight."

Manny nodded, and as he did, the small diamond stud in his left ear sparkled in the light. His mustache was trimmed precisely and seemed to gracefully merge with the closely cropped beard hugging the entire lower portion of his jaw.

Beth returned to her place on the tree beside him. Just as they had done as children, the two swung their legs over the edge and enjoyed a companionable silence. Then Beth noticed scrapes on the swollen knuckles of Manny's left hand.

After a moment, she touched them, saying, "I guess we all have to work out our pain some way." Her eyes began to brim. "I think we're going to have to sell the ranch, Manny."

"Don't you worry none about me," he said. "Carl is going to help me talk to Jake about buying his garage. I've had my eye on it for some time now."

Her eyebrows shot up in surprise as she swung around to face him again. In spite of himself, Manny had a timid grin on his face.

"Really! How—"

He squeezed her hand, interrupting her question. "Still got the money from my ma's insurance. Been saving up, too."

Beth breathed a sigh of relief, feeling as if a load had been lifted off her shoulders. Tears came readily then. "That's wonderful, Manny. It'll be one less thing on my mind when making some decisions."

"Good," he said, reaching up to brush away her tears. "I knew after y'all had to let the others go, you were probably worried over me. But I'll be just fine."

Beth lowered her head and silently sent up a prayer of thanksgiving for that. "You've been just as much a part of this ranch as me. The one good thing is that Daddy didn't have to see us sell." She turned away briefly. "You ever felt like you've lost something—something you can't put a name to, Manny?"

Manny shot her a curious glance. "Can't say as I have."

She forced a smile. Manny couldn't possibly understand how she felt. Neither could most of her other friends, who had all moved away from the sleepy town of Plover Creek. Although she had been popular in high school, she never really felt included and had lost touch with most of her friends.

She pondered the raw sensations of abandonment hovering over her. She had experienced it as a child when Carl and David left for college and when her mother died, as well as her friend Shannon Ware. Having just lost her dad, she almost felt as if God Himself had turned his back on her. She had wanted to prove to her dad that she loved him, to make things right between them again. But she had waited too long.

She shrugged. "Daddy had a knack for running things. I guess losing all our clients has gotten me spooked. Feels like I've got a load of buckshot waiting to explode in my belly."

Manny looked deeply into Beth's eyes. She sensed that his superstitious nature had come to fore. For an instant, she wanted to laugh. "That's your sixth sense," he whispered, conspiratorially. "Maybe you already knew something was going to happen with your pa."

"Don't be silly, Manny. That's just superstitious nonsense."

"You got a sense of things like this, Beth. One you keep denying," he said. "Maybe you just need a fella to take your mind off things."

"A fellow! No thanks."

Manny shrugged and let out a quiet grunt. "Need to tell ya I ran into Mike this afternoon."

Submerged memories surrounded her grief like a swarm of bees. Her breathing became labored, her eyes dilated. Like distant shadows, she saw the red strips of a satin dress strewn about on the ground. She felt the sting of Michael's hand against her cheek. She felt the shame and guilt of having an unwanted experience forced on her.

She started as Manny shook her. "Beth. It's all right."

Beth wrapped her arms around herself and began to rock. "I can't stop the memories, Manny. They're so real."

"You're shaking like crazy. Probably some kind of panic attack. Calm down. Michael will never lay another hand on you. I promise you that."

Beth forced herself to slow her breathing. She saw her friend's angry face and knew that the hatred she felt for both Michael Baker and George Tubbs couldn't possibly outrank what she saw in Manny's eyes.

"I've wished him dead a million times," she said, her voice dripping venom.

Michael Baker had been the one thing that had kept her and her father at odds. Years ago, the idea of marrying him was so intense she had allowed herself to become his puppet. Her dad had warned her that they weren't compatible, but she was too deep into rebellion to listen to him until it was too late. Then too proud to let him know that she knew he'd been right.

Four years ago, Beth vowed to never let another man blind her to reality. She didn't need a man to validate who she was. If she had to remain single the rest of her life to avoid men like Michael, then so be it. And the less she dwelled on her lack of a social life, the better.

Manny tightened his arm around her shoulder. "I don't take kindly to what he done to you. Told him so, too. But you can't go wishing death on folk just because you forgot how to live."

She knew Manny was right. She had lived in a virtual prison, one she had made for herself. The end result was isolation. It wasn't, she had decided, too much to pay for being so naïve about Michael and alienating her dad. She watched as Manny shook dust and gravel from his boot before slipping it back on. "I'm not that same gullible girl, Manny. Maybe I'm better off alone."

He turned to face her; his dark brown eyes had become angry slits. "I have never liked Mike. But it's not his fault you stopped living. It's not his fault you holding onto the past like you doing either. He had a hand in it, but it's not his fault."

Beth moistened her dry lips and shrugged. "I guess I do want to have somebody, but I'm scared. Sometimes the longing for a family of my own is so strong my dreams are filled with children."

"Can't have children without a husband."

"I know that," she said, bumping his shoulder with her own. "But I'm so disconnected from everything. Almost like back in high school when Daddy wouldn't let me go any place." She sighed. "I've been so busy trying to keep things going around here I never made things right between us." Her voice broke, but she quickly regained her composure. "I hurt him when I got engaged to Michael. And I never told him he was right. I wanted to. And now I can't even manage to hold on to his most prized possession."

Manny's brow knitted into a scowl. "Your pa loved you. And the ranch wasn't his most *prized* possession. It was just a possession. Your mind just got so tangled up with trying to please him that you forgot how to be his daughter. Managing the ranch, keeping the books, you even got out there with the rest of us and got dirty. It's been a lot on you and Carl. And you have a full-time job to boot."

"There's nothing special about that. I just did what had to be done. I still didn't do it well enough."

"You did fine, but you've got to come to terms with that for yourself," Manny said, scratching his chin. "Imagine David will come home for the funeral."

Beth nodded. She thought about the accusations Michael had hurled at her four years ago. *"Maybe I'm just not enough like David Spencer. Is that it? Do you dream of him when you let me kiss you?"*

"Remember the first time he brought us up here?" Manny asked, drawing her away from her musing.

Beth managed a smile. "I sure do."

They had tagged along while David roamed about sketching in a large tablet. She and Manny had climbed trees, and raced each other. From that day on, the southern ridge was her favorite retreat.

As they sat on the sycamore, Beth closed her eyes and leaned against the standing oak. "I feel so at peace out here. Walking through the trees and tending my flowers—I can collect my thoughts...sort things out. At one time I felt so invincible when I was here. Remember when this sycamore was straight and I fell out of it and broke my arm?"

"*That* what you think you lost, Beth?"

She was surprised Manny had really heard her. "Maybe. Some parts of it. Seems I closed the door on a lot of simple pleasures just to grab hold of something I didn't really want."

"Things change, that's all," Manny said, rising to his feet. "Carl told me what you're thinking about George. Shock has a way of putting funny notions in folk. You might want to watch your mouth about that. At least until you've had time to grieve."

It was two in the afternoon when David finally pulled himself away from his computer. He closed his leather briefcase and glanced across the office where Bree sat coloring at the conference table.

Anxiety washed over him as he remembered the promise he had made just that morning. He would stay with his son at a Friday evening birthday party rather than just drop him off. He wasn't looking forward to it. He'd probably be the only adult male there.

His son had been unusually clingy lately. David was concerned that he was beginning to feel more conscious of being without a mother. The guilt he had been struggling with intensified, and he swung his chair around to mouth a brief prayer.

Lord, please help me be a better father. Help me find the right mother for him—the right wife for me. I don't want Bree growing up without a mother.

The ringing telephone interrupted his entreaty. When he swung around to answer it, Bree was standing beside him.

"Who could *this* be?" he asked, winking at his son.

The child leaned against his father's chair, one foot atop the other. "Maybe it's God, Daddy." David smiled and picked up the phone.

"David Spencer."

"Dave! I'm glad I caught you," Carl said. David frowned, noting a slight quiver in his friend's voice. "I'm afraid I've got bad news."

David held his breath, mentally bracing himself for news he guessed had to do with Ray McDade.

Ray and Clara McDade had taken him in at fifteen after his own parents had died in a house fire. They had raised him right along with Carl and Beth. "Is it Ray?"

"Yeah," Carl managed. "He passed away a few hours ago."

A quiet groan escaped David's throat. The news struck like a hammer blow. Shock and grief hastened tears he didn't want Bree to see. "I'm sorry, Carl," he whispered, trying to steady his voice. "I thought he was supposed to come home tomorrow."

"He was. But he went into cardiac arrest early this morning. They couldn't bring him back."

Trying to swallow past the lump in his throat proved difficult. His stomach contracted into a tight ball as he slumped lower into his chair. He had to be strong for Carl and Beth now. David wiped away the tears from his eyes and glanced toward his son. "God, I'll miss him," he whispered. "How's Beth taking it?"

"She's spouting off something about George and murder. I can't seem to calm her down. Maybe she's just in shock. You know how headstrong she can get. I guess that, mixed with grief, is making her a little irrational."

David blew his nose on a handkerchief and frowned. "George Tubbs?"

"Yeah. George dropped by her office about a week ago, offering to buy the ranch. It was right after the bank turned us down for a loan. She suspects he convinced the bank to reject our application, and then upset dad in the hospital to produce the heart attack."

"Is it possible?"

"I don't see how, Dave," Carl said. "But Beth has been so caught up trying to keep things going around here that she's hard to reason with. She's been working overtime at the office, and keeping the books for the ranch at night. And she was tireless with Dad, even during the outbursts he aimed at her." Carl paused to collect himself. David could hear the tremor in his voice. "When I mentioned that George stopped by to see Dad, she exploded. Wouldn't even leave the office to come to the hospital. She was already half-crazed by George's visit to her office."

"Where is she now? Up at the ridge?"

"Yeah. Manny's out there with her," Carl said, a smirk in his voice. "Those two are still pretty much like each other's shadow."

The reference to the two friends aroused a degree of proprietary envy in David. Although he knew Manny was Beth's friend, *he* at one time had been her hero. She had told him so each time she hugged him good night, clear up to the day he had left for college.

His mind went back several months to when he and Bree had gone home for Christmas. Beth had kept herself busy baking and visiting the older people in the community. She had taken Bree along on some of her excursions. He had longed to take a walk with her the way they used to do, but David sensed resentment toward him.

Beth was about seventeen when he had married Deidre. Seemingly, that was all it had taken to sever the bond they had once shared. He shook himself. Why was he thinking like that? Beth was a grown woman now, and the last thing she needed was a secondhand hero.

"I'll be home tomorrow morning around eleven, Carl. Meet me at Garrison Field."

TWO

The next morning Beth waited for David in the lobby of Garrison Field, a small privately owned airport ten miles from the ranch. She felt ill at ease. Airports still produced a sinking sensation in the pit of her stomach. She had felt it the day Carl and David flew off to school many years ago.

She gazed up at the sky through the wide glass doors. The morning was bright and crisp, the blue of the heavens streaked with clouded paths made by airplane traffic. David had once told her they were called contrails. It seemed to be an odd tag for condensed water.

Maybe some day she would muster the nerve to actually take a flight. But for now, grew queasy at the very idea of being so high off the ground.

David now piloted his own plane and was the owner of a small architectural firm in Seattle. She was anxious to see him again. As with her father, she had not made things right with David. She was seventeen when he made the decision not to return to Plover Creek, but she had to let him know that she was now an adult who respected his choices. That included his wife.

She closed her eyes, fondly remembering his place in her childhood. David had been particularly patient, taking the time to do things like teach her to fish and swim.

She still had many of the pictures he had drawn for her and Manny. He had sketched a picture of her sitting on a log at Tatum's pond. It had been one of those special times when it was just the two of them. Her mother had liked the drawing so much she had it framed.

Leaving her reminiscing behind, Beth turned just as the double glass doors were closing. David strode toward her, his muscled body

She had seemed able to gauge honesty in people beyond the ability of adults around her. It was as if she could see into the heart without even trying. Bree's instinctive awareness sometimes reminded him of Beth.

David remembered the time she had begged her father not to leave for Galveston to deliver several horses. David and Carl literally had to peel the howling child off her father. That was the day the bridge was out between their home and Shanty Town. Ray had very nearly plowed into it.

"Wanna talk about it?"

She shook her head. "Not really. But thanks."

Her short answers and the way she had whisked Bree up at the airport suggested that the wall she had erected between them was still very much intact. She obviously wasn't going to make things go very easy—even now.

On the way downstairs the next morning, Beth's eyes fell on the mule collar hanging on the upstairs hallway wall. The house was filled with similar artifacts her parents had collected over the years.

Though she had slowly modernized the house with new furniture and carpeting, it retained a traditional quality that reminded her of her mother. She had succeeded in making changes without displacing the cozy, comforting atmosphere of their home.

She moved down the stairs, glad to have David and Bree home. In many ways, it was like old times. Carl had been a little annoyed with her for her suspicions about Mr. Tubbs. But David's presence seemed to soothe ruffled feelings. Deidre had never felt the need to come home with them. And though she wouldn't admit it aloud, Beth was glad. At times she still wished David hadn't married.

She vaguely recalled how, as a teenager, her brother had gone through a rebellious stage, which he had promptly outgrown once his best friend moved in with their family. Everything seemed to change for the better after David came. Even at the young age of six, she recognized and embraced the difference his being there made. Despite the passage of time, some aspects of David being a part of their family remained unchanged.

She was fifteen when her own defiant phase surfaced, her mother had already died and both Carl and David lived away. Although he was a busy pastor, her father tried to curtail the rebellion raging in her. Michael had been all too ready to convince her that her father's stern restrictions were harsh and outdated.

Her anger toward her father had become so intense she could barely think straight. She now realized that she had been influenced by Michael's constant taunting, as well as the other kids teasing her about his strict ways.

The kids weren't really all that cruel, but the teasing made her feel even more separated from her classmates. The more they ribbed her, the angrier she got. Her father became less encouraging and more restrictive. But it only served to intensify her desire to get away from him and Plover Creek.

Beth turned into the kitchen to start breakfast and found Carl already there. "Hey, what are you doing up so early?"

"Thought I'd grab a cup of coffee and check on the horses," he said without looking at her. The naked grief on her brother's face made her even more determined to shelve her own. She thought of Carl's words when she blurted out her suspicions about Mr. Tubbs. *"As always, you're being irrational."*

She could almost understand why Carl thought she was operating in a mode of hysteria. After all, it was crazy to point fingers at a man who had always been kind to them. He had even sat with her father for hours at a time playing checkers. She was hesitant to let her doubt go, but perhaps she should be more careful about sharing them.

"I need to talk with you about George," Carl said, finally looking up. "I'm sorry he took it upon himself to come up to your job. But he didn't mean any harm, Beth. I talked with him. He admitted that John at the bank mentioned we were having financial problems and might be willing to sell. George probably already had his suspicions about that. After all, he's been coming around here for years."

Discarding her earlier resolve to keep quiet, Beth frowned. "What I can't understand is how John Wagner could be so unethical. How could he even fix his mouth to publish our business?"

Carl took another sip of coffee. "I don't know. I'm not surprised by the things people do anymore. In any case, we don't have the time or money to legally chase it."

"I've been thinking about that," Beth said, pouring herself a glass of juice. "Have you approached anyone yet?"

"I haven't officially put it on the market, but I did talk to your boss. I'm not sure how serious he is, but Taylor mentioned taking a look at it."

Beth sat her glass on the table and pulled out a chair, surprised. "Taylor? What would *he* do with a ranch?"

"*Does* seem a mite unlikely." Carl hesitated before looking up again. "That's why I was thinking of approaching George. We already know he's interested. I wanted to see what you thought about it."

Beth's eyes flashed. "You already know what I think."

"Dad told me a while back that George had been after him for years to sell, Beth."

Beth felt her stomach turn. "Did Daddy know we were in trouble?"

"I think he had suspicions, but I hadn't talked to him about it." Carl raked his stubby fingers through his hair. "I remember after Mom passed, Dad was thinking of selling. I didn't think about it at the time, but I remember him mentioning that he really didn't want to sell to George."

Beth was shocked. Hearing his words somehow convinced her that Ray McDade also had misgivings about his supposed friend. "That was a long time ago. Ten years. What happened that he didn't sell?"

"Got a loan at the bank."

"Don't you find it odd that Mr. Tubbs and Daddy have been friends for years and he didn't want to sell to him?"

"As you say, Sis, that was a long time ago. And no, I don't really find it odd. So don't go making anything of it. The only reason I mention it is because I needed to see what you thought about going against ten-year-old wishes…and approaching George. You do realize we need to sell as soon as we can."

Beth finished her orange juice and pondered her brother's words. She wanted to be fair and think with a level head. "Maybe you should pray about it," she finally said. "I personally want to see if Taylor is really interested. If not, I would like to try and find another buyer before approaching Mr. Tubbs."

She closed her eyes and tried to suppress her mounting apprehension—an unspecified premonition of sorts. She thought of her childhood and all the plans she and her friend, Shannon, had made as they sat on the southern ridge. She thought of the family she had craved, the crush she once had on David and her desire to become a pediatrician.

Then she began considering where she would live after they sold the property. Although a small surge of excitement penetrated her rising panic, countless unanswered questions hovered ominously. Delicate issues drifted about aimlessly, bursting without resolution. Her next remark, then, was more in observation than query.

"How can a person know what God is directing him to do?"

Speaking with a certainty his sister didn't share, Carl said, "What helps *me* stay on track is the matter of seeking Him daily. You thinking about your future?"

Beth nodded. "I'm a little scared. I've been thinking about returning to school. But I'm not sure that's the direction I want to go."

"Pray about it, Sis. You'll get your answer. But try not to get impatient."

THREE

The next two days were filled with funeral preparations and related events. Despite all the activity, Beth was unable to erase the doubts lingering in her thoughts. And with Carl and David out running errands and Bree down for a nap, she had more time than was healthy to dwell on them.

She walked aimlessly through the downstairs, chilled by the very idea of solitary silence. Everything she looked at or touched reminded her of her father: His old Bible beneath the coffee table; his silver-handled cane behind the kitchen door; and the old Chevy pickup parked beneath a tree in the backyard. She unwillingly started focusing on questions raised by her father's unexpected death.

Could she be wrong about Mr. Tubbs? But he was aware of her father's illness. He knew that his condition could be agitated with unpleasant news or badgering. She frowned and bit into her lower lip. If her dad reacted to upsetting news by having a heart attack, Mr. Tubbs would be free and clear to buy the ranch. Still, she couldn't figure out why he had approached her about it beforehand? Had he not realized it could bring suspicion on him? That's a clear motive for murder, in her opinion. He wants the ranch. But does he want it bad enough to kill for it?

Beth made her way into the kitchen, panic still clinging to her. Nothing was making sense. Her mind kept going back over the fact that they were preparing to bring him home from the hospital when George Tubbs visited. Minutes later, he was dead. She shook her head and moved woodenly to the counter and switched on the radio to break the silence.

More than likely, Carl was right. It was just happenstance. Her long dislike for Mr. Tubbs, combined with the shock of her dad's death, had probably magnified her animosity toward him. Still, he had opportunity. But even *she* had a hard time believing that his lust for the ranch would be motive enough to actually hurt her father.

Her mind turned to Manny's words. *"Shock has a way of putting funny notions in folk. You might want to watch your mouth about that. At least until you've had time to grieve."*

Mansfield Jefferson was her best friend, and one of the gentlest men she knew. They had told each other everything for many years now, but every now and then he still surprised her. She could hardly believe that he had actually approached, and brawled with, Michael. It also surprised her that he had talked to Carl about Jake's garage. Beth inwardly shrugged. Perhaps she had been so wrapped up in herself that she hadn't really been there for Manny.

She thought of the anger in his eyes when he mentioned running into Michael. What had happened, she wondered.

Just before graduating high school, Manny's dad had simply walked off. He hadn't even returned for his wife's funeral. Beth admired her friend's strength, which was evident at a very early age. In spite of his unsophisticated demeanor, he was remarkably insightful. His tendency to spend so much time alone made him seem peculiar to some. When he was with anyone other than Beth, it was more likely the elderly. She shuddered involuntarily as she recalled the gloom that enveloped them both the year they graduated high school.

Manny had been shaken by the death of his fiancée, Charla Welch, who had been killed by a hit-and-run driver. Three days before that, Shannon Ware, a young girl Beth had befriended, was found dead by her brother, Leonard, who was now a deputy with the sheriff's office.

She abruptly stopped this train of thought, telling herself that this was no time to be dwelling on such deeply troubling events. She then forced herself to redirect her attention. An old seventies tune by Marvin Gaye played on the radio. Beth smiled and began cleaning out and rearranging the food pantry. She had been so distracted lately that she hadn't done any grocery shopping. This would give her a chance to make out a list.

The back door was suddenly pushed open, startling Beth. Lena Hall marched in, chattering to herself and carrying an armful of bags. "Sorry, girl," she said with a smile. "I didn't mean to scare you."

Beth grabbed one of the bags and placed it on the table. "What's all this?"

"Food," Lena answered, eyeing Beth ever so briefly. "You don't look so hot. Sit down and talk to me while I get your supper going."

Lena briskly began putting things away. Beth moved aside, unsure how to react. "Really, Lena. I appreciate your kindness, but you don't have to do all this."

Lena looked up then. Having already stepped out of her shoes, she was now tying the apron Beth kept on a hook beside the stove. Beth could see she had been weeping, and briefly turned away to still her own emotion. "I know I don't, Beth. But if you don't mind, I'd like to."

She had paused in mid-knot, clearly waiting for Beth's consent. Beth nodded her agreement and began helping put things away.

Lena worked in administration at the hospital and had been instrumental in getting their father care after his stroke. She was a few years older than Beth, but had initiated their friendship about three years ago. Beth had noticed her watching Carl with an undeniable gleam in her eye. But Carl, wrapped up in his countless responsibilities, hadn't seemed to notice her subtle hints. She suspected Lena's unexpected interest in her had much to do with her attraction to her brother.

"Actually, I'm glad for the company," Beth said, turning off the radio. "My mind has been rolling down memory lane all day."

Despite her notion that Lena had an ulterior motive for befriending her, Beth had benefited from the relationship. Lena's culinary skills and knack for teaching were exceptional. She was tall and big boned and had a round, pretty face. Her eyes lit up every time she spoke, and her low, rumbling laugh was extremely infectious. Beth had seen bystanders, unaware of the conversation, be amused solely by the sound of Lena's laughter.

"Where is everybody?" Lena asked, glancing around.

"Carl and David are out running errands. Bree is down for a nap."

"I take it his wife didn't come this time, either?"

Not looking the least bit sorry, Beth answered. "No. I suppose it's all right, though. She didn't really know Daddy well. It wasn't for a lack of trying on this family's part, though. Naturally, Daddy was like a grandfather to Bree."

Beth recalled the last time she had seen Deidre. David had brought her home the summer Bree was born, four years ago. Bree had been so tiny, and she had longed to hold him. But she had been so out of sorts that she spent most of their visit finding somewhere else to be.

"Beth!"

The sharpness of Lena's tone gave her a start. "Girl, where are you? I've been standing here talking to these walls. I can't find any cornmeal. You got any?" Beth smiled as she watched Lena search through their pantry.

"There should be some in that canister on the bottom shelf, right behind the sugar."

"So what's on *your* mind?" Lena asked, reaching for the container. "I figured you needed a woman to talk to. Manny's ears can bend just so far, you know?"

Beth smiled at Lena's kind offer to listen. "You know how it is, Lena. Shiny memories and gray ghosts. Even though I've taken a few days off work, there's not enough to do to keep my mind off things."

"Hmm. Thinking about Shannon and your mama?"

"Yeah. Among other things. Shannon and I were pretty close for a little while." She covered her mouth, giggling. "We made some pretty outrageous plans a long time ago."

"What kind of plans?" Lena asked, pulling a large bowl into her lap as she dropped into a chair at the table.

"For one, *I* was going to marry David Spencer and have two children—a boy and a girl."

"David?"

Beth grinned and watched Lena's surprise melt into a wide smile. "I was living in a fantasy world, me and Shannon both. Sometimes, though, I think those were the happiest times of my life."

Lena smiled and gazed up at the ceiling. "Ah, the simplicity of childhood dreams. There's a place for it, you know. Innocent dreams are the rod and staff of God."

"Is that in the Bible?"

"Nah. My mama used to say that all the time." Beth watched as her friend's eyes misted. "I sure miss her. I think it must be a natural thing at a time like this. Our minds just run toward the past." Lena visibly shook herself and stood.

"Yeah," Beth said, nodding understandably at the notion. "Like I said. Shiny memories and gray ghosts."

"So did Manny like Shannon?" Lena asked. "The two of you have been friends for so long, I can't see him letting somebody else squeeze him out."

Beth chuckled at the odd question. "Manny was still around. But there were times for just us girls, you know?"

—∭—

The morning after the funeral, Beth rose early, her mind in its usual cluttered state. The sun was just peering over the horizon when she stepped out into the dampness. The backyard could stand to be mowed, she thought, moving toward the barnyard. Tiger and Gus rushed up as if they had been summoned. A sense of melancholy gripped her when she looked northward, where the stables and empty bunkhouse stood. Change was never easy.

She could remember the ranch being alive with the rowdy whistles of the hands, dust, horses and the rushing excitement of hard work. But it would never be like that again. Despite that realization, the ranch was still very beautiful and peaceful.

She stopped at the metal gate leading to the west meadow and turned to balance her weight on the lower rail, the way she had count-less times before. Resting her chin on the top of her hand, Beth eagerly awaited the brightening eastern sky. She loved this time of day—the moment the sun dawned and touched the drops of dew with a golden kiss.

Then she thought of the service for her father and the beautiful eulogy Carl had started. But he had broken up before he could finish, so David had left her side to conclude the tribute. She had felt exposed by his absence and immediately pulled Bree onto her lap.

David's delivery was powerful. She wondered whether other mourners had been as moved as she.

The dogs trotted off toward the meadow and Beth hurried to catch up with them. She had just settled into a comfortable pace when she heard her name and swung around to see David coming after her. She watched in wonderment as the sun gilded his athletic frame, fleetingly suggesting the image of a tall heavenly being depicted in a very old Bible.

David moved through the gate, hurrying to catch up to Beth. After talking to Carl, he was anxious to see where her head was. "You running from the pleasure of making us all a big breakfast?"

He moved up beside her and matched her pace. The sun shone against her face, highlighting her creamy, brown-sugar complexion and the haunted look in her eyes. It tugged at his heart. He longed to reach out and touch her skin without inviting questions he couldn't answer.

She smiled broadly. "I was just giving myself some thinking time."

"Mind if I join you?"

"Not really going anywhere," she said, continuing toward the west paddocks. "If breakfast was over, I would probably ride up to the ridge." She pointedly evaded his gaze.

"You still like it up there, don't you?"

She offered a small smile and at last relaxed a little. "I used to think it was…sacred, especially during a rain shower. The thunder would rumble just over the trees and my whole body would shake with the vibrations. I was almost sure it had some mysterious meaning. Sometimes I actually thought I understood it. It's funny when I think about the things I thought about as a child."

"Interesting," David said, lifting an eyebrow. "What did it feel like?"

She shrugged absently. "If I were a kid again, I could probably tell you without feeling stupid, but…"

"Tell me anyway," he said, intrigued. Beth had always had the ability to stand alone, never taking the time to decide the safest or most popular course of action. She simply did what she felt was right at the time. He had always admired that.

"I would say it felt like my belly was turning flips and enjoying it…free and happy. Like free-falling off a cloud." She turned to look up into his face. "You know what I mean?"

He smiled, surprised that he did. "Ray used to tell us you had a special ear for God's whispers."

Beth stopped, her eyes showing surprise. "When did he say that?"

"A long time ago. I guess you were about seven the first time I heard it. Right after you warned him against taking the horses to Galveston." Thinking about the feisty little girl she had been, David threw back his head and laughed. "You were such a busy little hen."

He saw her try to hide a shudder by stooping to pick up a stick. "Why haven't I ever heard that?" she asked. "Do you know what it means?"

"I don't know. I just thought of it when you mentioned the sound of thunder. At the time, Carl and I just thought it was a father's pride talking. He really was very proud of you, Beth."

"What does that have to do with thunder?" she persisted.

"Did you know that thunder represented the voice of God in the Bible?"

A stray tear rolled down Beth's face. "So you're saying I can actually hear the voice of God and not know what He's saying?" She quickly brushed the tear from her cheek. "Daddy was obviously pulling somebody's leg."

"Maybe so," David said, as they fell back into a stroll. "But I wouldn't be a bit surprised if there was something to it. You about ready for that talk?"

She shook her head. "Maybe later."

"How about heading back toward the house?"

"Sure," she said, turning back. "I've been thinking about those times a lot lately. Back then God was the basis of all my fantasizing. Maybe I'm just trying to recapture it."

David weighed her words. "You're longing for the past. Maybe you don't want to admit it, Beth, but you might be craving for that connection with God again. What if somehow your dad was right?"

She forced a smile. "You'd better be careful. You're beginning to sound as idealistic as I am."

"Hear me out," David said, stepping in front of her, his hands on her shoulders. "I believe God plants a longing in all our hearts. I can see it in Bree right now. Ray obviously saw it in you. Don't dismiss that as nonsense."

Her face suddenly twisted in anguish. "If that's so, wouldn't I be able to hear Him now?"

"Not necessarily. As a child you heard his voice in the thunder." He paused and cleared his throat. "When we become adults, we tell ourselves its naïve to trust that kind of sensing. We move on to more reasonable ways of thinking."

"You're making too much sense," she said, studying his face.

He kept his eyes on hers. "You used to have this uncanny knack for detecting trouble, Beth. In spite of all the stuff going on now, you still have it. A lot of us do. We just won't be still long enough to listen."

She shook her head. "I'm almost afraid to be still."

"Why?"

"I'm afraid I won't like what I hear, or see."

David felt a chill as he watched the intensity in her expression turn grave. He wanted to smooth the frown from her brow, erase the fear from her eyes and quiet the pain in her heart. "God will prepare you before He shows you what you need to know."

FOUR

Once the house was filled with the aroma of breakfast, they all found their way to the kitchen table. After the blessing, the room gradually began buzzing with lively reminiscing. Part of Beth's mind was still on her earlier talk with David. They had lingered outside before being interrupted by Bree's excited chatter. She sensed that David had wanted to tell her something more, but he hadn't. Still, she couldn't stop thinking about it. Could it be possible that God was actually talking to her?

"Bree, would you like to go into town with me this afternoon?" Beth asked.

The child nodded excitedly, his mouth filled with syrup-soaked pancakes. "Manny still pretty much stays to himself, doesn't he?" David asked. "What does he do for leisure?"

Beth offered a casual, no-details answer. "He still hunts and takes part in shooting contests." Then she turned toward her brother. "Carl, he told me you were going to help him negotiate with Jake for that garage."

Carl placed another forkful of eggs into his mouth. "Yeah. Jake's been trying to sell it for a couple of months. I think we can talk him down a little more, though."

"I hope he gets it. He deserves it, and he's good with cars."

Carl shook his head sympathetically. "He could stand a break. That's for sure. I hated it when Tom up and walked off like he did several years back. Manny's mother didn't last much longer after that. They tried, but they couldn't even locate him for the funeral."

Beth grew quiet, mulling their strange alliance. In elementary school, Manny had rescued her from a spider another student had tossed too close. His father, Tom Jefferson, had been the meanest drunk in Plover Creek. In snubbing Tom, people in the community had inadvertently rejected Manny. But he had adapted well to rejection and outside insults.

She recalled how relieved Manny had been when Tom left, but she had no intention of sharing that with Carl and David.

She took a sip of juice and dabbed at her mouth with a napkin. They were teenagers when Manny told her the reason for his limp. She had been complaining about her dad's restrictions at the time. He was only four when Tom came home drunk and beat him with a piece of firewood. Looking down at Bree, her heart warmed to his obvious attachment. He ate with his right hand, while his left hand clutched her shirt. She couldn't bear the thought of someone hurting him the way Manny had been hurt.

She saw David smiling at them. He obviously didn't mind the budding connection between her and his son. "I've been thinking about doing something special for Lena," Beth said, turning back to Carl. "She's been very helpful to us through all of this. What do you guys think?"

"That would be nice," Carl agreed. "I told her last night how much I appreciated all she's done."

Beth giggled, remembering how Lena had been so taken aback by Carl's attention that she had mumbled several inscrutable words and shrunk back into the shadows like a discomfited teenager.

"I go to the bathroom," Bree announced, jumping down from his chair.

"Do you need any help?" Beth asked.

"No, I do it." And with that he was gone, leaving the three of them chuckling for several long moments.

The unexpected ring of the phone interrupted the lighthearted moment. Carl went to answer it. Beth stood and began clearing the table. "I think my son is smitten," David said, peering over his coffee cup.

She smiled tentative agreement and moved back to sit across from him. "He's a real little charmer."

A look of incredible satisfaction came over David's face. "He *is* a good kid. You're really good with him, Beth. I love seeing the two of you together. How many kids do *you* want?"

Beth tried desperately to keep her focus on Bree, and not on the child nobody knew she had lost. But her breathing quickened, and she found it difficult to meet David's gaze. She cleared her throat and laughed softly, placing her trembling hands into her lap beneath the table. "If they could all be as sweet as Bree, I would have a hundred."

"After the first nine months, I'm sure you would change your mind about that."

"When do you have to head back to Seattle?" she asked, deliberately changing the subject.

"Sunday evening."

"So soon?"

"I have a meeting first thing Monday morning," he said, resignedly. "Ted could probably handle it, but I think I need to be there."

After breakfast, Beth saddled and mounted Midnight while David and Carl selected a pony for David to ride with Bree later. The question of children had given her the sensation of walking on quicksand. The subject had come up so easily, and if the truth were known, it was something she wanted more than anything in the world. But she couldn't trust men, and she refused to dwell on it.

She rode hard, trying to empty her overcrowded mind and heavy heart. A familiar sense of guilt rose from the depths of her soul. Unsettling images entered her mind's eye, conjuring emotions better left buried. The more she struggled to push them aside, the more vivid they became.

Twisted visions of children, her parents, Shannon, and Michael danced tauntingly in her head, pushing her closer to the edge. The wind briskly dried her tears as she raced through the meadow toward the southern ridge.

After reining in Midnight beneath the canopy of trees, she dismounted and tethered him to a nearby bush. She went straight to the flowerbed she had planted four years ago when she returned to Plover Creek.

Confusion cut through her soul like a cold wind, but seeing the smooth sycamore somehow calmed her. Its very existence was a miracle. It had been struck by lightening the same year she and Manny graduated high school—the year she lost Shannon and Manny lost Charla.

She knew it was a childish notion, but she almost believed God had commemorated their deaths with the thunderstorm that split the tree in two. Though it was perfectly healthy, one section of the tree served as a sort of couch she parked on beneath the other foliage.

Unsure how to channel the mixed emotions consuming her, Beth sighed and began weeding the flowerbed with her bare hands. After a few moments of this, she moved to the edge of the cliff and gingerly looked down into the deepest point of the very creek that bore the town's name. The steep drop consisted of jagged rock formations and stunted cedars jutting out from the sides.

A rabbit scurrying from beneath a wild holly startled her. She closed her eyes, loving the calming sound of water as it rushed around the rocks below. On sultry days, there was nothing sweeter than choruses of birds in the branches, or the sound of their wings flapping against an upper wind.

She peered down at the water again. The sparkle combined with the sound of calling birds was hypnotic. Cicadas buzzed against a soft breeze, and Beth casually kicked a mud clod over the edge. She watched the fading ripples, seeing the scene as a precise representation of her world—a black hole of vanishing swirls.

She snorted in facetious retrospect. Life as she knew it was fading away. Everything was changing. There was no longer any reason for her to continue juggling the finances, and trying to keep the ranch from sinking. Her whole way of thinking had to change.

Many years ago, she had dreamed of marrying David and having his babies. Perhaps Michael's accusations hadn't been far off the mark. Maybe she still had fantasies about David, but it was wrong. David was married now, with a child.

After he married Deidre, Beth had appropriately pushed that dream aside. Becoming a pediatrician had replaced it. She smiled, thinking of Shannon's dream to be a model. They had sat together in this very spot and planned futures that were not to be. A warm calm came over her as she imagined Shannon's blonde strands blowing in the breeze. She inched forward, sensing a peculiar hush that was as still as darkness.

Suddenly, a large hand grabbed her from behind and snatched her back from the ledge. Her heart lurched in her chest and her breath came in short, panicky gasps.

"What do you think you're doing?" David shouted, shaking her a little. His accusing eyes burned into hers without wavering. Her head came up quickly. Several long seconds passed before she could speak.

"David...I wasn't..."

Although she didn't want him thinking she was about to harm herself, anger won out over abashment. She pulled away from him in a huff.

"Go away!" she yelled, heading beneath the trees. He followed, almost stumbling over a black plastic bag protruding from beneath the smooth horizontal sycamore.

Beth was burning with discomfiture and was anything but inviting. David sat next to her on the tree anyway. After what seemed like hours, he began to speak. "I'm sorry," he said, wiping the sweat from his brow. "I didn't mean to jump to conclusions. It just scared me to see you so lost in thought...so close to the edge."

It amazed her, as it always had, that he was even there. "I was just looking down into the water." Out of the corner of her eye, she could see him poking at the black plastic bag with the toe of his boot. Her throat felt tight and swollen, but she took a deep breath and gestured toward the flowers with her head. "My gardening tools. I wrap them so the weather won't ruin them."

"Won't they sweat and rust?"

"I poked holes in the plastic," she said. Her heart was still slamming against her ribcage. And her stomach was curling into a tight ball.

His gaze seemed to bore holes in her. She glanced away, ashamed at what she was thinking about a married man. "I didn't realize you had planted a flowerbed up here, too," he said.

"David, you said I had a knack at knowing things. Could I have somehow caused Daddy's death?"

The question took him by surprise. "What?"

"Nothing," she said, turning away. He turned her chin so that her gaze once again met his. His own was intense but kind.

"What's going through that head of yours, Elizabeth McDade?"

Beth swallowed bitterly and lowered her eyes. "Could I be an evil force?" she whispered. "I know it sounds childish, but I've been thinking. Maybe I cursed Daddy."

She clamped her mouth shut when she saw the look in his eyes. "Whatever gave you an idea like that?"

"Something I overheard Mr. Tubbs say when I was a kid. When we were talking earlier, I thought about it again."

"I remember. Your mother told us about it. Honey, you're not evil. Faith has been pumped into you from the womb."

Beth thought she hadn't heard right. "Mom heard him?" she asked incredulously. "I didn't think anybody knew about that."

"You can't believe that nonsense, Beth. What's really got you going?"

She shrugged, sensing her emotions were about to blow. "I just don't think God hears my prayers anymore, David. And I don't mean to hate anybody."

"Of course you don't."

"It's just..." She stopped and looked up into his eyes again. "Daddy died before I could tell him how much I loved him. And the fact that we're losing the ranch doesn't make me feel all that warm and fuzzy."

"Beth, do you really believe what you're saying?" David asked, grasping her shoulders. "You didn't cause any of this. This isn't about you."

She moistened her dry lips. "Obviously, I've lost touch with reality. I need to get away from Texas and get on with my life. But I don't really know how."

"Your mother told me something once that might help you now," David said. "It was after I decided I wanted to be an architect."

Her curiosity piqued, Beth looked full into his face. David released her and leaned back against the standing oak. "There are lots of things in life that will catch your eye, but only a few will catch your heart. Go after those."

Beth was stunned by the depth of insight in her mother's words. The words Lena had quoted from *her* mother were similar, and Beth recognized that this was one of the ways God spoke to His children. Her stomach tightened. Maybe, just maybe he was speaking to her. A sense of elation mixed with sorrow came over her. "Thank you for telling me that."

David straightened and looked down at her again. "Can you remember any of the things that caught your heart, Beth? More than likely, you had them as a child. God put them there."

"I think maybe I've already messed up my chance for those things."

"Do your dreams have anything to do with children?"

Beth suddenly felt the blood drain from her face. "What are you talking about?"

He gazed at her intently. "This morning when we talked, I saw something in your expression. I know our friendship suffered after I married, but I'll always be here for you. You and Carl have been my family for a long time."

She wasn't surprised by his remarks, but wasn't sure how to respond. Despite her reluctance to intrude on Deidre, her heart melted with gratitude. As a child, she had so enjoyed her connection to David and had felt betrayed when she needed to break it.

"Promise?"

"Promise," he said solemnly, placing her face between his palms.

The moment was heavy with something she couldn't identify, something magical. It startled her, and she immediately regretted having succumbed to the need for his reassurance.

"I'm sorry. I'm behaving like a child. I have no right to—"

"You have *every* right," he interrupted, lifting her chin again. "I care about you, Beth."

She thought for a few moments, her emotions tangled and impassioned. Her hands began to shake slightly as she cleared her throat, needing to pull away from the intense moment. "Is it possible God is angry with me?" She looked up into his eyes, waiting for her question to register.

"Does this have anything to do with the hatred you mentioned?"

She lowered her gaze, and despite the reluctance to speak of it, she did. "Hating Michael Baker, Mr. Tubbs, and destroying an unborn soul. Could I have messed up my chances to have a real family?"

"Hate is a strong admission, Beth."

"You know Daddy never forgave me for getting engaged to Michael."

David let out a long heavy sigh. "Honey, it wasn't about Michael. Ray thought he had failed *you,* that he hadn't prepared you to steer clear of the wrong influences."

"People like Michael?"

"Yeah. He didn't trust Mike. *You* knew that. But you're still beating yourself up over a rebellious phase. That wasn't anything new to Ray. He had already gone through it with Carl."

"I remember."

"Ray just wanted to point you in the direction he saw God leading you, as I've got to do with Bree while he's still young and teachable. Remember what we talked about earlier?"

She nodded as a fragile hope floated up into her thoughts. "I loved Daddy, but I hadn't told him in a long time," she said, her voice quavering. "I thought coming home and helping Carl run the ranch would be enough to show him."

"Your coming home was supposed to be temporary, Beth. I think it was more of an escape than anything else, don't you?"

Her head shot up. "What?"

One of David's eyebrows lifted slightly. "I'm not saying Ray wasn't the reason you came home, but he certainly wasn't the reason for you staying." Beth gasped and looked away. "What do you have against Mike, Beth? And what unborn soul could you destroy?"

Beth smiled in spite of the naked shame raging through her. She pulled a handkerchief from her back pocket and wiped her eyes and nose. She scooted back then on the horizontal sycamore, and leaned back against the oak. David brushed back a tuft of her hair that had fallen over her eye.

"Do you still want to marry Mike?"

She peered up at him, momentarily confused. "What?"

"Michael. Do you love him?"

"How can you love someone you're professing to hate?"

David shrugged. "Women say that sometimes when they're mad about something."

Beth stood and began pacing the length and breadth of the clearing. "There's something terribly dark about Michael. I could never love him again."

"Has he hurt you?"

She stopped a few feet away and looked at him. His voice was strong and reassuring. She swallowed dryly, averting her eyes. "The night we broke up. He just got a little rough."

Beth turned back in time to see David's lips curl in utter disgust. "Mike never struck me as the type to do anything in a *little* way."

Beth took a deep breath and lifted her chin. "You sure you want to hear this?"

"Beth, something other than the past few days is eating away at you. And, I want to hear it."

Fresh tears streamed down her cheeks. She moistened her lips, still tugging on the handkerchief. David took her hands and drew her back down onto the sycamore.

By the time she opened her mouth to speak, it was little more than a whisper. "It was Valentine's night, four years ago. I don't know why I didn't follow my first mind and cancel the date, but I didn't. Michael had taken to bullying me into agreeing with his way of thinking…on some things. I was so dense not to see it at the time." She glanced up. "David, why didn't I have the courage to admit my mistake?"

"Pride is a powerful thing." He squeezed her hand, giving her the courage to go on.

She straightened and began again. The tremors were coming in waves now as she visualized that horrible evening. "I guess I knew I was in trouble when Michael pulled into a wooded area behind the dorms."

Pure rage shook David to his core.

"He *raped* you?"

She nodded, her eyes brimming. Looking into the distance, she leaned unsteadily against the oak. Intent on keeping her calm, David gathered Beth into his arms. He couldn't believe the unspeakable horror she had hidden for years. With great effort, he maintained control of his own rage and let her weep on his shoulder.

The savagery of Michael's crime overwhelmed him, and he deeply regretted that she had not told him sooner. Still, Beth had held up well under the burden of such a secret. But he knew appearances could deceive. He vowed to reassert the sense of protectiveness he had always felt toward her.

"Stop blaming yourself," he murmured against her hair. "It wasn't your fault. It's a terrible way to learn a lesson, but that's where you've got to put the experience. You were young and gullible. Don't let it keep dragging you back."

When she spoke again, her words came in muffled whispers. To hear her he had to release his hold. "When I knew I was pregnant, I was so hurt and scared that I didn't even think about taking care of myself. I was even angry with God. I hated Michael. I hated the child he had forced on me." She paused and wiped her face again. "I lost the baby in my first trimester. That was right after Dad's stroke. So it was a good time to come home."

As his understanding grew, David tightened his arms around her, uncertain which of them was quivering more. Even though their relationship had changed by the time Beth graduated high school, the strain she had been feeling was more evident in the last few years. She had been cool and detached, and it was quite an undertaking just to get a couple of focused words out of her. He had known something was eating at her. Bree had been the only subject she would discuss with him.

Naturally, he'd assumed part of it was because of the old rift born of his marrying Deidre and moving to Seattle. He had noticed her growing self-reliance and confidence, but in actuality it was all a part of the coping mechanism she had devised. She had been isolating herself, locking herself away.

She was indeed a strong woman. Her perspective was a little off-kilter, he thought, but he supposed guilt and shame had done that. He couldn't imagine how she had been able to muddle through alone for so long.

"David, why did it happen?"

He placed a finger to her lips. "Shh. You probably have questions only God can answer for you. He will when you're ready to hear them. Then you will find a way to move on."

Beth lifted her head and ruefully touched the wet spot on his shirt. Her pain-filled eyes resolutely evaded his gaze. She stood then and started walking toward the horses. "I know I'm supposed to forgive him. But I don't know if I can."

"I know," he said, swallowing hard. He felt incapable of giving her sound advice in the area of forgiveness. He still didn't know if he could forgive his ex-wife, much less Michael Baker.

"Please don't say anything to Carl."

"Beth, you're going to *have* to talk to your brother about this, sooner or later. It's time to stop hiding from things that can't hurt you anymore."

"Not now," she said, continuing to move toward Midnight.

FIVE

"Gee-de-up!" Bree shouted, leaning back against his father.

David beamed with delight and pride. "Not just yet, Son. Wait till Carl gets mounted."

"Hope you don't mind me taking Midnight, Sis," Carl said. "Couldn't catch Aster."

"No problem," Beth said, smiling up at Bree.

The child's excitement ignited infectious laughter. Beth giggled, enchanted by his enthusiasm. A pleasant sensation came over her as she watched him with David. She wrapped her arms around herself and headed back to the house, remembering her own first ride.

Telling David her ugly secret had somehow quieted something inside her. She seemed able to concentrate better and could even feel a greater degree of hope stirring in the trenches of her soul. Hiding the truth all those years had inhibited her in more ways than she cared to admit.

After the dinner dishes were washed and put away, Beth's earlier sense of foreboding resurfaced. The ringing of the doorbell jolted her back to reality.

"Hello, Beth," Taylor Steele said.

Her boss grinned, looking like the proverbial cat. "Come on in, Taylor," she said, smiling. "We just finished up dinner a little while ago. Can I offer you a glass of iced tea?"

"Sure," he said, stepping past her. "Sounds good."

Beth showed Taylor into the living room as she pulled her apron over her head. "I'll be right back."

Almost as tall as David, Taylor was dressed in jeans and a yellow pullover that made him look more casual than usual. He was tanned, with piercing blue eyes and a bad-boy smile, and he wore his long black hair combed back. She had been surprised that Taylor was actually interested in looking at the ranch. She had teased him that he just didn't know what to do with all the old money hanging from his pockets.

Returning to the living room, she placed his glass on a coaster and sat down on the sofa beside him.

A wave of mixed emotions rolled over her and she swallowed hard. Things were happening so fast. "I didn't know you were coming out today."

"Didn't your brother tell you I wanted to look at the property?"

"Yeah, he did," she said, shrugging nonchalantly, "but I didn't think you guys would move on it so quickly."

She knew by his next question that he had noticed her hesitation. Placing his tea back on the table, Taylor slid forward and turned to face her.

"I don't mean to be presumptuous here, Beth. I need to know how you really feel about my interest in your property."

She stroked the air with a dismissive gesture. "Don't mind me. I'm still reeling from all the changes. I'll miss it, of course, but I'm looking forward to a new beginning. We have to sell. In light of that, I'm grateful you're interested."

"Do you feel up to showing me around the house?"

"Sure."

Beth hadn't shared her family's financial problems with her employer. But since the morning he became a believer, he and Carl had occasionally spoken on the phone. She assumed their relationship had evolved into one that led to a discussion about having to sell the ranch. After walking him through the downstairs, Beth showed him the second and third floors.

"You won't be uncomfortable working with me if I decided to buy, will you?" he asked as they walked back down the staircase.

She paused and looked back at him. "Taylor, why in the world would you want a ranch?"

"Don't you need to sell it?"

The phone interrupted them, and Beth continued down the landing to answer it. "Beth? This is George Tubbs. Is Carl there?"

"No, I'm sorry, Mr. Tubbs," she said, biting her lower lip. "He and David are out riding. Can I help you with something?"

"Well, I might as well tell you. I'm a mite upset by y'all's decision to sell without giving me first dibs. You knew I was interested. Heck, I talked to you only a couple weeks ago."

Beth groaned, wondering how he knew they were going to sell the ranch.

"Mr. Tubbs—"

"Doggone it. Carl told me I shouldn't have come by your job like that, and I'm sorry. But this is business. You just have that brother of yours call me."

By the time she'd thought of a comeback, he had already hung up. She stared blankly at the phone for several moments before Taylor noisily cleared his throat behind her.

"Everything okay?"

"Yeah," she answered pensively. "Thanks. Just the town pharmacist wanting to speak to Carl. You were telling me why you're interested in buying a ranch. It seems a little sudden."

"You sound a lot like my father," Taylor said, laughing lightly. "But I'll have you know I've got a lot of plans. I understand Mr. Spencer is an architect. I'd like to talk with him about them."

They slowly made their way back into the living room. Beth moved to the chair so she could look directly into Taylor's face as they talked. "Yeah, but David lives in Seattle."

"That's okay. I want someone that cares about the property and not just about making the money. He *does* have a personal interest in this ranch, doesn't he?"

"I suppose, but…"

"Hello, Taylor," Carl interrupted, taking giant strides across the room, his hand extended. "It's good of you to come out."

Bree skipped in, chattering excitedly about his first ride on the big horse. After noticing the stranger sitting on the sofa, he scampered over to Beth and climbed possessively into her lap.

"Taylor, this is David Spencer and his son, Bryson," Beth said. "David…Bree, this is my boss, Taylor Steele."

Beth sat in the chair with Bree on her lap, hardly believing her ears. Practically without taking a breath, Taylor outlined his detailed plans for a boy's ranch. His eyes gleamed with excitement and passion as he talked about some kids he'd met while attending a charity function several months earlier. The openhanded part of Taylor's character had developed into something she didn't quite recognize.

He wanted to break up the remaining acreage into a campground and retreat center. Listening to him talk almost made her as excited as he seemed to be.

The three men left to look around the property, leaving Beth behind in Bree's make-believe world. Absorbed with the new toy truck Manny had bought him, Bree didn't seem to notice when Beth moved to the sofa.

But unexpectedly, he looked up from the floor, his eyes quite serious for a child. "Me and Daddy leaving tonight, Beth."

"I know," she said, motioning for him to come sit beside her. Bree climbed up and instinctively slid over close to her. "But you probably enjoy riding in the plane with your daddy, don't you?"

"Yeah," he said with a slight frown. "But *you* won't have me no more."

Beth gave the child a noisy kiss on the cheek. "I'll miss you terribly," she whispered. "But I'll see you again real soon. And we'll talk on the phone, too."

"My daddy, too, okay?"

She giggled at his earnest request. "Okay. I'll miss your daddy, too."

"I luvoo," he said in the sing-song mode they used with each other. "Will you be my mommy?"

Touched and secretly pleased, Beth cooed, squeezing him fondly. "Oh, Bree, you're such a dear. You already have a mommy, though. How about I be your aunt?"

At that moment, she heard the sharp sound of gunfire in the distance.

Alarm shot through Beth like an arrow, shattering the special warmth of the moment. She froze, briefly hoping she had imagined the sound. Then, the distant shouting of men confirmed her fears and galvanized her.

In one motion, she snatched Bree and clutching him to her chest rushed to the small shoe closet under the stairs.

"What's the matter?" Bree whined, looking frightened. "B-e-t-h!"

Beth heard more shots in the background.

"Bree, listen carefully, now," she said, stooping to his height. "I need you to stay right here. I won't be gone long. But don't leave this closet until your daddy or I come get you, okay?"

"Beth, I scared," the child wailed. "Where's Daddy?"

"He'll be back soon, honey. I'll find out and come back for you."

Beth closed the door and raced to the kitchen window. She nearly fainted when she saw the men galloping furiously through the dust into the corral, pushing the horses hard. The horrifying scene and the sound of rifle fire scared her speechless. Someone was obviously firing on them. Nauseating surges of adrenaline rushed through her veins. She could see Carl racing toward the barn on Midnight, with David and Taylor right on his heels.

Another shot rang out and Midnight stumbled forward, throwing Carl from his back and collapsing on top of him. Beth screamed and, without thinking, ran out the back door. Moments later, David and Taylor pulled Carl from beneath Midnight and rushed through the gate.

"Get back inside!" David yelled, as they hurried toward the house carrying her brother.

She quickly returned to the enclosed porch and held open the screen door for the men. They laid Carl on the kitchen floor. He was writhing in pain. His leg was clearly broken. Taylor rushed for the phone and Beth went to Carl's side.

"Beth, where's Bree?" David asked.

"In the stairway closet," she said, looking worriedly at Carl. "What's going on?"

"I'm sorry, Sis," he said, his face twisted in pain. "Midnight's hurt pretty bad."

Her heart sank as the implication of her brother's words hit her. Her head spun with questions, but she would have to wait for answers. "What can I do to help?"

"Just stay right here," Carl said, reaching for her hand.

David walked back into the kitchen, Bree in tow. She wondered if Midnight could possibly survive the fall. Bree pressed in beside her, as David swept past carrying a rifle.

"Where are you going?" she demanded, leaping to her feet. David continued walking and pushed through the back door without a word. "No, David! Please...don't."

"Let him do it, Beth," Carl said, trying to recapture her hand. "Midnight's hurting."

Without conscious thought, Beth rushed after David. But Taylor grabbed her around the waist just before she made it through the door.

"N-o-o-o!" she screamed, covering her ears to shield the sound that was coming.

The sun had gone down by the time Sheriff Bill Harper and his deputy, Leonard Ware, arrived. Taylor had stayed with her and Bree, who was now asleep in bed. David had taken Carl to the hospital. Leonard smiled quietly as he stepped up beside the sheriff. His shifting blue eyes reminded her of his sister, Shannon.

"Sorry it took us so long, Beth," the sheriff said, "but all the cruisers were out on other calls. Seems to be a busy evening."

Beth watched them pull the car around back and through the wide gate to the meadow. When they turned the spotlight on, it seemed to illuminate the entire acreage on the eastside of the woods.

"What if the shooting had taken place during Bree's ride?" Beth whispered, her heart pounding in terror. "What if he had been hurt?"

"Thank God, that didn't happen," Taylor said, handing her a glass of tea she hadn't requested.

"What's going on?" she asked, her eyes heavy with sorrow. "Why did this happen?"

"I don't know, Beth," Taylor said, his brow furrowed. "It seems you're having quite a few snags out here. Does anyone else have a bid on your property?"

"No. We haven't really put it on the market. You're the first one to know about it. Except…"

She paused, recalling the call from George Tubbs. She didn't want to mention it to Taylor before she had talked to Carl and David. "Nothing like this has ever happened around here before."

"It's a nice piece of real estate for what I want to do. If y'all still want to sell, I'm ready to make an offer. I'm sorry about your gelding. I know how attached you were."

The overwhelming sense of loss suddenly exploded in Beth's chest. She hadn't expected anything like this, especially after all that had already happened in the last week.

Beth's mind bounced around the events of the past hours—the past week. Fear and confusion mixed in a flurry around her. Everything, including her family unit, her home and her very life, was spinning out of control. Welled up tears began flowing unchecked down her anguished face.

David had reminded her that misfortune visited everyone. But everything seemed to break apart around her. Maybe she would've been more prepared if her dad, or even Midnight, had been expected to die. But these deaths were sudden and unfathomable. They didn't feel normal.

She soon felt extreme exhaustion setting in and swayed a little. Taylor moved closer and wrapped his arms around her quivering frame, holding her steady. She closed her eyes, just wanting to rest. There was nothing to say.

Taylor was still holding her when the sheriff and Leonard returned to tell them they had found nothing.

SIX

Early the next morning, Beth was in the passenger seat and David was driving her car as they headed for the airport. He had said good-bye to a cranky Carl, who was trapped in a cast all the way up to his hip.

The memory of the events of the day before had settled in Beth's stomach like a cement block. Uncertainty and dread danced wildly in her thoughts. The sun was just coming up, and a few scattered clouds seemed to echo the ache in her heart. She regretted David and Bree's departure. It seemed she was saying good-bye much too often of late. Out of the corner of her eye, she noticed David's stiff movements. She would miss both of them.

A shiver ran down her spine as her mind tried to dissect the trau-matizing events of the past few weeks. She thought of her initial suspi-cions in regard to her father's death and grimaced. She must have been out of her mind with grief to lash out with an accusation as she had. Still, there had been too many flukes around the community for her comfort. And George Tubbs seemed to be at the center of most of them.

His knowledge of the bank's loan denial, his assumption that they would sell to him, and his presence at the hospital before her father's death—the images kept scrolling through her mind. And it wouldn't take much of a leap to factor in his involvement in the shooting yesterday. After all, she had just told him that the men were out riding in the meadow.

Both Carl and David had dismissed her implication when she told them he had phoned just before the shooting started. And he'd had plenty of time to set up an ambush between their returning with Bree and going back out with Taylor.

She felt a smidgen of regret for not having made more of an effort to dispel her harsh feelings toward the man. But he had shown his true colors the day he visited her at the office. She recalled the annoyance in his eyes when she told him that the ranch wasn't for sale. She realized her distaste for the man was born in the mind of an impressionable youngster, but she couldn't seem to dismiss it.

Beth shook herself mentally and looked back at Bree, who was nodding off again. She half-wished she could fly away with the two of them, but Deidre would more than likely resent her intrusion. After all, she had already shared her family an extra night.

David's wife had always been somewhat detached. She had only visited twice and was to some degree unapproachable. Her last visit had been just after Bree was born. After that, she had always sent him alone with David, claiming her work schedule didn't permit extended travel. Mulling this over, Beth felt a peculiar pinching in her gut. Was there something she should have noticed? A notion stayed in the back of her mind, but she couldn't quite pin it down.

"Penny for your thoughts," David said, casting a questioning look at her.

"Nothing, really."

Then in a flash, she recognized what had been nipping at her subconscious. Deidre hadn't once called during her family's visit, and Beth suspected they hadn't called her. She sneaked a look at David, hoping to find a clue to this mystery. But he was looking straight ahead, his mind probably on some aspect of his business.

He hadn't been very talkative since putting Midnight down. Her horse had been more than a pet. He had instinctively understood her feelings, and she had learned to sense his moods precisely. She had developed such a kinship that sometimes riding him was like gliding through the air with the perfect dancer. But she didn't blame David. It would take a while to get used to the loss, but she understood. She had lived around horses all her life. Her muted grief once again rose to the surface.

"Will you be able to make your meeting?" she asked, wondering if something else entirely was bothering David.

"Nah. Not with a clear head. I spoke with Ted last night. He knows the gist of the presentation, and I e-mailed him the notes I had. I'm sure he'll do fine."

"It's been a bizarre week, huh?"

"That's an understatement if I ever heard one. I really hate to leave with things so up in the air. How do *you* feel?"

She sighed wearily. "I don't mind telling you, it's all a little weird. I can't help thinking, the shooting has something to do with us selling."

"Beth, I really don't know about that, but the timing *does* seem a little strange."

She shrugged, drumming her nails on the armrest. "You already know I suspect Mr. Tubbs had something to do with it. I know it doesn't make sense to you and Carl, but that's how I feel."

David lifted an eyebrow. "You've been making some strong allegations with nothing to support them other than his visit to the law office."

Feeling trapped between her imagination and common sense, Beth felt rising irritation. "You've gotta admit...something's not right here, David." It was exasperating, constantly trying to convince everyone that she wasn't crazy, especially Carl and David. They consistently challenged her logic. She glanced at the back seat. The high strained pitch of her voice had awakened Bree. "I'm sorry," she whispered. "But sometimes you and Carl still treat me like a child."

David parked and opened his door. "I know you're not a child, Beth. And I have a lot of respect for your intuition. But you've gotta admit this is way out there."

The airfield was nearly empty. Bree held Beth's hand as they walked toward the lobby. Annoyance and grief stuck in her throat, so much so she had difficulty swallowing.

"Hold me, Beth," Bree said, lifting his hands to her waist. She obliged and hugged him close.

"Don't you forget, you're my little big man," she whispered, kissing the top of his head. She sat with Bree while David checked out the plane and put their bags on board. When he returned to the waiting area, his son was still sitting on her lap with both arms wrapped tightly around her neck.

Bree turned to see his dad approaching and immediately began to whine and cling more tightly to her. "Beth, you come with me. P-l-e-a-s-e."

"Maybe next time," she whispered into his ear. "I have to stay here and take care of Carl."

David's return had signaled for her to stand. He wrapped them both in a protective hug. "I want you to be careful. Remember your promise not to go back out on the ridge and to keep your suspicions to yourself."

"I'll be fine," she said, trembling a little. "It only stands to reason our imagination can run a little wild."

David pulled back and looked at her. Her attempt to ease his worrying was transparent and weak, considering her earlier statements. She was scared out of her mind. And he had to admit, so was he. Something was indeed wrong.

"To some degree I'm inclined to accept your first impression," he said. "The timing of the shooting is suspicious. But I think it's highly unlikely George was involved."

"Maybe it was just some kids fooling around," Beth said.

"It's more serious than that. And that's what worries me."

He saw fear mixed with relief and astonishment in her face. Her reaction would have seemed odd, except that he knew how much he and Carl had drilled her about rushing judgment. Maybe they hadn't taken her notions seriously enough, especially in light of her keen intuition. But he felt her suspicion of George was way off the mark. They knew him. Beth was upset about a lot of things and was simply letting a childhood memory influence her judgments.

"Carl said he intends to expedite the sale," Beth said calmly. "And he and Lena are talking about having a party for the Fourth. I'm sure everything will quiet down. Taylor is in no hurry to take possession, and will give us time to find a new place."

"That's a month away, but it doesn't give you license to be reckless," David said, playfully catching her nose between two of his fingers. "Be careful."

He lifted Bree from her arms and handed over her car keys, giving her a perfunctory kiss on the cheek. The clean, fresh scent of her perfume made him want to linger a moment longer. Bree began to whimper, anxiously holding onto Beth's blouse. This pulled at David's heart, and he found himself tempted to stay one more day. But that wouldn't make it any easier when it came time to leave again.

"I should be back in four weeks—just in time for the party. I'll have plans for Taylor to look at. Will that be too soon to hope you will have found another place?"

"Girl, you go on to work," Lena said, pouring water into their old-fashioned coffeemaker. "I had already taken the week off, anyway. I don't mind staying around here today to help out your brother. Besides, we don't want that nice-looking Mr. Steele to think you're taking advantage of his kindness."

Beth smiled knowingly and quickly gathered her things to leave. She turned back and looked at Lena, already busy preparing breakfast. "Thanks for all the things you've done for us, Lena. We both really appreciate it."

Beth wished Carl could see Lena as more than a means to organize functions and lend a helping hand. She giggled, remembering the time her friend had taken clippers and cut her hair as close to the scalp as she could get, hung large loops in her lobes and marched into church as if nothing was different. It took some getting used to, but the short style was actually perfect for her quirky personality.

Lena was a loner, yet could connect with anyone. It wasn't at all strange to see her totally engaged with a group of children, or sitting quietly on a porch chatting with an elderly couple. She was very attractive, and obviously crazy about Carl. She had tried so hard to get his attention. But for the last four years, he hadn't noticed anything outside of the ranch, their father and church business.

Lena was gone by the time Beth returned home. Supper was on the stove, and Carl was propped up on the sofa with pillows beneath his encased leg. She hoped he had at least been civil to her friend.

"Hey, Sis," he said in a cheerful tone, which immediately got her attention, since he had whined all night about the pain.

"Hi," she said, settling down in the chair opposite him. "I take it you're feeling pretty good."

"Yeah. Just took something for the pain. Lena said to call if you needed anything."

"I'll get changed and go take care of the horses," she said, heading for the stairs.

"No need. Manny said with so few horses, it doesn't take long for chores." Giving her an I-told-you-so look, Carl added, "George stopped by. He bought the remaining horses, both trailers, and Dad's old pick-up."

Beth couldn't conceal her surprise or her befuddlement. "I noticed when I drove up that the truck and trailers were gone. He wasn't upset about the contract with Taylor?"

"Didn't seem to be. Paid cash for everything. Said he had bought the land adjoining the old Tatum place. He's talking about putting in a riding stable. Beth, this will almost get us out of hock with the banks. George will even pay us to board the horses until he finishes getting his place ready, probably around the Fourth of July."

Beth bit her lip as a muted sense of apprehension moved through her. Why was he being so nice all of a sudden? She ran upstairs and changed into jeans and a shirt, and then left to find Manny. Gus and Tiger raced to welcome her home with wet slurps. Tiger stood with his front paws on the fence. He looked as though he was pleading with her to let him follow as Beth moved through the gate. But she ignored him. The dogs were not allowed near the high-spirited Aster.

"What am I going to do about those two?" she asked, approaching Manny from behind. "I know I won't be able to keep them in…"

Before she could finish the sentence, Manny's face lit up like a strobe. He dropped the pitchfork he had been using and limped toward her.

"If it's okay with Carl, I'll take 'em, Beth."

"Carl won't mind," she said, incredibly relieved. "He thinks of the dogs as more mine, anyway."

Manny's excitement was catching, and Beth found herself chuckling. He would probably work wonders with them. She had hesitated to ask because he already had a couple of hunters.

"Congratulations on your new garage," Beth said. "Perfect timing, huh?"

"Yeah. Carl helped a lot," Manny said, excitedly. "Bought me a used wrecker today. Already got a couple of contracts."

"I'm glad, Manny," Beth said, poking at a pebble with the toe of her boot. "Okay, I've waited long enough. Who is she?"

"Who is who?" he asked, grinning slyly.

"I can tell you've been courting. Who is she?"

"Kia Paine." A huge grin lit up his face. "Pretty, ain't she?"

"That she is," Beth agreed. Manny's good news lifted the emotional dark clouds that had been besetting her. "Maybe that quality for attracting a companion will rub off on me."

He playfully rubbed her head. "There you go. You can now step out and find yourself a fella."

After a little chitchat, the two sat on the water trough and settled into a companionable silence. Leaning back against the fence, they watched the setting sun. It was beautiful. Bright yellow bowed to a subdued orange, then to pink, and finally to purple.

"Manny?"

"Yeah."

"Don't you think it's odd Charla died right after Shannon seven years ago?"

Manny's expression changed slightly. She hoped she hadn't dampened his delight in courting Kia by reminding him of Charla.

"Oh, I don't know, Beth. They say disaster always grabs for three."

Her eyes widened in alarm. "That would mean two more things are due to happen around here."

Manny turned and saw the fear in her eyes. "Not if you count losing Midnight and the ranch. And don't forget Carl's broken leg. With Rev'n Ray passing, I'd say y'all were overdue for a blessing. But it's just like you always say, Beth—a silly superstition."

"Do you know if the sheriff ever found out anything in Charla's case?"

"Nah. Even though your pa kept after him, he drug his feet 'til all the clues dried up. I don't spect it's his fault. Folks were too scared to talk. They still like that."

Beth searched her friend's face. "Scared of what?"

"Of the law."

"But it's the law that helps. Right?"

"Not out here. I understand your thinking so…working for a lawyer and all. But black folks out here feel like Bill Harper don't follow through on our complaints."

Beth's face burned with indignation. "That's ludicrous. He's the sheriff."

"Exactly. He calls the shots. Has he gotten back with you after the shooting? He'll close the case without coming up with anything, just like he does all the others."

—᠊ᘛ᠊—

He stumbled into the dilapidated shanty and hurled a half-empty bottle against the wall. It shattered. The sound only served to enrage him more. He grasped the knife that stood wedged in a tree stump in the center of the tottering structure and paced around the cramped space, frenzied.

He spit onto the dirt floor, kicking at an empty can. "I've gotta do something," he said aloud. "Those McDades can't do this. I won't let 'em." He paused as a thought occurred to him. A crooked smile grew into a grin. "Maybe they just need a little more persuading."

He laughed aloud and hurled the knife into the drenched wall.

SEVEN

David jerked up, disoriented and uneasy. To his relief, familiar surroundings came into focus. He was in his own dining room, his hand still wrapped around a mug containing cold coffee.

He remembered now. He had been looking over drawings for Taylor when reverie had given way to sleep. His mind had been filled with thoughts of Beth—the scent of her, the soft feel of her. He had wanted so much to kiss her lips in the lobby of Garrison Field, but he couldn't. It probably would have shocked her even more than everything else going on. After all, she didn't even know he was divorced.

He recalled the moment he walked back into the lobby and found her and Bree so comfortable together. The scene made a perfect portrait. But of what? Was he letting his concern over Bree's motherless situation influence his emotions?

David sat up and rubbed his eyes. He had been dreaming of her, too. She had appeared in his dreams a lot since his return to Seattle. But this time, it was more of a nightmare; she had been in some kind of danger. He shook himself. He was being much too dramatic. Still, a lot was going on in Plover Creek. He just hoped Beth wasn't planning to share her suspicions about George with anyone else. He and Carl had talked to her most of the night, but they clearly had failed to convince her to back off.

David rubbed a hand over his face in an effort to stop his shaking. It's just a dream, he thought. Beth is safe. His fears and uncertainties had merely woven nocturnal sketches into his subconscious. That was it. Yes. That's all it was.

Lord, please keep her safe. Keep them safe.

He stacked the sketches he'd been working on in a neat pile on the table. He knew he had to get a hold of himself. Since leaving Plover Creek, he hadn't spent one day without Beth crossing his mind. At least now he understood what had caused that haunted look in her eyes, that defensive coolness in her manner. And he was relieved that she once again felt comfortable enough to confide in him. But he couldn't help wishing she could talk with her brother about it—get spiritual guidance.

He scanned his surroundings again. The dead air around him was stifling. The television in the next room was tuned to a station that had signed off for the night. His calves, pressed hard against the rung of the chair, were tingling. Sighing, he started to stand, but for lack of circulation in his legs dropped back down.

It had been a difficult couple of weeks. He had spent as much time as he could with Bree, but his work had kept him extremely busy. He knew that his home life *and* work were suffering.

He opened his eyes, absently looking at the mug. He had worked fourteen hours straight, traveling from site to office, then off to another site, then on to a scheduled meeting. New opportunities were constantly pouring in. Ted was picking up a lot of the slack, but he had to think seriously about hiring more people.

Moving mechanically through each hour of his down time, he had tried to keep his mind off Beth, tried to meet the needs of his son. He had to force himself not to call Carl daily on the pretext of checking on his injured leg. It didn't help matters that Bree constantly asked to talk to her.

He winced, wondering what was happening to him in regard to Beth. His normally friendly manner seemed to be changing into something else, something he wasn't sure he was comfortable with.

"Lord, the protectiveness I once felt for Beth is intact," he prayed aloud. "But there's something more now. Please arrest anything that shouldn't be there. And give her the peace she needs to move healthily through the phases of grief. She's trying to deal with Ray's death, as well as with financial pressures and troubling memories. It's no wonder she's agitated and consumed by suspicions. Help me leave the care of her to you and focus on my son and business."

They were one week closer to the big celebration at the ranch. Beth was in the kitchen about to start breakfast when she heard a soft knock on the back door. She tightened the robe around her and peered out. It was Lena.

"Lena! What are you doing out so early on a Saturday morning?"

Carl and Lena had been working tirelessly on the upcoming festivities, so her visits were more frequent than usual. Lena brushed past her and dropped down into a chair at the kitchen table. A sense of urgency gripped Beth as she sat across from her friend. "Girl, I'm as nervous as a mouse in a house full of cats."

Lena's agitated state unnerved Beth. "What is it? You're shaking!"

"It's just awful, girl. But you need to know." Lena dabbed at her misting eyes. "Mr. Baker's been out looking for Mike all night. Did you know he was in town?"

Beth nodded, trying to appear indifferent to the news. "Manny told me." She suddenly realized what else Lena had just said, and frowned. "Why is Mr. Baker out looking for a grown man? Maybe Michael stayed with a friend overnight. I'm sure it's nothing to worry about."

Lena forcefully shook her head. "Sheriff was at my door this morning at five. They found Mike's car parked down the road with the motor still running."

Beth blinked as a feeling of dread took hold of her. "What!"

Lena's eyes were wild now. "You know, Terry and Felix disappeared the same way. You remember how close those three boys were. People called them the Three Musketeers."

"But those two disappeared over five years ago," Beth said, remembering the rule of three that Manny had mentioned. "Surely, this has nothing to do with that. Michael probably had too much to drink and went to sleep under a tree somewhere."

"They've looked all over for him, Beth. The sheriff said he'll be coming around to talk with you, too, seeing as how the two of you were engaged."

Beth could feel the adrenaline pumping through her. "I don't know anything. I haven't seen Michael in four years."

"Why did you two break up anyway?" Lena asked, grabbing the saltshaker on the table. "Did it have anything to do with his friends?"

Disconcerting notions invaded Beth's mind, as she watched Lena taste the salt she'd sprinkled on the back of her hand. Her thoughts drifted back through the years. "Terry and Felix went missing during our second semester at TU. Come to think of it, Michael got real nervous around that time."

Lena placed the saltshaker back and turned to face Beth. "Caused quite a stir around here, too. People still whisper about it. It's been real noticeable that Mike hadn't come home but a few times since y'all went off to college. And even then, he didn't stay long."

A peculiar catch in Lena's voice made the hairs on the back of Beth's neck stand up. She considered the probable reason for his irregular visits. Perhaps he assumed people were aware of what happened between them, and he just didn't want to face the music. But that was years ago. Where was he now?

"Lena, do you think somebody might be after him?"

"Like who? He doesn't even live around here anymore. If I'm remembering right, Felix went out to get his folks a newspaper and never came back. A few days later they found his car parked on the side of the road with the key still in the ignition."

Beth shivered. "What about Terry?"

"*He* never made it home from the barbershop over in Shanty Town. It was just like something swallowed them both alive. And now Mike."

Beth listened intently as Lena went on about how frightened Mr. Baker was. "But it's been a long time since those boys disappeared, Lena. What do you think *really* happened to them?"

"I don't know. But it sure is odd how we've never heard anything more from the sheriff about their disappearance. He'll more than likely sweep this one under the rug, too."

Beth felt a sudden chill. Those were the very words Manny had uttered. "Sweep it under the rug? Why? Has he completely closed the case?"

Lena shrugged. "I don't know. Like you say, it's been years since those boys come up missing—just a month apart, too."

Beth shook her head, mystified. "Such strange happenings for so many in Manny's and my high school class."

"I hadn't thought about that," Lena said, her back straightening. "Let's see. Shannon Ware and Charla Welch died. All three of the musketeers now have just vanished into thin air."

The women grew quiet. Hearing the names of her ill-fated classmates sent an eerie wind keening through Beth's soul. Her mind spun as she recalled the sight of Manny's angry eyes and scraped knuckles after he had run into Michael. Although she hadn't questioned him closely, she was certain the run-in was not a casual one. Why had they tangled, she wondered. She knew Manny was protective of her, but she couldn't imagine him harming anyone—especially after having scolded *her* about her death wish for Michael.

She suddenly felt icy cold. Manny could never hurt anyone. She knew him.

Beth made sure Taylor's office door was still closed. Hopefully, Tricia Peters would keep him tied up for a few minutes, giving her time to make a phone call. As she nervously dialed the Plover Creek sheriff's office, she couldn't help wondering what kind of legal help the elegant Ms. Peters could possibly need. Dressed in a gray business suit, her long dark hair pulled back from her face, she was a head-turner.

The instant the sheriff picked up the line, Beth pressed the phone closer to her ear and spoke softly into the mouthpiece. "Sheriff, this is Beth McDade."

"Well hello, Beth. How ya doing?" She could hear a creaky sound in the background, and was certain it was the sheriff's chair crying out against his weight as he leaned backwards.

"I'm well, thanks. I never heard anything about your investigation into the shooting at the ranch. Have you closed the case?"

There was a long silence. Her question had obviously taken him by surprise. "I wouldn't exactly say it's closed, but I don't have any leads. You suspect somebody?"

Beth thought of Carl and David's warnings. "Well, no. I was just curious as to why we never heard back from you."

"I told Leonard to come out and talk to you folks…see if he could scrape up any other leads. Maybe he got tied up. We've been kinda busy around here."

Likely story, she thought, rolling her eyes upward. Her mind once again turned to Mr. Tubbs' call just before the shooting. Her eyes misting, she thought of never again being able to brush down Midnight's coat.

A wave of impatience overtook her when she heard the sheriff's prelude to dismissing her call…and her concern. She'd been troubled ever since she realized the possibility that he neglected his duties in the black sector of Plover Creek. She balled her free hand into a fist, causing her nails to dig into her palms. Her voice betrayed her growing impatience.

"Sheriff, you don't seem to be taking any of this very seriously. Carl's leg was broken, and we had to put down my horse. Continuing the investigation is important to us. Why can't we have a little more cooperation?" She allowed her words to sink in before continuing. "What about Michael's disappearance? Do you have any leads on that? Is it tied to Terry and Felix in some way?"

"I know the folks out here are worried, Beth. Those boys disappearing the way they did is peculiar. David called me yesterday all the way from Seattle. He was shocked to hear about Mike."

"David called?" Her eyes narrowed. So David *did* have suspicions of his own.

"Yep. Wanted answers…same as you, but I'm sorry I don't have any to give you right now. We're doing the best we can. Folks out here just won't talk, and there's very little we can do without the cooperation of possible witnesses. The same thing goes for the Baker case. I don't have any leads or witnesses."

Beth felt surging indignation. "Just like Charla all over again," she blurted out. "How could so much happen, and so many people go missing, within a seven-year span and nothing be done about it, Sheriff? Did you run any lab tests? Check fingerprints? *Anything*?"

Beth heard a low, mocking chuckle on the other end. It infuriated her. "What, you turning into a crime-scene investigator now, Beth?"

She ignored the facetious remark. "What about my father?" she blurted out. "Do you realize he may not have died of natural causes?" The sound of the squeaking chair came over the line.

"What are you talking about?" he demanded. "You're beginning to sound a little obsessive. What do you think you're doing?"

Beth's head spun with frustration. "I'm not doing anything, and by all appearances, neither are you. I'm just curious as to why you don't follow through on our cases."

"Our! Are you accusing this office of anything in particular, Beth McDade?"

She gulped, realizing she had already said more than she had intended. She didn't want to ruin her chances of getting information from him later. "I'm sorry. I guess I'm just aggravated over the whole situation."

"I know it's hard to let things be. After all, you *are* a McDade. Your daddy was persistent, too. God rest his soul. But I'm warning you, there is no need poking your nose where it don't belong. Let us do our job."

Agitated beyond her ability to cover it up, Beth slammed the phone down and slapped her hands to her head. "Augghh!" she shrieked, swinging around in her chair to face her computer. Then she saw Taylor and his visitor watching her from his office doorway.

"I-I'm sorry," Beth stammered, visibly embarrassed. "I didn't mean—"

"I take it you're having some problems with the sheriff?" Taylor asked, curiously.

Beth glanced skeptically at his visitor. "It's okay," the woman said kindly. "Please go on. I'm very interested. I'm the assistant district attorney for Plover Creek."

Several hours later, Beth drove her car through the wide metal gate to the ranch and breathed a sigh of relief. The entire drive on a moonless evening felt thick with unnerving question. She smiled in spite of herself as she thought of the phrase her father had coined for the nights of a new moon. *A country-dark night can fold itself around the light of seven suns just to smother a plain thought.*

It was true. With so many scenarios competing for space in her mind, the drive had worked on her nerves. Even the path created by her headlights in the dense darkness caused the trees to resemble giant sentinels. The spectacle her mind displayed had intensified the dread that crept through her like an army of ants.

She had stayed late talking to Taylor and his friend, who had insisted that Beth call her Tricia. She seemed genuinely eager to help. Beth was surprised by her own willingness to reveal her suspicions, especially after the sheriff accused her of being obsessive. Maybe talking freely was the result of someone actually listening to her without making her feel silly for having unproven suspicions.

Tricia, intrigued by Beth's conviction that the sheriff's office was selectively negligent, agreed to inspect all unsolved and open cases. Beth mentally shook herself. Hopefully, she hadn't bitten off more than she could chew by getting Taylor and Tricia involved. This could very well turn into something more serious than a few misgivings.

Rather than pull into the garage at the front of the house, Beth drove the car around back, near the porch, to unload the grocery bags, allowing easier access to the kitchen. Still jittery from the drive, she slammed the car door shut with one foot and struggled to control her cargo. Seeing how dark the house was, she grimaced, stumbling up the steps to the screen door. It was early for Carl to have already gone up to bed.

Beth froze the instant she pushed through the back door, having heard movement. A prickling sensation shot up her back, conjuring visions of mice nipping at her bare feet. Without conscious thought, she let out a scream, dropped both bags and scrambled for the nearest chair.

Just then, the lights came on. "Sis, you okay? Why are you standing on that chair?"

"Don't you dare be funny, Carl Avery McDade," Beth shrieked, momentarily blinded. Cautiously stepping down to the floor, she fumed as she stooped to gather the scattered food items. "Look what you made me do. Why are you standing here in the dark, anyway?"

"I'm sorry, honey. I didn't hear you drive up. You go on upstairs. I'll put the groceries away."

She laughed sardonically. "You're still hobbling around here on crutches. How—"

Beth halted the instant she caught sight of Lena peering around her brother's stout frame. Her eyes flitted from one to the other, her jaw dropping.

"Oops. Sorry you two. I didn't…I mean…."

"I'll put the things away," Lena offered, moving around Carl. "You go on upstairs and relax."

Beth stood and rushed toward the stairs, giggling to herself. She hadn't known what to say, but was thrilled at the possibilities.

Lena had been doing most of the organizing for the Fourth of July event. Carl wanted an elaborate celebration that combined the holiday, an all-class reunion and a farewell to the ranch. Lena loved being in the middle of that sort of thing. Even though Manny had dropped Miss Virgie off each morning, Beth had noticed Carl being more helpless when around Lena.

She started preparing for a nice, relaxing bubble bath. But the phone rang just as she pulled on her robe. She hurried to grab it before the lovebirds downstairs could be disturbed. "Hello."

"Beth!" Bree said. "What you doing?"

Thrilled to hear his voice, Beth settled down on the bed and curled up against the pillows. She reveled in the pleasure the child's voice gave her.

"Hello, my little big man. I just got home from the store. What are *you* doing?"

"Daddy read me a story," he said with excited innocence.

"Which story did he read?"

"Jonah in the well." Beth laughed lightly at how loudly he spoke into the mouthpiece and how he turned whale into 'well'.

Cradling the phone on her shoulder, she closed her eyes and imagined she was in Seattle, sitting next to him. She could almost see David's wide smile as he proudly gazed at his son.

"Is Daddy a good story reader?"

"Yeah," he answered, adding in a whisper, "But not good like you." She could almost see his sparkling eyes as she heard the merriment in his voice. Oh, how she envied Deidre. She quickly curbed the thought and shook herself back into reality.

"Oh, Bree, I love you."

"Luvoo, too" he sang. "Can you come over my house?"

The moment had ended, and she didn't have the energy to yet again explain the distance between them. She closed her eyes and saw his curly hair. He was such a bright kid for four; affectionate, too. "We'll see, okay?"

"Wait…wait!" the child squealed, giggling irrepressibly. "Daddy's taking the phone, Beth. I not through, Daddy." Based on the sounds she was hearing, David was tickling Bree to get him to release the receiver.

"Beth?"

"Hey, mister," she said, having succumbed to the child's infectious laughter. "What are you doing to my little big man?"

"Oh, we're just hanging out. I took the afternoon off to spend with him for a change. I hope we didn't disturb you."

"Nah. I just got home, actually. Carl's still up. I'll get him." She was about to rush for the door when his reply surprised her.

"Actually, I called to talk to *you*. Do you mind?"

This was a change, she thought, puzzled. David called every few days like clockwork. He and Carl would talk like two old women gossiping over a backyard fence, often past her normal bedtime. Occasionally, she would get to speak to Bree. For *that,* she was grateful.

"Well, no," she said hesitantly. "It'll give me a chance to apologize for my stubborn inclinations. I know I shouldn't be so suspicious. And I don't mean to push my way of thinking off on you."

David abruptly cleared his throat. "I have to admit, I have my own misgivings about things, Beth. I talked to the sheriff yesterday after Carl told me about Mike's disappearance. They still don't have anything. So you stay away from them and keep your opinions to yourself. Please."

Beth felt a tinge of guilt as she recalled her chat with Taylor and Tricia. "Well, you didn't call to talk about me," she said. "What's up?"

She listened as David stumbled over meaningless words. Something inside her seemed to flip an alarm, causing her to cringe as it slowly spread through her.

"Does anything have to be *up?*"

Her mind was racing. She recalled the evening of the shooting when Bree had asked her to be his mother. She thought it odd at the time, but in all the excitement she had forgotten to ask David about it. And it was odd that no one seemed to be mentioning Deidre. Why wasn't it Deidre who read to Bree? Why did he find it necessary to take off work to be with his son?

She was thankful they had revived a degree of their friendship, but she felt a little awkward talking cat-and-mouse with a married man, even if he was a close friend. She would never intentionally do anything to make his wife feel uncomfortable. They were both adults now, and she was astute enough to know that their relationship could never be the way she had perceived it as a child, or even fantasized about as a teenager. Too much had happened.

"Do you think you'll be able to bring Bree back when you come next week?" she asked, hopeful.

"I suppose I could. He would probably scream for a month if I didn't. Do you have any idea yet about your plans after Taylor takes possession of the property?"

"Probably get an apartment in Dallas. That shouldn't take more than a day or so."

"What do you think Carl will do?"

"To be honest, I think I can hear wedding bells in the distance."

"Lena?"

"How did you know?"

"He told me a while back he thought he might be falling for her."

"He did?" she asked, surprised. "Y'all sure know how to keep a secret."

"How would you feel about that?"

"I think it would be wonderful. Carl needs a good wife."

"What about you?" David asked. "What do you see in your future?"

Beth felt the stirring of panic. "Actually, I've been thinking a lot about what we talked about on the ridge—going after the things that have caught my heart. I certainly want more than *this*."

"A big part of that is listening to God for some kind of plan. Are you ready to hear what He has to say?"

Though her anger toward God had softened, Beth hadn't been very committed to spending any time in prayer. Nightmares were becoming a real problem for her, too. They had grown so unsettling that sometimes they left her barely able to catch her breath when she awakened.

"I think so."

David was silent for a long moment. The lull was nerve wracking. She was just about to end the conversation when he continued. "You really should think about going back to school. I think you would make a wonderful pediatrician."

Beth held her breath a moment. "I don't know, David. Maybe I've outgrown that particular dream. I don't like the idea of going back to school. Too much has happened. Too much is still happening."

"Beth, did Manny know about the attack in Austin?"

She hesitated, feeling a sour taste coat her mouth. "Yeah. Why?"

"Just curious," he said. "Are you doing all right with Mike's disappearance?"

"I don't really know how to feel about that," she admitted. "I'm a little jumpy, I guess. We all are."

"It's all a little too strange for my comfort, honey," he said. Beth warmed and shuddered simultaneously at the sound of his endearment. "Listen, tell Taylor when I get there we can ride out and take another look at the site. I have the plans ready. He should get an outfit to do boundary and topographical surveys."

"David?"

"Yeah?"

"Where's Deidre?"

Beth heard an unmistakable break in his breathing just before a heavy sigh. "She doesn't live here anymore, Beth. We've been divorced for a little over a year now."

For the next several moments, energy seeped out of her like air from a punctured balloon. Cold shock ripped through her depths. She felt a perplexing mixture of relief, betrayal and sadness. Well, maybe not relief, she told herself, but something deeper—something she was certain she'd never experienced.

"I-I'm so sorry," she managed.

"I'm not," David said matter-of-factly. "It had been a long time coming."

His voice was edged with a coldness she had never heard. It frightened her a little. "How could you keep something like that from me? Does Carl know?"

"No. It just never seemed like the right time to dump it on you guys. You were inundated with Ray, and…"

"That's no excuse, David," she said, her voice cracking. "What happened? Can you talk about it?"

"Not right now. Prince Charming wants to say goodnight. I'll talk to you in a couple of days. Okay?"

"Sure," she said, her heart sinking lower. She grasped the phone tighter, trying to choke back the sobs. After managing to say goodnight to Bree, Beth succumbed to the agony and lay back on her bed and wept.

Everything from the loss of the ranch, her dad and Midnight; the nightmares, Michael, and now Bree and David came crashing down around her like a top-heavy tree on a rain-saturated hill.

In his own innocent way, Bree had been sincere when he had asked her to be his mother. He had been without one all this time. Perhaps this was the root of the sadness she had seen in David's eyes. She hated seeing a family torn apart like this.

Beth struggled to regain her composure, but thinking of Bree made her ache all the more. She lay for a while, pondering what David could've meant when he said he wasn't sorry for the divorce. He was angry, but what about? She snatched a couple of tissues from the box on her nightstand and dried her face.

In all the time he had spent comforting her and Carl, David hadn't once complained about his own pain. She marveled at how different things could look when one took his eyes off himself. Closing her eyes, Beth bowed her head in prayer.

"Lord, I don't really know what David is going through. I don't know what Bree understands about it all. But you do. You love them both more than any of us possibly could. Please give them joy and peace."

EIGHT

David eyed his son curiously as the child, a serious look on his face, trotted over to the leather chair in the living room and climbed up.

"What's the matter, Bree?"

"Can we pray for Beth, Daddy? She misses me bad."

David was pleased his son was learning quite a bit in Sunday school. "It's nice you want to pray for her. Did she ask you to?"

"She crying."

"You mean at the airport when we left? That's pretty normal. It's hard to say good-bye to people you love."

"No, Daddy!" he said. "Tonight…she cry tonight."

Then David remembered that Bree was extremely perceptive for his age, and he now had no doubt his son had sensed Beth's disquiet. He himself had heard it in her voice. But she would never intentionally cause Bree distress—unless she was so troubled she couldn't entirely suppress the source of her anguish.

He slowed his accelerated breathing, determined to hide his concern. "Are you sure she wasn't laughing with you? Laughter sometimes sounds like crying. And you *are* a funny character, you know."

"D-a-d-d-y!"

After much talking and steering the conversation to lighter matters, David finally got Bree calmed, bathed and tucked in for the night.

The evening was finally his. He turned off the lights in the living room, opened the drapes and sat down on the sofa, exhausted. He took pleasure in watching the lighted city just beyond his balcony. It had been too long since he had totally relaxed and enjoyed it. He leaned back against the overstuffed pillows and inhaled the distinctive smell of

Italian leather. Beth would like Seattle, he thought. And he would love showing it to her.

He was relieved the news of his divorce was finally out. Maybe now he could work on doing something about the path his thoughts had taken of late. He couldn't seem to erase the image of Beth sitting in the airport holding Bree. It had looked so perfect. He actually had to look away when he'd returned to the lobby to collect him. He recalled glancing back through the doorway to see her looking small and alone, her arms wrapped around herself. It had taken all his willpower to keep walking.

He had never thought of her in any way except as the kid sister of his best friend. But she wasn't a kid anymore. She was a woman—one, to his amazement, he could easily fall in love with.

David stared at the phone on the lamp table, trying to decide whether to call and see if Bree was imagining things. But Beth would probably be asleep by now. Besides, he couldn't in good conscience put much weight on a child's assessment, despite the boy's unusual sensitivity. Still, he knew Beth's mood had changed after he had told her about the divorce.

David stirred restlessly, his mind infused with visions of her tear-stained face in the woods. His throat constricted, and he felt a dull, empty ache in his gut. He would never upset her, not intentionally. He felt guilty that she'd had to draw out information he should've given over a year ago. Hopefully, she didn't feel deceived, especially after she had shared her own secrets. He would have to call and talk to Carl tomorrow.

"Daddy."

David lifted his head and turned to see his son staggering toward him and rubbing his eyes. "Bree, I thought you were asleep?"

"That well wet in my bed," he said. "Can I sleep with you?"

"What kind of well?" David asked, discreetly checking Bree's pajama bottoms.

"He's big and yellow...and he got jelly all over his face. He eat me like Jonah."

David smiled, making a mental note to watch the stories he read at bedtime. Bree moved to the sofa and climbed up. In one smooth move, he stretched out on his back and laid his head in his father's lap.

"Daddy?"

"Yes, Bree."

"I luvoo."

"I love you, too, Son."

"Is it okay if I love Beth?"

David frowned, wondering where this peculiar line of questioning was going. "Sure it is."

"Is it okay that I asked her to come here?"

"Mmm—hm," David answered, buying time.

"Is it okay I asked her to be my mommy?"

Realizing what was coming out of Bree's mouth, David straightened, his heart skipping a beat. Perhaps this was what had prompted Beth's question.

"When did you do that?"

"At her house," he said, yawning. "Tell me another story, Daddy."

Manny and Beth were once again visiting on the back stoop at the ranch house. Manny leaned back against the top step and glanced over at Beth. "I hear the sheriff paid you a visit about Michael."

"Yeah, he did. I don't think he's all that pleased with me right now, though," Beth said, thinking back to the visit from the sheriff and Leonard. She had been thankful that Carl wasn't present. Leonard had acted a bit skittish, rubbing an old scar on his forehead that he had gotten in school. He had graduated with Lena, and had regularly gotten beat up because of his fondness for racial slurs. Beth was surprised at the time that he didn't seem to mind Shannon spending time with *her*.

After she had answered several routine questions, the two had left her to her thoughts. She had not been asked the reason for the breakup with Michael. This was something else that didn't seem to fit normal behavior. Yet, everyone was simply accepting the sheriff's laxness.

"It's a scary thing. Everybody in town is going on about it. Just like those other two. For his parents' sake, I hope he'll turn up soon."

"Manny?"

"Huh."

"What did you two fight about?"

Avoiding her eyes, Manny looked toward the barn. "Told him not to come round here…is all."

Beth looked at her friend incredulously. All she could think to say was, "Oh."

"I heard the Bakers are having all Mike's personal belongings shipped here," Manny said. "The sheriff told them not to touch anything when it arrives…not until he goes through everything."

Beth's eyes narrowed. "Wonder what he hopes to find? It just seems odd that Michael would disappear so long after Terry and Felix. And right on the heel of Daddy's passing."

NINE

The next day, Beth, her anxiety and apprehension unabated, decided to visit Miss Virgie on her way home from work. She needed the old woman's encouragement, as well as information about what was going on in their community. If anybody would know, Miss Virgie would.

As she made the turn onto Milsap Road, a comment Taylor had made came back to her. *"I've asked Tricia if her secretary could run a paper trail on the history of the ranch for me. Didn't want to send you to the courthouse, knowing that you and the sheriff are at odds."*

She had stood motionless, trying to sound unconcerned. "Why are you getting a history? Is there a problem?"

"Not at all," he said with a smile. "Just curious." And that's all he had said.

Beth turned off the dusty road and into Miss Virgie's yard. The older woman was sitting under a large shade tree. A gigantic maple covered the side and back yards. Miss Virgie was shelling peas in a pan that rested in her lap. The sandy clearing beneath the tree looked cool and inviting.

Beth sat in the car, quietly surveying her surroundings, wrinkling her brow ever so slightly. Chester, the old gray hound, slowly dragged himself from beneath the house. She giggled as she listened to his long mournful bellow.

"Little slow, huh, Chester?"

The large structure was set on bulky cement blocks and was high enough off the ground to serve as a storage space, as well as a cool refuge for dogs. Her quiet giggle turned into hearty laughter as Chester suddenly lost interest in her and moved off toward the open field just beyond the yard.

"Elizabeth! You gonna sit out there in the sun, or come help me shell these peas?"

As usual, Miss Virgie had a large wad of tobacco packed into her jaw. The woman's antiquated habits could still surprise Beth, but she always enjoyed the special way she felt in her presence.

Beth got out of the car and hurried toward the tree, pausing a moment when she saw the large ugly stick Miss Virgie used as a cane. In spite of differences, it reminded her of her father's smooth brown cane with the silver handle and wide rubber tip. Her brother had taken to using it since graduating from his crutches.

Beth moved toward the lawn chair and bent down to kiss the woman on the cheek. "Hey, Miss Virgie, how ya doing?"

"Doing just fine, baby. Been missing y'all since Carl come off them crutches. How you getting along?"

Beth dragged a chair closer to the woman, put some of the green vegetables into the lap of her navy skirt, and began shelling them into the pan Miss Virgie held.

"We could always use your help, Miss Virgie. You know that."

"Carl still limping around there pulling on Lena's pity?"

Beth grinned and gazed into the woman's face. "Yeah, he is."

"What are you doing out here, gal?"

"I just thought it was about time to pay one of my favorite people a visit."

"O hush your foolin," she said, throwing her head back in laughter. Beth couldn't figure out how she did that without tobacco juice sliding down her throat and strangling her.

She sat for a while, making small talk and thoroughly enjoying the woman whose laughter shook her entire body. When there was a lull in the conversation, Beth began her inquiry.

"Miss Virgie, why don't people speak up about the problems out here with the law?"

"I was wondering when you'd start asking questions. But you might as well talk plain with me, Elizabeth Ann."

"What do you mean?"

"Did you know I help bring you into this world?"

Beth had heard the story a hundred times, ninety-eight of those from Miss Virgie herself. Her father had been away ministering or hauling horses, and her mother couldn't get to the hospital. Carl had gone to fetch Miss Virgie on horseback.

"Yes, ma'am. But…"

"Even though you was born veiled, you didn't give your ma a bit of trouble. Just came on like you was s'pose to."

Beth closed her fingers around one of the unshelled beans. "I've always heard you mention a veil when you tell me about this, Miss Virgie. What exactly does that mean?"

"Your folks didn't tell you 'bout your gifting?" she asked, her voice taking on a conspiratorial lilt.

"I don't remember anything like that. What does it mean?"

"Honey, you come with the sac…saw it with my own eyes. Ol' folks say that's a sign of blessin'. You a special gift from God to your folks. And if the truth be told, to this here community, too."

Beth knew the story of her birth, but had never understood this part—never thought it significant enough to ask. A strange giddiness came over her. It reminded her of the things David had told her about being able to hear God's whispers.

Beth grunted cynically, thinking of the long ago words of Mr. Tubbs. "With so much going on around here, for a while I thought I was a curse."

"Curse?" The old woman gawked at her in disbelief and chuckled aloud. "What kind of fool idea is that?"

Beth glanced at the woman out of the corner of her eye. "I heard tell that some folk thought I was cursed, I mean."

"Some folk weren't there. I was," Miss Virgie said. "Nah, baby, you blessed. God put a special knack in you. He gives us all knacks, but some never grow in 'em."

She leaned forward, straining to see the older woman's eyes. "I don't understand."

"You got a knowing in you, child. Ain't you ever noticed your spirit knowing thangs your head don't?"

Beth suddenly felt as if a million butterflies had been let loose in her stomach. She was so relieved to hear those particular words a girlish giggle rose up in her throat. She wanted to leap and dance and sing, all at once. But she wasn't sure why she hadn't felt that way when David told her practically the same thing. She suppressed all the tangled sensations so that she wouldn't miss one word Miss Virgie had to say.

"That knowing…how do I get it to my head? What am I…"

"Folks out here generally don't trust the sheriff because of all the bad treatment some have gotten. Best to just pray and stand clear if you can."

As usual, Miss Virgie jumped subjects so quickly, Beth couldn't focus on the other questions she had. For an instant, she had actually forgotten why she was there. Reluctantly, she returned to her original intent, which was exactly where the woman's train of thought had gone. She made a mental note to shelve the *knowing* questions until later.

"Do you believe bad things happen in cycles?"

"Sometimes they do. But God is still on the throne, baby. Nothing sneaks up on Him."

"With Michael coming up missing like he did, I'm having a hard time sleeping at night. It's just so aggravating how bad things are happening all around us and nobody's doing anything about it."

"You sound just like your daddy," she said, shaking her head. "It's aggravating, all right."

"Manny thinks the sheriff doesn't investigate black folks' cases. But he can't do that if nobody out here will talk with him."

Miss Virgie had always had a funny way of selecting what she heard or chose to answer. Today was no different. Before Beth could get an answer, she had reverted to the previous subject.

"You got to be still before the Lord, child. Your gift—that knowing on the inside—is on the move. You got hurt and pulled away from

God. You need to move back. Things ain't right out here in Plover Creek, and God intends to fix it. I been praying."

"But how?"

"You need to hear God and get on with living, Elizabeth," she said. "You young folks can do a lot more than us older ones could. With *your* eyes and your brother's wit, you can make this a livable community again."

"What do you mean?" Beth asked, more anxious than she had been before she came. "What am I supposed to do?"

"Your daddy died before his time, Elizabeth. Both you and Carl are part of him," she said. "You better get on home now and fix your brother's supper."

Beth hesitated, feeling more confused than ever. She frowned, trying to remember the questions she had put on hold. But somehow, they didn't seem to matter now. When the old woman began humming a hymn, Beth knew it was a form of dismissal and stood to leave.

After supper, she showered and crawled into bed early. But her mind kept rehashing the old woman's words. After running everything through her mind again and again, Beth found herself wondering what she meant by "they could do more." And why had she said that her dad had died before his time?

Could she be suggesting something sinister about her dad's death, too? Beth rejected the notion, realizing that she was probably letting her overactive imagination run rampant. She frowned. But Miss Virgie didn't have much imagination, much less an overactive one. Her misgivings about her dad's death didn't seem so silly now.

Despite having let it slip out to the sheriff, she knew she would have to keep quiet until she found a more logical motive of some sort. And she was grateful Taylor and Tricia were obligated to consider her discussion with them confidential. Once she got some real evidence, she would approach Carl.

Beth fluffed her pillow, lay back and began to pray. "Lord, I repent for staying distant from you so long. I feel lost and scared. I'm not sure why I'm so curious about all that's going on. But I assume you're leading me to question things, to dig at them. Everyone says I need to be still before you. I guess you already know I don't feel comfortable with that. But I will. I just need you to show me how."

The phone rang just as she started dozing off and she reached for it without opening her eyes. After a foggy salutation, her eyes flew open at the sound of David's voice.

"Beth?"

She instantly sprang up in bed. "Is Bree okay?"

"Bree's fine," he said with a light chuckle. "I called to talk to you."

"Obviously," she said with a yawn that popped her jaw.

"I wanted to apologize for keeping y'all in the dark about me and Deidre. I didn't want to add to your distress. I figured you guys had enough on your minds."

"I sure wish you and Carl would stop trying to protect me," she snapped.

Beth heard a slight intake of breath and inwardly chided herself for sounding surly. She had blundered, she thought in despair. She hadn't wanted her anguish to surface like that.

"There's really no need to apologize," she continued, softening her tone. "The news just took me by surprise. I was more bowled over that Carl didn't know, considering you guys talk so often."

"I don't think you understand," he said hesitantly. "My reasoning for keeping it a secret had more to do with ego than anything."

"What?"

"Deidre was…well, she was seeing someone else, and my ego was involved. It's not an easy thing to admit. Not even to close friends." He paused. "I know I'll have to forgive her at some point. But it's not easy. Even after all this time. I've been praying about that."

"I know. Sometimes forgiveness is the hardest thing to give. Even when you know better." Understanding seemed to swell between them through the line. "What about Bree?"

"Deidre's friend didn't want children. They live somewhere in Canada now. I haven't seen or spoken to her since she left."

"That's pretty rough on him, I'm sure. Not to mention what you've gone through. If Carl and I had only been aware, we could've offered some sort of support. Just knowing you have people in your corner sometimes is a help."

"I know," he said. "And I'm sorry. I did talk to Carl earlier today. He really said some things that helped. But Bree and I are doing all right now. I'm very grateful that he seems to have gotten used to her not being here. As I said, it's been over a year."

"What happened between you two?"

She could almost feel the anguish infusing his brief pause. "A lot of things. It had been coming for a while. I just ignored all the warning signs, hoping they would work themselves out."

"I see," she said, puzzled.

"Deidre wasn't really a believer, so her ideas were...well, different."

"Ideas about what?"

"About marriage, for one," David answered. "I found out about her affair by accident, really. I was supposed to fly out one evening, but the plane had some problems. I didn't have a chance to call, so she wasn't expecting me back home. When I arrived, she was...entertaining. Bree was at the sitter's. She at least had the decency to keep him away from it all. Or maybe her companion couldn't stand the sound of my child."

Hearing the hurt in his voice was distressing, and she yearned to say something to comfort him. But what? She didn't know anything about having a relationship. Not a real one.

"I'm sorry you had to go through that. It must be hard. Bree is still just a baby."

"I honestly never realized how hard it would be raising him alone. I love my son and don't regret for one minute that I have him. It's amazing that something so good can come from something that's not. I-I just don't want the divorce to have any negative affects on him."

"It's already affected him," she said, wishing she hadn't the moment the words were out. "I'm sorry. But you can see that he's craving attention."

"I know. But we just couldn't hold it together after he was born. She never wanted children, and blamed me when she accidentally got pregnant. I wouldn't let her abort him. Things went downhill from there."

Beth heard a pause and the faint cry in the background. "Beth, I've gotta go. Thanks for listening. I'll see you in a couple of days."

She hung up the phone, enjoying the excitement she felt at seeing Bree again. But then, she found herself wondering if it was actually Bree's father she was so anxious to see.

TEN

It was the last Friday in June. Beth had awakened with a vague sense of something weighing on her mind. She finally zeroed in on exactly what was plaguing her. It was the anticipated visit of David and Bree. She wondered whether she could actually be falling in love with her brother's best friend.

After work, Beth was in the supermarket working her way down Lena's shopping list when to her surprise, she saw Leonard Ware strolling down the aisle toward her. She was stunned that he actually walked through the busy store with a smile on his face. As he came closer, he took off his hat and looked directly into her eyes. Leonard rarely smiled. And he never looked anyone straight in the eye.

Her jaw dropped and she froze in place. Leonard had never had a lot to say to her, not even when she was at his home visiting his sister, Shannon. After awkwardly stammering a greeting, he came right out with what he wanted to say. "I hear you've placed your property on the market. George mentioned that he'd be mighty interested in making an offer."

Beth frowned, confused. "Actually, we never placed it on the market, and Carl already talked to George. In fact, he bought Daddy's truck, trailers and the remaining horses. Didn't he tell you? My boss is buying the property."

Leonard's eyes registered surprise. He leaned against the shelving as if the wind had been knocked out of him. "Nah. He didn't say a word to me about it. You mean he don't want the land anymore?"

Beth shrugged and placed the jar she'd been holding into her basket. "He seemed pretty satisfied with what he got," she said, curious about his jerky movements. "Leonard, are you all right?"

"How long ago did he buy the horses?"

"A couple of weeks. When's the last time you talked to him? I saw him just yesterday driving the pickup. He was hauling one of the trailers behind it, too."

"I can't believe this. George tells me to make sure y'all know he wants first dibs, and I find out he's already talked to ya. Don't that beat all? And he's satisfied, you say?"

"He seemed to be."

The veins in Leonard's neck stood out in tight ridges. The more he mumbled to himself, the more agitated he became. She casually moved her cart a little past him.

"Thanks, anyway, for inquiring, Leonard. We were really stretched and glad to unload it. By the way, have y'all found out anything more about Michael's disappearance?"

"Nah," he answered, his mind obviously elsewhere. "What does he aim to do with it? Your boss, I mean."

"He's planning to make quite a few changes actually, but I'm really not at liberty to discuss them."

"I'm sorry," he mumbled, lowering his head. "I-I didn't mean to pry. I was just so sure George would buy it."

Beth gave the man a long, searching look, wondering why he seemed so disturbed about a transaction that had nothing to do with him. "Once he found out somebody else had placed the contract on it, he seemed satisfied."

"So it ain't completely sold?" New hope sprang into his face. She wanted to let it go at that, but couldn't bring herself to mislead him needlessly.

"Well, *technically* it hasn't changed hands, but…"

"I guess I'll let you get back to your shopping," he said, slapping the hat back down on his head. "I know you probably getting ready for the big shindig everybody's talking about. I'll be seein' ya."

Leonard quickly walked back down the aisle and disappeared before she could say another word. He could be so strange at times, she thought.

Fifteen minutes later, Beth was placing her bags into the trunk when she noticed Leonard sitting in his pickup watching her. Suddenly, he pulled out of the parking lot and headed back toward the town square. Still puzzled by their exchange in the store, she shook her head, closed the trunk and started for home.

The trees were a vibrant green, thanks to the rain. Water stood four feet high in the trenches on either side of the country road. It made twin canals, evoking a surreal feeling as she sped toward the ranch. The sun shone against a gentle breeze, taunting the emptiness of her soul. She was lonely. But she didn't want to give in to it. Not now.

Her mind traveled back to Bree, and her spirit soared. They were due in tonight. She had already purchased two new children's books, and couldn't wait to read them to him. She smiled as she reflected on the child's sweet nature.

"Oh, Lord," she whispered. "Is it possible for David to care about me in the way I'm beginning to care about him? I would love to have a family of my own."

She began to sing along as the radio blasted her favorite tune. Finding out Bree had been without a mother for so long made her feel even more maternal toward him. She enjoyed the feeling—she needed it. She only hoped she wasn't letting her concern confuse her into thinking she was falling in love with David. But it was obvious Deidre wasn't concerned at all. According to David, she had been gone over a year without any contact.

Passing the road leading to Tatum's pond, Beth remembered the times she and David had gone fishing there. Even though they had two ponds on the ranch, they weren't stocked. She heard the sound of thunder in the distance, and her stomach tightened with uneasiness. She looked up at the sky, but it gave no sign of an approaching storm. Perhaps she had imagined the sound.

Hold firmly to the faith you profess.

The quiet words floated into her mind, startling her. Beth's car suddenly lunged forward, just as a deer sprang into its path. She instinctively slammed on the brakes, swinging wildly to miss the animal. The car spun out of control toward the cement guardrail.

A sense of helplessness closed in on her as she fought to keep the car on the road. It came to an abrupt stop on the edge of the opposite side, causing her head to slam against the steering wheel. She could tell the rear end was hanging off the edge between a gap in the rail. She could barely move her head and found herself fighting to stay conscious.

Gradually, the car started sliding downward. Fear rose in her throat as she screamed out, shielding her head with her arms. Her eyes were tightly closed, but Beth could feel the rotations as the car flipped down the embankment and into the water. She could hear the sounds of crunching metal and breaking glass.

When the car stopped tumbling, it was right side up in the trench fifteen feet below the road. The smell of wet grass mixed with gasoline drifted past her nostrils. Cool water rushed in over her ankles. Though dazed, she could tell that the steering wheel had her wedged against the door. She tried to turn her head toward the sound of someone calling her name. But she was unable to move, and was too confused to make out who was calling to her.

Her head hurt, and everything was spinning in slow motion. She tried to reach her cell phone, but it was like bumping around in the dark.

Hold firmly to the faith you profess.

"I'll hold," she whispered, as darkness closed in around her.

"*Beth!*"

It sounded more like an echo this time. Beth forced open her eyes; the brightness was blinding.

"David?"

There was no answer. Was she dreaming? Had David come to rescue her? She *had* heard her name.

The water was so cool on her feet. Had she gotten everything on Lena's list? The shrill sound of a scream recurred in her consciousness and she instinctively began to struggle. "No…no."

"It's okay, Beth," Carl said, gently squeezing her against him. "Calm down. I'm right here."

"Carl?" She opened her eyes to find a blurry figure looming against her, holding her. Inadvertently, she drew back.

"You're all right."

She reached anxiously for his face and pulled it toward her. "Help me. Make it stop." She struggled to swallow, knowing she had to make Carl understand that she was in danger. He didn't act as if he could even hear her.

"You're okay, honey. Lie back."

"No," she said firmly. "Still moving. Hold me still."

Carl lowered the metal rail and sat on the side of the bed. He put his arms back around his sister. "Sh, sh. You're all right now."

Beth closed her eyes against the excruciating pain. It felt good to have someone she trusted close by. She was tired, and the room wouldn't stop spinning. "Don't leave me?"

"Beth, you're safe. You're at the hospital."

"Where's David?"

"He'll be here soon."

"Where am I?"

"County General. You've been in an accident. Lena called me the instant you were brought in. She was wailing like a siren."

"Let's go home," Beth said, squeezing her eyes shut against the nausea. "I don't want to stay here."

Carl gently squeezed her. "Beth, why are you so frightened? You've got to calm down."

Her stomach finally settled and her vision began to clear. She could feel herself relax a little more. "I'm okay?"

"You gave me quite a scare, Sis," he said, gently stroking her shoulder. "I don't know what I'd do if something happened to you right now."

Beth lay back then and let a lazy smile light her face. "Would next month do?"

He chuckled, happy to hear her wit again. "The next hundred years would be even better."

"A deer…jumped right out of nowhere," she said, straining to remember. "Bumped my head. It hurts."

"I know. You have a slight concussion."

"Did I hurt anybody, Carl?"

"Nah. Leonard said you swerved to miss the deer and ended right side up in the ditch, but nobody else was involved."

"Leonard?"

"He was coming down the road behind you. He saw the whole thing."

"Are you sure?" she asked, feeling her stomach lurch. "I thought…I thought I saw him going…Are you sure I'm all right?"

"Of course, I'm sure. Now why don't you try and get some real rest? It's a good thing Leonard was there. As low as those trenches are, you could have been down there unnoticed for days. He and a passer-by pulled you out after the car flipped. You have a concussion and a couple of bruised ribs where you banged up against the steering wheel. Your face is a little uglier than usual, too. But you're alive and safe."

"Ugly!" she shrieked, despite the lingering headache.

"Just making sure you were listening," Carl said, placing a kiss on her forehead. "You're very fortunate. God was looking out for you."

"I think I heard Him, Carl. Right before the accident. I think I heard words…more like felt them than anything. I can't remember exactly what they were. But I heard Him."

Carl gazed at her, a puzzled look on his face. "Heard who?"

"God."

"Okay, honey," he said, pushing her shoulders back down onto the bed. "The doctors want to keep you a couple of days."

"No!" she said, struggling to sit up. "I wanna go home. I promised Bree…"

Once again, Carl placed a restraining hand on his sister's shoulder. "I'll take you tomorrow, then. But you'll stay here tonight. Now lie there and be quiet."

"Carl—"

"Beth, use wisdom. You've been in a car accident."

She lay back and closed her eyes against the burning tears, submitting to her brother's instructions. "But I wanted to be home when Bree and David got there."

Carl wiped away the trail of tears that had reached her ears. "Don't worry. You'll see them tomorrow."

"Do you love Lena?" she asked. He sat back down on his sister's bed and gently brushed the hair back from her face as if giving himself time to come up with an answer. Her eyes never left his face. He looked content and happy.

"Very much," he said. "For a long time now."

Squinting in the bright lights, she asked, "Why didn't you tell her? Why didn't you tell *me*?"

"I thought you would think it inappropriate."

"I'm not a child, you big ape. I know ministers are human. And why should you care what I think?"

"I've always cared about what you thought, little sister."

"It means a lot to hear you say that," she said. She suddenly felt sleepy again, and her thoughts were becoming confused.

"You sacrificed so many things to come back home and take care of Dad. I've been so preoccupied with things that I hadn't realized your engagement was one of them until Mike disappeared."

She squeezed her eyes shut. "That was no sacrifice, Carl. It was over before I came home." She inhaled carefully and slowly reopened her eyes. "To be honest, I didn't just come home to take care of Daddy. I sort of *ran* home."

David walked through the door of the small private room and glanced around. He felt like a man on the verge of madness. His stomach was in knots after stopping by Manny's to see the damage done to her car. He was certain she was more injured than Carl had let on.

It was only by the grace of God that she'd gotten out of that car alive. He frowned as he thought of the mangled wreck. There was something more unsettling about it—something he couldn't quite put his finger on.

Carl had warned him that Beth would probably be knocked out until morning, but he didn't care. He had to come. He blinked as he scanned the room. It was quiet and dimly lit. Muted tones of coral adorned the walls and window. He examined her soft features, wincing at the sight of the bruises marring them. It was quite unnerving seeing her so still. Her arms had cuts and bruises, too. These were minor blemishes considering what she had been through. They would heal, but he hated seeing her hurt, be it physically or emotionally. He never wanted her to hurt again.

Seeing her this way made the nightmare he'd had about her being in some kind of danger seem that much more real. He leaned in close and tenderly brushed a stray wisp of hair from her face. The fuzzy shadow her lashes made against her cheek resembled the smudges beneath the eyes of a quarterback.

On impulse, he bent and kissed her forehead. Suddenly, the core of his affection spilled out, seemingly swallowing him alive. He stepped back, stunned by his response. He had to get a hold of himself. Beth was obviously and understandably dear to him, but he was clearly letting his desperate need to find a mother for Bree distort his thinking.

"Beth!"

He almost felt foolish whispering her name. But somehow it calmed him. She was his best friend's sister, his adoptive parents' daughter, which somehow made her untouchable. His beautiful caged butterfly. She had always produced a protective posture in him. He felt it now. It would likely tear him apart if he were required to let her fly away.

"What's going on in that pretty head of yours?" he whispered, ignoring her swollen and bruised face. Very gently, David brushed kisses on her cheek, her nose and her chin. He watched the peacefulness of her sleep, wishing she would open her eyes and argue with him. Carefully lifting one of her hands, he kissed her fingertips. After a few moments, he sank into the chair beside the bed and whispered a prayer.

Physical and emotional fatigue brought out the headache he had been fighting. He closed his eyes and leaned back on the chair. Just for a minute, he told himself. He was simply worn out, his energy utterly depleted.

He was tired of being alone and angry, tired of mistrusting women. He thought of Natalie in Seattle, who had tried without success to build a relationship from a friendship. She was an attractive woman, and smart, too. But he just wasn't interested in her that way. He hadn't allowed himself to become vulnerable to another woman since Deidre. It was as if his heart was sewn up and unyielding to the opposite sex.

He had wondered many times if discouraging Natalie's advances had been a mistake. But after the divorce he had vowed to never again become involved in a relationship in which Christ was not at its center. Although Natalie professed to be a believer, she didn't seem to live like one. Somehow his oath seemed to keep romantic avenues completely out of his range. Besides, unlike Beth, Natalie wasn't the nurturing type. He certainly had to think of his son.

He chuckled a little under his breath. How in the world had Beth gotten through that hard core of his? Maybe she hadn't. Maybe he was just confused.

Suddenly, Beth began to stir restlessly, making sounds as if she was frightened or in pain. He sprang to her side and placed a hand over hers.

"Beth, it's David. I'm here. Rest."

He stood there gazing helplessly into her face. Maybe his ties to the family had already placed Beth there in his heart. Without conscious thought, he once again brushed his lips against her chafed cheek. She remained quiet.

"Please give her peace, Lord…from whatever might be troubling her."

Just as David decided that it was time to leave, Beth called out his name in her sleep. It had come out in such a soft murmur he'd almost missed it. He froze in stunned silence, wondering if he had only imagined it. Why would she call his name in a drug-induced state, one in which she had to literally fight to withdraw?

On the ride home, he let his mind drift back to Beth talking in her sleep as a child. But somehow his heart wanted this to be different. He thought of how she had looked up to him as much as she had to Carl. It had done more to make him feel alive after the death of his family than anything else.

He reflected on the time he and Beth had gone fishing in the pond on the far northwest side of the ranch. Although there were no fish in it, they had gone. It was one of those times Manny hadn't been with them, and she had fallen in. She'd screamed his name as if she thought the very sound of it would save her from drowning. That's when he'd decided to teach her to swim.

He had been the first one she told when she became interested in her first beau. He smiled, thinking of all the questions she had asked him, such as what she should do if the boy tried to kiss her.

Maybe he was making too much of her calling out his name. Her subconscious mind was probably responding to his having spoken to her moments earlier. Still, he couldn't let it go. For some strange reason, the very idea made his hopes soar.

He smiled, remembering how gentle Clara McDade had been in trying to curb her daughter's unpredictable nature. But Beth was never much in the house around her mother. Clara was frequently ill, and Beth being a bit of a tomboy had grown up without many of the gentle qualities one normally finds in little girls.

Being a part of a pastor's family had been hard on both Beth and Carl. After losing his own parents to a fire, David had managed to escape *that* particular impasse. He had grown up fast in many way and hadn't struggled to overcome the typical 'preacher kid' syndrome like Carl and Beth. He laughed out loud now as he drove Carl's pickup through the gates of the ranch. Beth had been so annoying back then, so demanding. And on several occasions, he had been tempted to brush her off. But he just hadn't had the heart to do it.

Had it not been for Ray and Clara McDade's kindness, he could be just about anywhere now. Being a part of their household had been his salvation in many ways. Now, he found himself wanting to be a real family member. Walking into that hospital room had clinched it in his mind.

Perhaps he had already fallen in love with Elizabeth Ann McDade.

ELEVEN

Beth opened her eyes and immediately shut them again. The brightness was blinding and painful. Her head felt as if someone had clobbered her with a baseball bat. Her muscles ached, and it hurt to take deep breaths. When she re-opened her eyes, she saw the worried face of her best friend.

"Hey, Manny," she said, reaching for his hand. "Where's David?"

"Stayed at the house with Bree."

Lena breezed in and shooed Manny and Carl out so Beth could get dressed. A little while later, they were all in the car headed for the ranch. Relieved to get away from the hospital, Beth put her head back and in no time had dozed off. When she awakened, David was lifting her from the car.

She shook her head gently. "Put me down. I can walk."

David smiled down at her. "I know. But this might be the only way we can be sure you won't overdo it."

Manny quickly moved to open the front door while Carl and Lena remained outside. Their blank stares made her feel exposed. Were her feelings written all over her face?

"Where's Bree?" she whispered, glancing around expectantly.

"Upstairs playing with a toy truck. I asked him to stay put until we got you settled."

The minute they entered the house, the familiar aroma of home hit Beth full in the face. She inhaled deeply, relishing the moment. Even though she had been gone just overnight, she was relieved to be back in her own home. A comforting sense of security and devotion swept over her, and her body shook involuntarily.

"You okay?" David said, pausing in his tracks.

Suddenly feeling exhausted, she relaxed in his arms. "Just good to be home."

"It's good to have you home."

Manny rushed up the stairs ahead of them. "I'll make sure your room is ready."

"Thanks, Manny," David said, holding Beth's gaze. "I know you're your own woman. But surely you can let us take care of you for a couple of days. Besides, Bree is anxious to see you."

Beth ambled over to her bedroom window the instant David put her down. She was still a little unsteady on her feet, and tried to hide a near stumble. Carl and Lena were on the front lawn locked in a passionate kiss. She felt a hint of envy, but resisted it. Her brother and Lena deserved to be happy.

"I'll go check on the horses," Manny called, heading back downstairs.

"I'll see you later," Beth said without turning.

Sensing rather than seeing that David was very near, Beth closed her eyes and held her breath.

"He's more content than I've seen him in years," David said, glancing out over her shoulder. The warmth of his breath tickled the hairs on her neck.

"I know," she said quietly. "Lena, too, I think."

David's hands settled on the tense muscles of her shoulders. Again, she shuddered involuntarily. "Beth?"

She closed her eyes, enjoying the way his breath made her hair dance around her ear. "Hmm."

"Are you in any pain?"

She turned, alert to his grave tone. "Not a lot," she said, frowning. "It's dulled by the meds they gave me."

David very gently drew her into his arms. She felt a prickle of intense expectation as she placed a finger on the cleft in his chin. "Would it hurt if I kissed your lips?"

Beth's heart hammered in her chest. Her skin tingled everywhere his body touched hers. The unexpected appeal had not only surprised her, it had also answered a precise longing. Without a single word, she lifted her chin and accepted a very gentle, very warm kiss. She relaxed in his arms, sensing a restrained storm pulsing through him. The tenderness of his touch seemed to silence a long-standing craving.

David slowly guided her toward the bed. "Now, Miss McDade, you should follow doctor's orders and rest. Shall I send Bree in?" Having glimpsed her reflection in the bathroom mirror at the hospital, Beth hesitantly looked up at him. Her face was discolored and swollen. David playfully rubbed the wrinkled spot between her brows. "What's that?"

"Bree. Don't you think my appearance will frighten him?"

"Nah," he said with a smile. "I've already explained."

Shortly, Bree tiptoed through the doorway. Beth noted his restrained manner and assumed David had cautioned him to be extra careful. He crept over to the side of the bed and gently touched her cheek.

"There's my little big man."

"You hurt bad, Beth," he whispered, peering into her face. "I kiss and make it better. Okay?" He carefully climbed up on the bed and kissed her face. "I luvoo."

"I love you, too, Bree."

"Can I lay down with you?" he asked hopefully. "I be careful."

Beth pulled the covers back and let Bree scoot in beside her. After a moment, she picked up the remote and clicked the television on to the cartoon station. He lay quietly and watched without any fidgeting. It probably took everything in him to lie still like that, she thought affectionately. She leaned down to kiss his curly top.

She closed her eyes and willed the tears of sadness away. She could literally feel the yearning and love he had for her. It pained her to think he had been starving for the attention of a mother figure for so long. She gently squeezed him to her and once again kissed the top of his head. To her amazement, he had already fallen asleep.

David shaded his eyes from the late afternoon sun and squinted at Taylor, who rode beside him out into the open meadow. Rusty snorted and wiggled an ear as a large fly flitted around it.

The two men had brought along rifles and were being watchful of anything out of the ordinary. An unusual sound or reflected flash of metal would be enough for them to take defensive measures.

Manny had volunteered to check out the spot they believed the shooter had been in, but David couldn't quite dismiss his misgivings about the man. He had been wondering if he had anything to do with Mike's disappearance. After all, Manny knew everything about Mike's attack on Beth in Austin.

Beth had rejected the idea of telling the sheriff about it. Everyone knew Manny was protective toward her, and the sheriff would unquestionably consider him a suspect if foul play had occurred. David didn't want to tell her that. Knowing Beth, she would throw herself right in the middle of things. He had learned from the sheriff that Mike hadn't come to Plover Creek that often, and when he did, he stayed close to home. What if Manny snapped and did something to him?

Wariness and suspicion stalked him like an unseen enemy. He thought about the condition of Beth's car. He knew Manny wouldn't hurt her. Not intentionally, anyway. But there was just too much going on around her. He wondered if he and Carl could be wrong about George. He felt awful about what he was thinking, but decided he'd better keep his eyes on both Manny and George. *Keep her safe, Lord.*

"This is a beautiful piece of real estate," Taylor said, jolting David from his silent prayer. "I'm very fortunate to have known about it before it went on the market."

"Did you contact any surveyors?"

"S&J. They should be out here in a week or so. With the creek, ponds and the woods, they think it might take a couple of weeks to complete."

"Sounds about right. You'll have that extra acreage across the creek as well," David said, pointing southward. Immediately, his mind went back to Beth and her private retreat.

David half-listened to Taylor repeat his plans as they rode across the meadow. Out of the corner of his eye, he could see Carl driving alongside the fenced boundary in the pickup. Manny was riding toward Carl from the opposite direction on Aster, one of the remaining stallions.

The July sun was blistering hot, making David wish he was back at the house sharing a glass of iced tea with Beth. Despite the lack of substantial content, he had enjoyed their little chats of late. He simply took pleasure in being near her. He enjoyed taking care of her, too—a difficult task with someone like Beth. He'd already decided that he and Bree would stay home from church tomorrow so she wouldn't be alone.

He thought of the moment he heard her call out his name in the hospital. Then his mind moved to the kiss upon her return home. His own daring had surprised him, as did Beth's response. He prayed beyond hope that her feelings for him mirrored his for her.

He wondered about her stubborn ways. Perhaps that self-sufficient mindset was typical in rape victims, but she had once been so naïve and free. The innocence that had made Beth so appealing now placed her at a disadvantage. And now she harbored a lot of bitterness against both George and Mike. Although she had her reasons, he knew embracing resentments like that could be self-destructive. Something he was finally coming to grips with in regard to Deidre.

Frowning, he remembered something Carl had told him. Beth had been terrified out of her head when she had first awakened in the hospital. Was it the wreck that had frightened her? Her notions about Ray's death probably needed to be reassessed in light of the shooting and her accident. But Carl would likely think he was giving in to her suspicious nature. Maybe he would speak to Carl, anyway, about broaching the subject with Taylor.

He had promised Beth that he would watch over her that afternoon on the ridge. He had meant it. And the more he thought about it, the more he wanted to make it so. He laughed inwardly at his present train of thought, feeling a little absurd for being so dramatic. But he couldn't seem to stop his flow of affection for Beth. Despite her response to his kiss, would she welcome the way he really felt about her?

"What do you think, David?" Taylor asked, watching him curiously.

"About what?"

Taylor laughed out loud. "Where have you been? I was asking if you thought we could put some type of bridge across that creek and make it a usable asset."

"Oh, I'm sure we can," David said, a little embarrassed. "That *would* be a nice feature."

Taylor lifted a speculative eyebrow. "Someplace nice, I hope."

"Pardon?"

"Wherever you were—I hope it was someplace nice."

"It was very nice," he said, envisioning one of Beth's radiant smiles.

The men rode back to the house and went over the plans for another hour at the dining room table. Taylor had several changes he wanted to make and a barrage of questions. He left for Dallas just after looking in on a sleeping Beth.

Lena was busy preparing dinner and keeping an eye on Bree, who had to be restrained from popping in on Beth every few minutes.

Later, David quietly entered her room and sat in the rocker next to her bed. He watched the movement beneath her closed eyelids. Despite the harsh bruises, she appeared very soft. Very beautiful. God had truly watched over her in the accident. He scowled as he thought of her car tumbling down that embankment. That was enough to terrify anyone.

He glanced around the spacious room, seeing a reflection of Beth in its décor. Although the furniture was made of red oak, the four-piece ensemble wasn't bulky. The comforter was the color of sage, as were the pillows in the rocker he occupied. The curtains that fanned about the window were made of old-fashioned white lace.

When he had come in to collect Bree for supper the night before, both he and Beth were asleep. He smiled thoughtfully. They had been serenely snuggled together—like two best friends.

"Hey," she said sleepily, opening her eyes. "These meds keeps me too out of it."

"That's good," he said. "You need your rest."

"I know, but I don't think I'll take anymore. I want to be ready for the party on Monday."

"How do you feel?"

She yawned. "Like somebody hit me with a cement snowball. What are you doing in here?"

"Watching you sleep."

"I'm sure you have better things to do." Her delicate smile revealed dimples and sent a silent signal straight to his heart. "Where's Bree?"

"Lena has him tied to her apron down in the kitchen," he said, noting her inquisitive mood. "You need something for pain?"

"Nah. I'll be fine. How did Taylor like the plans?"

"He's got a few changes. I'll make them and e-mail them in about a week."

Despite her obvious grogginess, her eyes shone with an energy he hadn't seen in a while. "You really enjoy what you do, don't you?"

"Very much." He leaned forward and smiled back at her. "It was your mother who encouraged me to pursue it. She was a great listener. Why do you ask?"

She slowly sat up and leaned against the headboard, leaving the pillows at the small of her back. "Just curious, I guess. I'm glad you love what you do. That's important, I think."

"You can still do anything you want to, you know. You're still quite young. Me, I guess I was born with this in my blood. Remember how I used to sketch everything in sight?"

David stood and went over to the window, pulled back the lacy curtain and glanced down into the front yard. It was plush and green. He smiled knowingly, recognizing Beth's passionate handiwork with the flowerbeds. It would be hard for her to see it change hands. He could only imagine what Carl was feeling.

As he turned to walk back to the chair, his eyes were drawn to a framed picture on the wall above her chest of drawers. He walked over to it and took it down, looking into the innocent face of an eight-year-old girl with pigtails, sitting by the pond with a fishing pole. Her smile was faint, but the dimples were there. He had sketched it a long time ago.

He turned to comment that he was surprised she had kept the drawing, but she had already fallen asleep, her head resting against the headboard. He re-hung the drawing, walked back to Beth's bedside and pulled the cover back up around her shoulders. Unable to resist the quiet moment, he got down on his knees beside her.

"Thank you for protecting her, Lord," he whispered. "Please help her find her way." He looked at Beth's closed eyes and whispered to her subconscious. "I'm hoping you can find room in your heart for me, Beth."

Just as David lightly pressed a kiss to her lips, Bree strolled through the door. "Daddy!"

"Shh," David whispered, placing a finger over his lips. "She's asleep."

"I kiss her too, Daddy," Bree said, already racing toward the bed. David scooped him up just before he reached it and quickly carried him out of the room.

TWELVE

On the day of the big celebration, Beth put away the pain medication. She was still very sore, but she would gladly tolerate the pain in exchange for consciousness. She had always hated taking pills. Even the vitamins her mother had insisted she take had ended up in the trash.

With Lena's help, she covered the remaining bruises with just the right touch of makeup. She was even able to briefly move among their two hundred guests at the cookout. She was unwilling to challenge David and Carl any further by mingling too much, but it was nice to see so many old classmates and former neighbors.

Michael's disappearance had turned her mind even more to all those in the community who had been lost, including Leonard's sister, Shannon, Charla, Terry, and Felix, too. And Ray McDade, though she'd be the only one to add her dad to the list. Why hasn't somebody else seen the disturbing coincidences and alarming possibilities and investigate them?

There was an eeriness about it all. And it bothered her to no end that nobody except herself was willing to do any probing into these troubling events. It was not lost on her that Carl and David had avoided mentioning Ray's death to her. Maybe that was as it should be. She didn't intend telling them that she had talked to Taylor and Tricia about her concerns.

Beth surveyed the crowd and smiled warmly. Lena had done a superb job and was delirious with excitement. She had managed to get several sponsors through the church and hospital personnel. Taylor had even donated a handsome sum. She had gone the extra mile and found addresses for Plover Creek High alumni. The response was more than they could've hoped for. Despite the short notice after the accident, Lena had been able to get a group of ladies to do all the cooking.

At first, Beth had been reluctant to see old classmates, but having that talk with David had diminished the humiliation she felt for dropping out of school. Remarkably, she was beginning to realize that she could still achieve whatever God's window of grace allowed. She had begun to pray again, though she still sensed a wary distance.

She giggled when she saw her boss putting away ribs and baked beans like a hungry soldier on leave. He had brought along four teenagers from a Dallas youth center, and competed against them mercilessly in tests of stamina.

Beth greeted many familiar faces. Most were married and eager to introduce their families. She smiled as she watched Lena bounce around as giddy as a goose, making sure everyone enjoyed himself. Bree was having a great time with Millie Colbert's little boy, Sam. The two sat on the lawn near the platform, playing with little muscled action figures. She thought Sam was adorable, but not nearly as cute as her little big man.

She watched them for a while, intrigued by their amusing imagination with the toys. Soon she was laughing so hard she started to cough. She then caught David watching her intently. Despite being deep in conversation with former classmates, he was never far away. His constant attentiveness felt good.

When the band stopped to take a break, Carl moved to the platform, leaning heavily on their father's cane. Closing her eyes, she tried to dismiss the apprehension that had gradually returned after she stopped the meds. She hadn't once been seized by the familiar dread while taking them.

"Folks, I have an announcement to make," Carl said into the mike. Everyone began to move closer to the platform. Beth couldn't imagine what he was going to say. Everyone already knew they were selling the ranch. Then, it dawned on her. Lena was lit up like a Christmas tree, sashaying up the steps to join him.

Deciding to get a little closer, Beth carefully moved down the steps. Distracted, she was only vaguely aware of Bree pulling at her shirt. She couldn't take her eyes off Carl's face. He was beaming. David soon walked up beside her. She glanced up just in time to catch his wink. In a gesture that seemed both bold and natural, he draped an arm around her shoulder and let it casually rest there. Her heart skipped a beat.

"Are you doing too much?"

"I'll be fine. Thanks."

As more people closed in, David drew her closer in a protective stance. Beth felt a tide of unfettered joy wash over her. He had been wonderful the past few days. And she was behaving like a schoolgirl again. She smiled, hoping he couldn't hear the thumping of her heart.

Several people moved in front of them, unwittingly blocking Bree's view. "Pick me up, Beth," he said, stretching his arms upwards. "I can't see."

When she moved to lift him, David grasped her shoulder in protest. "You want me to send you to your room?" He reached down and swung his son up and around to his shoulders.

"Yea!" he squealed, looking around to see if his newfound friend was watching. "Beth, I taller than ev-vy bo-dy?"

"Yes, I know," she said, looking up into his overly excited face.

"Daddy, bend me down. I need to tell Beth something."

"I know, Son," David said, distracted.

Bree eagerly leaned toward her. "No, Daddy, in her ear." David tilted the child closer to Beth's ear.

"Daddy kissed you when you sleep," he said, placing a finger to his lips.

Beth's heart skipped a beat. Flushed with warmth and affection, she smiled and took the child's hand and kissed it. Though she had enjoyed David's gentle kiss the day she came home from the hospital, she had hesitated to dwell on it. Knowing that Bree had seen such a display was disconcerting, especially since she hadn't sorted it all out in her mind. She did not object to David's kiss, but it had been so unexpected it became suspect. Too good to be true. She was thankful Bree didn't seem to be bothered by the kiss he'd seen. In fact, the boy seemed downright pleased.

After a few words of welcome and several acknowledgments, Carl placed an arm around Lena's shoulders. "I feel privileged to announce that to my great joy, Lena Hall has agreed to become my wife."

Although Beth had suspected as much, her mouth still flew open in surprise. The roar of the crowd was so loud, she hadn't heard what David said as he moved closer to the platform.

"We will be wed in early September," Carl continued, "and of course, you're all invited."

Slowly turning away from the hooting, whistling crowd, Beth strolled around the house to the back fence and gazed out toward the grazing meadow. Though she was thrilled for Carl and Lena, their upcoming wedding was a reminder of the many changes in her life. There was no turning back now, she thought. She had to see her investigation through. She had to know what was going on in Plover Creek before she could make plans of her own.

Beth began to fan herself with her hand. It was much too warm. The sun felt as if it were boring a hole in the top of her head. She scolded herself for not wearing a hat. She leaned heavily against the fence, not certain she had the energy to go inside to get one.

Resting her chin on folded arms atop the gate to the corral, Beth squinted in the brightness and watched the remaining horses take a cool drink. She couldn't help thinking of Midnight. She imagined seeing her reflection in his big glassy eyes and enjoying his welcoming nuzzle. If he were here, she would sneak off to the ridge. But then, if Midnight were here, there would be no need for her to have to sneak. The restriction was necessary, of course. But she hated feeling like a prisoner in her own home.

Her thoughts did not stray from recent trauma: her dad and Midnight, the shooting, Carl's injury and her car accident. It was as if a representative from hell was bent on poking its ugly hand into her life to convince her that she indeed was a curse. And the lingering bubble of panic felt much as it had the weeks leading up to her high school graduation. Death and foreboding had been strong in her nostrils then, too.

"Beth."

She turned and saw Michael's father walking toward her with a small package in his hand. Her stomach suddenly became a tight ball. Her heart quickened with anxiety, but she kept her facial expression neutral. She had always liked Mr. Baker, but she wasn't sure how to respond to him now. She had managed to avoid both him and his wife at church. It certainly wasn't their fault Michael had strange moral lapses. Besides, they probably weren't even aware of his dark side.

She forced a wary smile as he drew closer. He looked as though he had aged since the last time she'd taken a good look at him. His bronze bald crown shone like a beacon above the silver gray; beads of sweat were sprinkled about on his head.

"Hello, Mr. Baker," she said, baffled. "How have you been?"

"We're doing all right, Beth. Thanks for asking." He pulled a hand-kerchief from his pocket and wiped the perspiration from his face and head, then moved to lean against the fence. "I'm glad to see you getting around so good after that car wreck. Do you need to go inside out of this heat? I'm sure it's not good for you."

"No, I'm fine. Thanks."

"I don't mean to bother you at such a festive time, but I found something when I went through Mike's things." His face twisted in anguish. It saddened her to see such raw grief and she instinctively placed her hand over his.

"What is it, Mr. Baker?"

"I know y'all weren't…I found these." He pulled a box out of a paper bag and handed it to her. "It's some of your letters. I didn't read them," he quickly added, embarrassed. "I didn't know what to do with them."

Beth took the box and lifted the lid. Immediately, she recognized the sweeping script on the top envelope as her own. A stack of fifteen to twenty letters was tied with a black shoelace. She winced as her fingers numbly toyed with the string. She had written and hand delivered these during their senior year. Holding them was like finding a lost doll she had long outgrown, but it also produced dreadful memories. She'd been so blind—or rather, so willing to be blind.

Nervously, Beth flipped through the first few envelopes, not really seeing them. Why in the world would he have saved them, she wondered. Lately, it seemed as if everything was dragging her back to the most wretched time of her life.

Mr. Baker cleared his throat as he straightened and stood facing her. "Beth, did I do the right thing by bringing those by? I didn't want to upset you. I know y'all been through an awful lot here lately. It just didn't feel right for me to keep them."

"Yes," she whispered in a quivering voice. "And you've been through a lot as well. Thank you for returning them."

The man patted her shoulder in a kind gesture and walked away without another word. The moment he was out of sight, Beth started ripping the letters one by one into little pieces and tossing them into one of the trash barrels that Carl and David had placed around the yard.

When she reached the last few, she came across an envelope she didn't recognize. It didn't have a return address. Curiously, she opened it and pulled out a sheet of paper.

"WHAT HAPPENS TO A THREE MUSKATEER THAT GETS TOO CLOSE TO A FLAME?"

She stared at the large block lettering. It struck her then that this might be some kind of threat. She turned the paper over and back upright, gazing intently at it as if the wording had magically changed in the last few minutes. Who could have sent him something like this?

Beth anxiously flipped over the envelope to see the postmark. It was dated February 8th—over four years ago—and mailed from Dallas. The letter apparently had arrived just before that awful Valentine's night.

She felt an icy chill and nearly swooned in the heat. Could this be the reason Michael went so crazy? She was folding the note to place back inside the envelope when a hand touched her shoulder from behind. Beth jumped and whirled around, stopping just short of screaming.

"I've been having the time of my…"

Halted by the apparent frightened expression on her face, Taylor instinctively pulled his assistant into an embrace. "Beth, what's wrong?"

Still trembling, she shook her head vigorously. "Nothing. You just startled me, that's all."

Taylor released her and carefully placed a finger on her cheek. Then he showed the wet finger to her. Tears. Realizing that she'd unconsciously been crying seemed to throw her into a state of mounting hysteria. She began whimpering, softly at first, then louder and louder. She couldn't stop. Unable to regain her composure, Beth moved back into Taylor's arms and began sobbing.

After letting her cry, Taylor pulled back and gazed into her eyes. Then he kissed her forehead and again on her cheek. "Why don't you go inside and rest, Beth? You've been through so much, and you're probably worried about Tricia's investigation, too."

"I'm okay," she murmured.

"You also have to remember you've suffered a concussion. You shouldn't be out here in the sun like this."

Grateful for the kind reminder and tender gestures, she nodded and watched him walk away.

Shock snaked through David's entire body. He slumped back against the stove, his eyes transfixed with disbelief and grief. He had watched through the kitchen window in helpless agony as Beth clung desperately to Taylor. This hadn't looked like a casual embrace.

He had come looking for her after seeing Mr. Baker drive off. He knew she'd probably be upset. And he had just decided to tell her exactly how he felt about her.

David reeled in astonishment, swallowing the acidic lump that had formed in his throat. Watching the two embracing, he felt his anger coming to a boil. He wanted desperately to move away from the window, but he was frozen to the spot.

Taylor's kissing of Beth had aroused a fiery possessive streak in him. His mind immediately went back to Deidre's deception. The pain of betrayal shot through him afresh. His hands turned into fists at his side, and he finally turned away.

"Why, God?" he whispered anxiously. "Why?"

He had to get hold of himself, he thought. Taylor was a good man, and Beth certainly deserved all the happiness in the world. But his mind went back to the moment she had responded to his kiss when she had come home from the hospital. What was happening here?

He sat down at the table and hit it in agitation. Why hadn't he told her how he felt about her? Why had he waited? He *couldn't* tell her now. He had lost her.

He bolted up from the table, feeling as if his whole world had fallen off a mountain. Maybe it was not meant to be, he thought. Maybe he was deceiving himself into believing he was in love with her because of Bree.

This leg of his business with Taylor was over, so he could get his son and fly back home tonight. Having made that decision, David hurried upstairs to pack, taking two steps at a time.

"I don't wanna go," Bree whined. "I stay with Beth."

David held his son's shoulders between outstretched palms. It was hard to see the disappointment on the child's face. "I know, buddy. But Daddy has to get back to work and Beth has to work, too. You know that. I wish things were easy, but most of the time they're just not."

When the taxi arrived, David trotted down the steps, luggage under one arm and Bree under the other.

"Hey," Carl called. "Where you off to in such a hurry?"

"I need to get back, Carl. Something's come up. Tell Beth I'm sorry we didn't get a chance to say good-bye. If necessary, I may be back in a couple of weeks to tie up loose ends with this project."

Carl placed a hand on David's shoulder, his brow furrowed with concern. "I could've taken you to the airport. Is everything all right? You look upset."

"Everything's fine. By the way, I'm real happy for you and Lena."

"Thanks, man," Carl said, giving him a couple of friendly taps on the back. "Have a safe flight back."

THIRTEEN

Beth was disoriented, straining to remember where she was. She calmed down as her vision began to clear. She was in the loft of the barn where she'd gone to be alone. She must have fallen asleep. Maybe the meds were still in her bloodstream.

Her right hand was still clutching the now wrinkled note, sent to Michael four years ago. She sat up straight and smoothed the paper out on her leg. After reading it once more, she refolded it and placed it in her pocket. Maybe she was too keyed up to be unbiased in her speculative assessment of the note's intent and purpose.

She stood up and gingerly moved toward the ladder, anxious to get David's take on what she thought were threatening words. Once on the ground, she looked around quizzically. A strange hush hovered over the place. Most of the guests had all left. She turned just as one lone car drove away from the backyard.

Beth stepped around the corner of the house and found Carl and Lena sitting at one of the picnic tables, chatting and sipping sodas. All that remained from the afternoon party was the trash around the yard.

"Hi, you two." She moved in next to Lena, attempting to hide her discomfort. Shallow breathing wasn't helping the burning in her rib area. "I didn't get a chance to congratulate you guys. I'm very happy for you."

"Thanks, Beth," Lena said, giving her hand a gentle squeeze. "Can you believe we're going to be sisters after all?" Beth stiffened. Lena pulled back and gazed intently at her. "You okay?"

"Yeah. Just fell asleep in an awkward position…in the loft, of all places."

"We thought after Mr. Baker left you were battle weary and went to rest in your room. Didn't think to ask David."

Carl's brow had knotted in annoyance the instant Beth mentioned the loft. "Don't you think that was a little ridiculous, considering you just got out of the hospital a few days ago?"

"I know," she said, waving her hand dismissively. "I didn't mean to go to sleep up there. I think I was more exhausted than I realized. Why aren't Bree and David out here with you?"

Carl and Lena glanced at each other, and then back at Beth. Her stomach fluttered as she held Lena's eyes.

"They're gone," she said.

Her smile waned as her heart plunged to its lowest depth. She felt as though she had been wantonly thrown into a black hole. "Gone where?" she squeezed out.

"Back to Seattle," Carl answered, taking another swig of his soda. "You must've been up in the loft when he went to check on you. Said something about making sure Mr. Baker hadn't upset you."

Lena nodded agreement and toyed with her can. "Hunted for you all over the place. It was right after Mr. Baker left."

"What could've been so important that he would rush off like that?"

Lena shrugged. "Just said something came up. He called a cab and left in quite a hurry."

Beth could feel the weight of her disappointment in the set of her shoulders. They seemed to droop a little lower with the realization that David had left, that he'd taken Bree without saying good-bye. She felt as if her heart had crumbled into little pieces. She looked away briefly, anxious to get her bearings before the two realized she was close to tears.

Bent on not advertising her distress, Beth kept her voice flat and emotionless. But inside she was in turmoil. "I thought he wasn't leaving until tomorrow evening."

"I think I'll go see to the horses. George should be by tomorrow to pick them up," Carl said, grabbing the cane. "Dave seemed concerned that Mr. Baker wanted to speak with you alone. Is everything all right?"

"Yeah," Beth said with a forced smile. "Everything's fine."

After Carl left, Beth sat for a moment in numbed silence. She peered around at Lena, who was openly gazing at her. In an effort to give her hands something to do and redirect Lena's attention, she grabbed her brother's soda can and drained it.

"What is it, Beth?"

"I think I need to go lie down for a while, Lena," she interrupted, standing to go inside. "Do you mind?"

"Of course not, girl. Do you need any help?"

"No, no," she said, raising both hands. "Keep your seat."

"Beth, what's going on with you and David? Did you two quarrel?"

"No," she said, with an empty chuckle. "I guess I've let myself get too attached to Bree."

"Maybe something was going on in Seattle with his business. He looked a little mad when he left. And that baby was kicking and screaming like a house-a-fire."

Later that night, Beth tossed in her bed as rejection curled itself around her heart and squeezed. She restlessly watched the hours tick by, wondering why David had left so suddenly. *Something came up.* That was only a frivolous excuse. Had he decided against pursuing the promise of their kiss? Had she made more out of it than she should have? Perhaps it was simply a by-product of witnessing Carl and Lena so completely wrapped up in each other.

Lena said that he seemed angry when he left. What could have happened so suddenly that he'd become angry enough to leave without saying good-bye? She hadn't even been able to tell him about the note. She carefully turned over on her other side. The intense love she felt for him had become a raw ache bumping against emptiness. She desperately wanted to tell him how she felt, but that would be foolish now.

Beth closed her eyes and tried to will away the headache. Her entire body seemed to retaliate for having pushed it the way she had all day. The pain was intense and she reconsidered her decision to stop taking the pain meds.

Her mind cast shadows over every thought, escalating the apprehension that seemed to seep into her soul by the moment. She longed to feel David's arms around her, hear his voice at her ear. When she could stand the ache of rejection no longer, she turned her face into her pillow and sobbed uncontrollably, trying desperately to muffle the sounds.

The ache of abandonment seemed to engulf her, conveying her back to the moment Carl and David left home for college. How odd that she still thought of that.

It seemed the tears would never end. Unwilling to answer the quiet knock at her door, Beth listened as Carl let himself into her room. He moved awkwardly around to the side of her bed and sat in the rocker David had occupied two days before. Bright moonlight poured through the lace-curtained window. "What is it, Beth? You in pain? You want me to get your meds back out?"

Not trusting herself to say much, she grasped her brother's hand and gently squeezed it. "Not now."

"Is it Dave?"

The question cut to the very quick of her being, but it was easy to evade. In reality, it was a combination of everything.

"I feel like I'm in the middle of everything that's wrong in this community." Her voice broke as she slowly sat up and pushed herself toward the headboard. "I don't want to live here anymore. It doesn't feel right."

"It hasn't felt the same since you came back from Austin, has it?"

Beth glanced up, startled. "How did you know?"

"Maybe just a lucky guess. Maybe looking at the driven expression on your face everyday." He paused and shifted in the chair. "When you came home...there was a sadness and a determination in you. I know now that it was probably because of your breakup with Mike, but that wonderful spirited wonder was gone."

She sniffed. "I grew up, that's all. I had lived in my dreams too long."

Carl sighed. "There's nothing wrong with dreaming, Sis. Life will steal our dreams if we let it. But it was God who initially put them there."

She smiled. "You know, sometimes you and David sound like twins."

"We had the same teacher."

"I *do* have hopes, Carl. But they float off in every direction. I'm a little uneasy about following any of them." She wiped her nose and leaned back. "Well, if the truth be told, I don't really know which ones to choose. I've already made such a mess of things."

"If you be still, God will show you what's real and what's not."

Her stomach tightened. "I don't know. He always seems to have a riddle for me to figure out. Why can't He just give me the real meaning of things?" She paused and gazed at the shadowy outline of her brother. "I guess you know I've been a little angry with the Lord. I know it's silly. But it's like wandering around in a desert. I don't have time to be still and figure everything out. His ways just seem so cruel."

"You have clear direction," Carl said quietly. "You just can't hear because you're letting other things drown out God's voice."

"Like what?"

"Unforgiveness, bitterness, even stress."

She lowered her eyes in the dimness. "David told me Daddy said I could hear God's whisper."

Carl chuckled reminiscently. "Yeah, he did."

"What do *you* think he meant?"

"That your spirit was wide open to God at that time. God could tell and show you secrets without making such a spectacle. You know, the way Mom could finish Dad's sentences, sometimes without realizing it. And he seemed to be able to read her mind just by looking at her."

"I remember feeling free. If God whispered secrets to me, I don't know what they were."

Carl chuckled. "Probably not in your head. But you knew in your spirit."

"Miss Virgie said something like that, too. I wish I could get back to that place with Him, Carl. I really do."

"I know, honey. But you might be too involved in other things. There might be some things you need to let go of, as well. Right now, your ear is not available to God's whispers."

"What do I do? Every time I get a glimmer of hope, it gets dashed. What does God want? What does He have for *me?*"

"You already have the answer, Beth. It's in those deep yearnings, those dreams. Before your mind can hear them, you'll have to get quiet. Put down all your defenses and listen."

"But how?" she asked with a desperation that surprised even her.

"The Bible tells us to avoid being conformed to this world, but to be transformed by the renewing of our minds. You've got to get back into the Bible, Beth. Meditate on the things you read in it, and expect God to show you things. He loves you, honey, and He knows what you're going through right now. In times like these, you have to let your faith settle you."

She blinked owlishly in the dimness. "What if I really don't have faith? Maybe I've just been going through the motions 'cause that's how I was brought up. Maybe Mr. Tubbs was right back when I was a kid."

Carl squeezed his sister's hand and breathed a mirthless chuckle. "Let that go, honey."

Beth grabbed another tissue from the box by her bed. "I don't remember exactly what I felt as a child, but there's something wrong about Mr. Tubbs. I don't hate him, Carl. Really I don't. I just don't like him."

"Beth, George has been good to us."

"I know, I know. I just can't help it. But then, what do I know?"

Carl cleared his throat. "We've all had moments when we doubt who we are. We lose our ability to accept God's uncomplicated truths."

Beth remembered similar words from David out on the ridge. "Why are simplicities so hard to grasp?"

"I don't know. We just have to press through the reasoning the world has taught us and believe God, no matter how we feel or what we face. You are a strong lady and God is with you. You can't forget that."

"I haven't been very faithful," she muttered. "And what if I don't want what He has in mind for me?"

"You can fix the unfaithfulness in an instant," her brother said, squeezing her hand again. "As far as wanting what he has in mind, I believe he placed the desire for it inside you. Just relax. You'll see. Everything will work out fine."

Carl rose from her side, giving her hand a final squeeze. "Carl?"

"Yeah."

Beth swallowed hard, knowing what she was about to do would be difficult. "There's something I need to tell you."

Manny stared incredulously at Beth. "What?"

"It surprised me, too," she said, hurriedly pulling out the note. "It has me as jittery as I've felt in a long time." Her voice was shaking and she paused to steady it. "Who do you think sent it? And why would Michael keep it?"

Manny read the ominous message, and something resembling panic moved across his face, but it was quickly replaced by annoyance. "Why are you trying to make something of all this? This is not a threat. Anybody could have sent this note. Have you shown it to anybody else?"

Beth shook her head and silently pried the paper from Manny's fingers. "No, I haven't. And to be honest, I'm sorry I showed it to you."

"If you start spoutin' off about this, people will think you've lost your marbles. I've lived with that feeling a long time and I'm telling you, you don't want it."

"I'm a little tired of everybody shoving my opinions back in my face," she said. "I'm working on getting hard facts before I approach anybody else."

Beth watched Manny's expression turn even more surly. Stress lines formed across his brow as he looked away. "I think you need to just leave things alone. Better yet, find something to do with your time. If you keep this up, you'll be accusing everybody."

"I thought you'd be just as convinced as I am that something's off here. But I see I was wrong."

Manny shook his head. "I don't know, Beth. You seem to be jumping from one strange thing to another. First you accuse Mr. Tubbs of doing something to your pa, and now you're thinking somebody planned to hurt Mike four years ago. How much sense does that make?"

Beth lowered her head as she tried to control her temper. "I admit it sounds bizarre, but there's got to be a connection somewhere. What if the sheriff is in cahoots with George Tubbs? What if Michael somehow betrayed Felix and Terry? Maybe they're the ones who sent this note. Did you notice it came just before Valentine's Day?"

Manny's eyes turned cold and hard. "I'm warning you, Beth, you're grabbing at straws. You'd better leave well enough alone."

FOURTEEN

David looked out over the city of Seattle from his fourteenth-floor office. From where he sat, the overcast morning did little to hide his anger—or disheveled appearance. He hadn't bothered to shave, and his suit looked as if he had slept in it. His sour mood was probably written all over his face.

To boot, Bree had not slept through the night since he was torn away from the ranch and his beloved Beth. David sighed, overwhelmed with guilt and anguish. The child had whined every evening to call Beth, and every evening he had been denied.

He rubbed his forehead, unsure why he was so angry. He was punishing Beth, as well as his son, for something they had nothing to do with. He had privately accused Beth when he hadn't told her how he felt about her. He hadn't even mentioned it to Carl. She had every right to pursue happiness with Taylor—or anyone else she chose. Reluctantly, he conceded that his anger was directed at himself. And he would probably throw himself into an emotional and confusing whirlwind like this until he willingly forgave Deidre.

He closed his eyes tightly, and then opened them again. The more he thought about it, the more he entertained the possibility that he didn't have those kinds of feelings for Beth after all. He should just wait on the Lord and not jump the gun simply because it was convenient.

Who was he fooling? There was no getting around the fact that Bree wanted Beth to fill the empty place in his small world. And, he had to admit, so did he.

He squeezed his eyes shut, recalling the sight of Beth in Taylor's arms. He had even kissed her. She was a bright and attractive young woman. Taylor obviously thought so, too. He leaned back in his chair, sighing wearily.

What was he doing to himself? What was he doing to Bree? He had overreacted by dragging him away like a raving maniac. He had to find a way to help his son through this.

David picked up his pencil and proceeded to finish up the sketches for the library in Bothell. When the phone rang, he automatically grabbed it. "Dave Spencer."

"Mr. Spencer, this is Maria."

His housekeeper, doubling as Bree's nanny, spoke into the phone slowly and deliberately. Her heavy inflections were crisp and refreshing, but sometimes he found it hard to sit patiently and let her get her words out. He constantly had to stop himself from rushing her.

"Yes, Maria," he said anxiously. "What is it?"

"Your son terribly misbehaving. He refuses to eat or let me help him get dressed. Please...you talk to him?"

"Of course, I will," he said, repressing another wave of guilt. "Put him on."

David heard his son pant timidly into the phone. "Hi, Daddy." He could easily envision him pouting, his eyes lowered. Based on the rubbery sound he heard, Bree was fidgeting as he held the phone with both hands.

"What's going on, Bree?"

"I don't want no oatmeal. And I wanna wear the shirt Beth bought me."

"Bryson, you and I agreed that you were going to do as you were told. Mrs. Sanchez has been very patient with us. Now you go in there and apologize to her, eat your food, and let her help you get dressed."

"But Da..."

"Bryson Spencer, did you hear what I just said?"

David realized he had spoken too sharply as soon as the words were out of his mouth. Bree tried to talk between broken bits of distress, but grew frustrated and apparently flung the phone down. He could hear him wailing as he ran back down the hall to his room.

He felt like a monster. He hadn't meant to do that. After all, Bree was only a child reacting to being separated from someone he loved. It was remarkable how strong the bond had become between him and Beth in such a short while. It was marvelous, actually.

He placed the phone back into its cradle and dropped his head into his hands. "Oh, God. I don't know how to handle this. Please help me."

By the time his secretary arrived, David had finished up the sketches, mapped out instructions for Ted, and was ready to head for a construction site. He would then go home and spend the rest of the day with Bree.

To alert Mrs. Sanchez that he had come in, David closed the door loudly. She rushed out of the kitchen, a finger to her lips.

"Asleep now."

He tossed his briefcase down on the sofa, pulled off his jacket and walked down the hall to Bree's room. As he moved over to the bed, David noted Bree's small, easy breaths. The child was obviously exhausted. Neither one of them had slept very well in the past several nights.

He eased himself onto the bed beside Bree, noticing a tear puddle on the bridge of his nose. As he gently wiped it away, Bree's eyes fluttered open. For a moment, a light shone that David hadn't seen in a week. But it disappeared as quickly as it had come.

"Hi, Daddy."

"Hello, Son," he said, stroking Bree's cheek. "I'm sorry I yelled at you. Will you forgive me?"

Clumsily raising up on an elbow, Bree leaned over and kissed his father's cheek. He then slowly climbed onto David's chest and gave him a bear hug. "I forgive you, Daddy."

After a marathon session of self-examination, Beth decided that she needed to be more realistic about moving on with her life. She had clearly fallen prey to her need for love and stability in her life. Consequently, she had unconsciously revived a semblance of an old crush. Evidently, she had mistaken David's friendly concern and kindness for some kind of romantic move.

She frowned as she recalled Manny's strange mood. It was the most unpleasant she had ever seen him. He had never made her feel silly for the way she thought. Maybe he had become more protective than was healthy for either of them. She might have to deal with him in the same reserved manner she had taken with Carl and David.

Still, she couldn't help wondering if she really was being obsessive and cynical. Maybe she *should* let things be. After all, if she couldn't distinguish between romance and friendship, she surely wouldn't recognize deception and deadly intentions. Who was she to question the skills of official investigators?

She smiled faintly, somewhat pleased that she had made a decision. But it didn't settle well. No matter how she thought about it, to her mind, things weren't right in Plover Creek. She sighed and turned to her packing. The church had already provided Carl with a small efficiency in town, and Beth was moving in with Lena temporarily.

Beth felt stronger than she had in quite a while, but she was still being careful to avoid wearing herself out. She sorted through several boxes in the attic, and was brought to tears when she found her mother's wedding gown and a set of diaries. Carl had enlisted several members of his congregation to help pack up the larger boxes and take them to the garage for the movers.

She had just placed the last of the smaller boxes out by the door when the phone rang. She wiped her hand on the towel around her neck and took a deep breath before answering.

"Beth, this is Tricia. Hope I didn't interrupt your packing."

A quiet unease gripped her. Despite her earlier resolve to back away from the investigation, she instinctively glanced around to make sure she was alone and whispered conspiratorially, "No, I needed a break."

"Good. I have a few items I need to go over with you."

"Did you find something?"

"The cases you mentioned never even made it to our office. But the sheriff has been forthcoming with his records. I'm finding a lot of unanswered questions. Also, I found some facts I thought you'd be interested in about George Tubbs. It's all a matter of public record…if one knows what to look for."

Beth tightened her grip on the handset and sat down in the hallway at the foot of the stairs. "I thought you were just checking on the sheriff and unsolved cases?"

Tricia paused. "Remember when you told us Tubbs was probably the last person who saw your dad alive?"

"Yeah?"

"Well, his name stuck in my mind. You know, Taylor had my office check the county records for the history of your property. A couple of names kept recurring."

"George Tubbs?"

"In a manner of speaking. It seems that at one time, sixty-five percent of Plover Creek was owned by one family—the Andersons."

Beth drummed her fingers impatiently against her leg. "Tricia, that's very interesting, but I…"

"Hear me out, Beth. George Tubbs is a direct descendant of Randolph Anderson. For years, Anderson maintained his property with people to whom he never paid wages. Soon after this was revealed to the authorities, he sectioned most of it off to the people who worked for him."

Beth frowned. "I don't understand."

"What I'm saying is that someone found out that Anderson owned slaves l-o-n-g after it had become illegal. He was forced to give most of his assets to them—all except the property you're selling to Taylor."

"My God, how long ago was this?"

"Anderson was the great grandfather of George Tubbs. This was approximately a hundred years ago."

Beth frowned in confusion. "What does this have to do with unsolved cases?"

"Beth, Tubbs was accused of assault with a deadly weapon fifteen years ago when he was recruiting for one of those small town hate groups."

"What? He's a white supremacist?"

"I don't see any real evidence of it being that organized," Tricia said. "I think it was more a Timothy McVeigh type thing. Just him and a couple of other guys. The group didn't last all that long."

"What do you mean by it not being deep-seated?"

"Apparently, he started this after he went to Memphis to a big family reunion and found out about his heritage. Ever since then, he's been obsessed with getting back all the land."

"No wonder he's been buying up so much property," Beth said. "That's probably why he befriended Daddy, too." Beth grew more excited by the minute.

"Do you think Tubbs would go so far as to shoot at Taylor and the others in the meadow, Beth?"

Feeling the creepy sensation of a spider crawling up her back, she hedged her response. "I have to admit I've been suspicious of that all along. But I've been warned a lot about spouting off. I'd hate to accuse him to an officer of the court without hard evidence."

"I can appreciate that. That's the main reason I'm calling. From what my investigation is turning up, I may have to look into a lot of things that may put you and Carl at risk of retaliation."

"What do you mean?"

"Since your concerns stemmed from the sheriff's department...well, they'll know if I go after Tubbs. Even though his group disbanded years ago, if he is still covertly committing hate crimes—"

"Actually, he appears to be an outstanding citizen," Beth interrupted with a snort. "As far as I know, nobody knows about his past."

"People have a habit of retaining only what makes things easy. Even if they detest something, they'd rather put up with it if it costs too much to confront it."

A random thought sprang into Beth's mind, and she instinctively cried out. "Uh, oh!"

"What?"

"George Tubbs is our town pharmacist. This is a man that the poorest of the poor visit instead of a doctor."

"I know," Tricia said. "I was surprised that he played such an important role in the community considering all the circumstances. And he seemed to be such a good friend of your dad's. He put himself through school by working with a realtor in Dallas."

"Oh?"

"That's the other thing I wanted to tell you. I hope you're sitting down. Tubbs worked for Davis and Associates, who, by the way, are no longer in business. Davis is the realtor that handled the transfer of the property to your parents. George Tubbs was the assistant that handled the details."

FIFTEEN

David edged his way through the crowd, realizing too late that it was probably a mistake to have called Natalie. When a patron in the pub bumped into him, he questioned his sanity for being in such a place. He spied his date sitting on a barstool, already sipping a drink. Relieved, he smiled and headed her way.

"Hello, handsome," she said, returning his smile. "I'm glad you could make it. Would you like to join me here or sit in a booth?"

"How 'bout a booth," he said. He didn't like closed-in places, the smell of stale liquor or smoky clothes. The last time he had been in a place like this was the night he walked in on his wife with another man.

He had suppressed the urge to smash the man's face. Instead, he had gone to a late-night pub, much like this one, and had drunk himself into oblivion. He couldn't even remember how he made it home.

"What would you like, sir?" their waitress asked.

"Cherry coke, please," he said, glimpsing amusement in his companion's eyes. "Do you want a refill?"

"No. I'm good," Natalie said, still nursing her drink. "Still the virtuous man of valor, I see. So how have you been, David?"

"Just great, Nat. How 'bout yourself?"

She eyed him curiously over the rim of her fashionable glasses. "I'm well. To what do I owe the pleasure of an invitation out?"

"I-I don't really know why I called, Nat. I'm sorry, I…"

"So, who is she?"

David did a double take, certain he had missed something. "I beg your pardon?"

Her smile broadened into a full grin. "Your heart is in your face where everybody can see it," she said confidently. "So tell me about her."

David tried to evade her gaze. "Am I that transparent?"

"Maybe a little. But I know I'm not your type, and you don't generally come to places like this. When you called, I knew you probably just wanted someone to talk to."

He nodded sheepishly, waiting for the waitress to set his drink down. "You're remarkable. I'm sorry. I didn't mean to mislead you."

Natalie waved her hand as if erasing his regret from a blackboard. "There's no need for an apology. I wasn't in the least misled. So, she really gotcha, huh?"

He took a swallow of his coke and leaned back. "Yeah, I think so. I'm just not sure she's aware of it." He was surprised when Natalie reached across the table and took his hand in hers. He looked up, baffled.

"Do you think this woman is right for you and your son?"

"I think she would be perfect. But I don't really know if I'm thinking very soundly these days. It's kind of complicated. Besides, I don't think she feels the same way."

She gave his hand a gentle squeeze and then slowly released it. "If you've really set your heart on her, I suggest you get out of here and go remind her who the better man is."

—w—

Beth woke without having to jump out of bed and rush into the day. It was Saturday, and she was at Lena's house. The small, cozy colonial was quite comfortable. It was a white frame house with black window shutters and a detached garage with tall oaks scattered about the front yard. Its front faced west, so Lena had placed pull-down blinds between the columns, though Beth had never seen her use them.

She could relax for another couple of hours. She was dog tired. Not just from the packing and moving but also of the small warning she sensed each morning she got up to go to work. Tired of not being able to express all her concerns and fears to her brother. And tired of keeping the threatening calls she had been receiving a secret.

Manny's angry outburst and Carl's dismissal of her misgivings had sealed her decision to keep things to herself. Perhaps when she had gotten some solid evidence and had pinpointed a credible motive, she wouldn't sound so fanatical to everyone. Manny had phoned her once, but hadn't been around in several days. She wondered if he was more upset by her persistent doubts than she had realized.

Her stomach flipped over as her mind turned to David. Though her heart was filled with love for him, the shock of his abrupt departure, followed by the lengthy silence, was painful. She had reached for the phone a dozen times to call. But what would she say? David didn't owe her anything. And she refused to let herself lean on him or any other man. She had accepted clear signs that there was no real hope for a relationship, and was determined to focus instead on the investigation.

Beth spent the next few days poring over records at the library, the city clerk's office and the tax assessor for any information she could find on George Tubbs or his family. Tricia had been right. Information was readily available to anyone who knew what to look for. She learned that her parents bought the ranch on a technicality.

Apparently, her father's miracle had come in the form of neglected taxes. After clarifying what she had uncovered with Tricia, Beth learned that the owner had been a gambler who had made the mistake of placing the whole ranch on the table. A wealthy man from Atlanta acquired it, but he traveled so extensively his tax notices went unopened. More than three years had passed when he learned of the sale. He declined challenging it because in Texas an owner had two years to redeem his property by reimbursing the new owner, as well as paying a 25 percent statutory tax penalty. After two years, the penalty increased to 50 percent.

In hopes that Tricia would seek a warrant to get a look at Mr. Tubbs' pharmacy logs, Beth agreed to hand over her dad's old prescription bottles for testing.

Between stressing over breathing phone calls, Manny's lack of support and her feelings for David, Beth felt as if she was near hysteria most of her waking hours. The phone calls were coming more often now. She shuddered as she thought of the man's whispers. *"If I were you, I'd quit snooping around like you've been doing. You could end up like the Three Musketeers."* Then he would hang up. Her nerves were tight and fragile. But at least she knew her suspicions hadn't been wrong. She was definitely on the trail of something ugly.

She wondered if Michael could be making the calls in an attempt to frighten her. But what would be his purpose? And why would he care if she snooped for a motive to confirm her suspicions about Mr. Tubbs?

Having taken the week off, Beth had some down time between visits to the library and courthouse. She was enjoying the quietness on Lena's front porch when she heard the telephone ring. She jumped up from the steps and ran into the house, not knowing if it was Lena's line or the one she had installed in her room.

It was Lena's. She hesitantly picked it up, hoping it wasn't another crank call. "Beth."

At the sound of his voice, her heart seemingly skidded to a halt and her body went limp. She almost cried with relief. The longed-for call was finally made. She wanted to be angry, very angry, with him. Instead she was experiencing a jumble of emotions that numbed her senses. It was good to hear his voice. But she was determined to keep her emotions in check. And no matter what, she wouldn't let him know how much he had hurt her.

She forced a smile onto her face, aware that he would hear it in her voice. "Hello, David."

"I need your help," he said. "It's Bree."

A sickening wave of panic grabbed her by the throat and she instantly straightened. "What's wrong?"

"He's having some trouble adjusting. H-he was pretty young when his mother left, and you…but…would you mind talking to him, please? He's been having bad dreams and asking for you, but I didn't want to impose anymore than I already have."

Hot anger flushed her face. "Impose? How could you possibly? Of course I'll talk to him," she said, realizing there was no real point asking him why he was behaving so strangely. He hadn't even apologized for leaving so abruptly, but then maybe he didn't think it necessary.

"Beth!"

"Hello, my little big man," she soothed, relieved to be able to talk with him. "I've missed you. How ya doing?"

"I wanna come with you," he pleaded without taking a breath. "Come get me. Okay?"

Beth smiled bravely and batted away the tears. "I would love to come get you, Bree. But what would Daddy do without you?"

"He's big," Bree said, his voice quivering with emotion. "You want me?"

"I want you more than anything in the world, darling," Beth said, taken aback by the truth of her words. "But so does Daddy. I'll talk with him and see if you can come in a couple of weeks. We can spend some time together, just you and me. Would that be okay?"

Her offer seemed to take his mind off his discontent, giving him something to look forward to. After the boy had talked a bit longer, David got back on the line.

"Thanks. I owe you."

"You're welcome," she said dryly, rising to hang up the phone. "And yes, you do."

"Beth, wait. You have a minute?"

She swallowed the fiery words on the tip of her tongue and breathed a sigh of relief. She hadn't really wanted to hang up. "What's going on, David?"

"I'm sorry I got off without saying goodbye, but I…I thought it best at the time."

"Why? What happened?"

"I've just had a lot on my head. I'd rather not go into it just yet. What have you been up to?"

Feeling the vein at her temple throb, she decided to voice her annoyance. "No. I want to know what made you sweep Bree away and not even allow him to call me." Her voice was edged with irritation. "How could you do that and not consider that I would need some kind of explanation?"

"I know, Beth. I'm sorry. I just got ahead of myself on some things, that's all."

"What things, David," she pressed. "Is it me?"

"I'll talk with you about it when I get it all sorted out. Okay?"

A familiar sense of rejection shot through Beth, and she wondered if their moment had reawakened his feelings for Deidre. Alarmed by that possibility, she quickly drove the thought away. Despite still feeling miffed, she proceeded to do something counter to her instincts—and to the vow she had made to herself. She told David about the note she had found among old letters to Michael and conveyed her concerns.

"Beth, try to stop worrying about things you can't change." Even though his voice was low, it pulled so intensely at her heart that she began to crave his embrace. "As far as the note...I wouldn't read anything sinister into it. You're predisposed for the negative. You've got to stop doing this to yourself."

Thankful that she hadn't mentioned the phone calls or her involvement with Tricia, she shifted gears and began playing down her concerns.

"I'm sorry, David. I didn't mean to hit you with this. As you can see, my mind is all wound up with no place to go."

"I don't mind listening, Beth. You know that. What's really going on? What's wrong?"

Her heart ached to tell him everything, including how she felt about him. She loved him desperately, but she certainly couldn't tell him. She couldn't take the expected rejection—not from David.

"Beth, you'll know what to do when the time is right," he said, clearly assuming she was upset about something else. Still, she was moved by the unselfish tenderness of his attempt to comfort her.

SIXTEEN

The sun had begun its descent. Beth and Manny sat on the top step of Lena's front porch, enjoying the breeze. She was grateful he had stopped by with the dogs. But he still seemed a little distant. The last time they had visited, Manny had insisted she had become obsessed with the threatening note she'd found.

Admittedly, she was extremely distracted by aspects of the investigation, as well as David's guarded explanation for his conduct. She glanced around at Tiger and Gus. They looked great; she could tell Manny had been working with them. They were unusually alert and very well behaved. She couldn't get enough of their wet greetings.

"Thanks for bringing them by, Manny," Beth said. "I'm glad to see them so well adjusted."

"I've been taking them out with me," he said without turning. "They train real good. It helped that they already knew me."

"No, you just have a way with animals."

Manny grew silent again, staring off into the open field across the road. Beth absently reached over and pulled a piece of straw from his hair. The movement startled him, and he recoiled from her touch.

"Sorry. Didn't mean to spook you."

He laughed hoarsely. "Just off into one of my dreams, I guess."

"What do you dream about?"

He turned toward her. "Lots of things…just like you. I just need to move on."

"But you have…you've got Kia, your garage, and…"

"You know I'll miss y'all when you move to the city," he said, interrupting her. "It feels strange. Kinda like my family is moving away and leaving me behind. Just brooding, I guess."

"Manny, you're my best friend. We won't ever lose touch with each other. I'll still be coming out here to church, and every now and then just for a visit. And you'll come see me."

"I know," he said, stretching his legs. "What's been bothering *you*?"

She chuckled a little, surprised by his abrupt change of subjects. "Nothing really. Why?"

"I saw it all over ya when I drove up. I hear you been digging around in county records, too."

Unwilling to discuss her search, Beth leaned forward and brushed an ant from her bare ankle. She found another trailing its path and stood to stomp around to shake off any that might've gone unnoticed.

"Did you know about Daddy investigating Charla's death?" She had hit a nerve. He looked straight at her, unblinking. Then his eyes moved down to his feet and out to the field.

"Yeah, I knew. He was getting pretty close to something, too. Told me so. Then he had that stroke. Couldn't seem to remember much after that."

"Why didn't you tell me?" she asked, a little annoyed. "And why did you get so testy when I showed you the note I'd found among Michael's letters?"

Manny looked around at her. "Rev'n Ray didn't want you knowing about things like that. Said you'd push your way into the middle of everything. Maybe even get yourself in some kind of trouble."

Beth briefly considered going to the sheriff with the note. Maybe it would be the lead they needed. But then, he might think she planted it. Maybe Manny was right. She was placing too much importance on a four-year-old note. After all, the sheriff had already gone through Michael's things.

"I wonder if Daddy talked to the sheriff about what he might have found."

"Yeah. Sheriff and Rev'n Ray had several disagreements over Charla, Terry and Felix. They just wasn't paying him any mind." Manny shrugged and lowered his head. "All they do is party around and strong-arm folk. I've tangled with 'em a time or two myself. They used to bring Pa home all beat up and tell Ma he'd been in a brawl. But Pa always said they'd beat up on him. He was a lot of things, Beth, but he wasn't no liar."

Beth felt apprehension creeping up her spine. "Does Sheriff Harper know his deputies are mistreating people?"

"He's gotta know. Probably sent 'em to do it. Folks 'round here are scared of 'em. They don't feel protected. And it just ain't nobody to *tell* without it flyin' back in our faces. Been feeling guilty 'bout saying anything about it to you before. I knew you'd go out and get something stirred up."

Beth's chest grew heavy and her breathing shallow. She could feel the heat of irritation warming her cheeks. "I wish I'd known Daddy had looked into all this."

Manny squeezed her shoulders in an embrace. "I'm sorry, Beth. He started back when Shannon and Charla died. He got interested 'cause they died just two weeks apart. The sheriff dismissed his suspicions because Shannon committed suicide."

"I've never been able to believe that, but I guess there's no other explanation." She looked away, as she was apt to do when revisiting pain. "Do you think Terry and Felix disappearing as they did could be a hoax? They could have had something to do with the shenanigans. They could've even sent that note to Michael."

"I s'pose anything's possible, but I don't see it. What would be the aim? Besides, those three were as thick as thieves."

Beth nodded. "I've been thinking about it a lot. Maybe Michael had done something to make the other two mad. Maybe if the three of them ran down Charla…"

"Could be Michael threatened to tell," Manny added, getting caught up in Beth's conjecture. "But if that was so…they waited an awful long time to pay him back."

Despite her relief that Manny was once again in her corner, Beth's agitated state intensified. "Manny, what if someone is looking to hurt *me*?"

"You!" he said, giving her shoulders another squeeze. "Why would you say that?"

"Don't you remember what the note said? '*What happens to a Three Musketeer that gets too close to a flame?*'"

"You're not a Three Musketeer."

"But Manny, everyone that's dead and missing was connected to me in some way. And somebody's been calling my job."

He sat up straight, shocked disbelief in his eyes. "Does Mr. Steele know about this? Does Carl?"

"No. I can't tell them. Carl doesn't think much of my misgivings lately. He says I'm letting my imagination run wild."

"Does this caller say anything?"

"The last couple of times, but usually he just breathes and holds the phone until I hang up."

"I don't know, Beth. You're playing with fire digging around like you are. Maybe you'd better back off this thing for a while."

"Maybe you're right. But I think it's already too late for that."

"You need to get yourself involved with something else." Manny whistled for the dogs, and they came running. "Come tomorrow, I'll be taking me a little vacation. I'll see you when I get back."

"Where are you going?" Beth asked. Just then Gus jumped into her lap and Manny grasped his collar.

"Down," he said sternly. Gus sat at Manny's foot and waited there patiently. Beth was impressed by the dog's obedience.

It didn't dawn on her until after he'd gone that Manny never said where he was going.

—m—

Beth moved through the next few days in a haze. With the phone calls still coming, she sensed impending doom. Terror was her daily companion, usually settling in the pit of her stomach. She couldn't be imagining things. Even Manny had recognized that she might be in danger.

Beth pushed in the drawer to the file cabinet and moved back to her desk. She had taken to locking the front door when Taylor was away from the office. It took more than a notion to even come in to work anymore.

She started wondering if the sheriff was somehow in cahoots with George Tubbs. There was no other explanation for why the disappearances hadn't been thoroughly investigated. Everything, the bank, her dad, the shooting, and the disappearances tumbled around in her mind constantly. She didn't know how George Tubbs could be linked to the Three Musketeers, but was certain everything was somehow connected.

Frustrated and admitting that she was in over her head, Beth finally decided to talk to Taylor and Tricia again. David would be home soon, and would make a good buffer when she explained everything to Carl.

The telephone rang. She flinched and stared at it for several moments before picking it up. "Taylor Steele's Office."

"I'm warning you," the whisperer said. "If you don't keep your land, you'll disappear, too."

The caller hung up, leaving Beth rigid with terror. She gulped spastically as vivid images of her death rushed into her mind.

SEVENTEEN

Beth sat at the conference table, her heart racing. Taylor was busy examining documents that she and Tricia had laid out before him on the table. Just as she was about to speak, Tricia spoke up.

"Beth, we checked the consistency of samples from your dad's prescriptions. I also spoke with your father's physician, a Douglas Conner?"

Beth nodded, her fingers gripping the edge of the table.

"I'm sorry, but the two don't jive."

She stiffened. "What do you mean?"

"Your father's prescriptions were not being filled according to the doctor's instructions. His high blood pressure medication, for one, was totally different. The others were laced with something that, if taken for long periods, could cause memory loss and sometimes death. Beth, your suspicions were right on. Your father was literally being poisoned."

The gratitude that filled her quickly faded. Though she was relieved to hear the corroborating revelation, she was also horrified. She thought of the calls she'd been getting. She couldn't just blow them off as cranks anymore. Someone was actually threatening her. Unexpectedly, she began to tremble as tears flooded her eyes.

Taylor looked at her worriedly. "Can you handle this?"

Beth nodded, quickly wiping away the tears.

"We sent the sheriff to arrest Mr. Tubbs," Tricia said. "But the drugstore was closed up. We can't find him. We've put out an all points bulletin."

Taylor took her hand and squeezed it. "Beth, you realize that this is no longer a question of whether you have a valid complaint, don't you? It's now a matter of life and death."

She felt cold but forced herself to continue. "Do you think the sheriff may be in on this?"

"That's where you lose me," Tricia said. "What motive would Sheriff Harper have in any of this?"

"I-I realize a lot of what I told you is speculation. But it's based on other things that have been going on for years—things I just recently got a real handle on." She turned toward Taylor. "What about the shooting? I thought you might understand that. Then there's Michael's disappearance, Charla Welch's murder and the other missing two."

"Who's missing?" Tricia asked, her eyes showing confusion. "What are you talking about?"

"Michael's two best friends," she said, opening her purse. Beth found the note, pulled it out and shoved it at Taylor. "It's significant because those three were real tight in high school. They were called the Three Musketeers. The postmark is four years ago."

By now, Beth was engulfed in tremors and a profusion of emotions. Taylor and Tricia looked at each other, bewildered, and then turned curious stares on her.

"Beth!" Taylor called out, his hands outstretched. "You're shaking like crazy. Tell us what you're talking about."

"Taylor, you know Michael and I were engaged back then. We were in Austin. Around the time he got this note, he was not himself...mean and frightened. I know it seems like several different cases, but deep down I feel like they're all linked," she said, her voice shrill with intensity. "You've gotta help me. Everybody thinks I'm obsessed, but something's got to be done."

Taylor placed several documents down on the table and pulled the note from Tricia's hand. "Maybe Carl will be more inclined to listen since we've uncovered Tubb's assault on your father." He read the words on the note again. "You and Michael had broken up prior to you leaving Austin, right?"

Beth didn't want to go into detail about their breakup, and was desperate to get back to her explanation. She wanted to say everything before she forgot something. She wanted to put things in the proper perspective. "Yes."

Tricia cleared her throat. "Were you still in love with him, Beth?"

Beth bit her lower lip. She thought about David and the things they had discussed on the ridge. "No."

Tricia shook her head. "You're right about something else, Beth. You seem to be talking about several cases in one, and they all seem to have one thing in common—insufficient evidence for prosecution. Your father's, however, has sufficient evidence to be ruled a homicide."

Homicide. The word seemed hard and earth shattering. Beth pressed hard to keep focused.

Taylor went over to the coffeepot and poured himself a refill. "Either one of you want a cup?"

"No, thanks," they replied in unison.

"I'm more interested in Tubbs and what made you suspect *him*, Beth," Taylor said.

"He's the pharmacist. He's probably feeling guilty about letting his family's property get into other hands when all along he had the means to recover it. He's been buying up a lot of land around Plover Creek. Said he wanted to put in a riding stable. Apparently, he'd been after Daddy to sell for years. But Daddy was strongly against us selling to *him*. I found that strange, given that they were friends."

Tricia smiled. "You're talking about the tax sale."

"Yes," Beth said.

Taylor stared at Tricia. "I've thought that odd ever since you told me about it. If his family owned it, why didn't he know about it?"

"Because he was raised by a single mother who hadn't disclosed his father's identity—not until several years ago—just before she died. For the first time, Tubbs went to an Anderson family reunion."

"Is that where he got the idea to buy back all the property?" Taylor asked with a smirk. "I've never heard of anything so ludicrous."

"It may be ludicrous to you, but Tubbs was serious," Tricia said. "His family even contributed to the cause. Maybe he's fixated. It would be an ideal maneuver to guarantee acceptance by a family that for years probably wanted nothing to do with him or his mother."

Taylor stared at Tricia for a long moment. "You want to tell me how you found out all this?"

"I have a lot of people who owe me favors—one is a private investigator."

The temperature was well over a hundred degrees, but it didn't faze Bree one bit. He bounced around in the back seat of the rental, chattering constantly about seeing Beth.

"How much longer, Daddy?"

Carl turned to look into the excited eyes of the child and smiled. David had picked him up at his Plover Creek apartment and they were now on their way into the thickly forested community for dinner at Lena's.

"Bree, I don't think I've ever seen you so excited. What's gotten into you?"

"I gonna stay with Beth," he chirped. "Beth loves me."

Carl laughed aloud and winked at David. "I know she does. But it seems to me...I saw a little tyke about your age running around with Beth about a month ago?"

Bree giggled and playfully fell back on the seat. "That was m-e-e-e! I wanna see her again."

David drove on, wishing he could express his feelings as unabashedly as his son. He was just as eager as Bree to see Beth. But being an adult required that he maintain a degree of reserve. He sighed heavily, unable to keep his thoughts clear of her.

"Dave, I didn't want to tell you until you got here. Taylor called me today. Apparently, a warrant has been issued for George's arrest. He said he would talk to us all about it once you arrived."

"Arrest!" David said. "For what?"

"Taylor wouldn't say. But I think it has something to do with Beth. I don't mind telling you I'm scared out of my gourd. Beth has been down at the courthouse digging up all kinds of things."

"Why?"

Carl shrugged. "She doesn't tell me anything. I hear what's talked about throughout the community."

David grimaced slightly, glancing at Carl. "Do you think Beth has been right all along, Carl? I've had my doubts, too. Especially since the shooting and car accident."

"I don't know. Taylor told me George was working for the realtor that handled the sale of the land when Mom and Dad first moved here. Several years ago, he found out that he was related to the original owner. Beth thinks that's why he wanted to get it back so badly."

"It makes sense," David said, making a mental note to question Beth about it later. "At any rate, Taylor is getting a good deal."

Carl nodded absently. "I'm surprised at how smoothly things are coming together, considering the scary start. It's Beth that's scaring me now."

"She's not getting in over her head or anything, is she?" David asked apprehensively.

"Nah. I got Taylor keeping an eye on her. But I'm not sure he knows she's going everywhere checking into George's past—tax assessor, city clerk."

"How's she been feeling?"

"Great. Just as active and fit as she was before the accident."

Agitated, David ran his hand over his hair, sighing. "My anxiety probably won't dissipate until all of this is over."

"What's *dis pa tate*?" Bree asked, stepping up between the bucket seats.

"Bree, didn't we agree you would stay in your seatbelt?"

"Yes, sir," he said somberly, sitting back down in his seat. He fumbled with the clasp of his belt until he managed to close it around him.

SECRET THUNDER

"I think I know what you mean," Carl said. "It's uncommonly quiet right now, except for the search for George. I'm almost scared a storm is brewing."

"You mean George has disappeared?"

"Apparently," Carl said. "Taylor said he's had a friend looking into the law enforcement out here. She's assistant to the DA."

David looked at Carl disbelievingly, letting out a long, muted whistle. "Are you ready for the antagonism their little investigation might stir up around here?"

"Anything is better than what we have."

The possibilities were enormous, and David considered that he might be feeling as anxious about things around there as Beth. Apart from his feelings for her, his concerns about the atmosphere and threat in the community had worried him a great deal. He decided to change the subject. "Will you and Lena stay in Plover Creek after you marry?"

"I don't know. We thought about moving into Dallas, but I'm feeling that's not far enough. I should have more of a warm feeling about home, but I just want a change—a new beginning."

"I'm surprised to hear you say that," David said. "Have you ever thought about moving to Seattle? I would love having you closer."

"I thought about it, but I need to stick close to Beth until I know she'll be all right. She told me she wanted to get away, too. By the way, she mentioned she wanted to talk to both of us later this evening."

David's heart leaped expectantly. "Did she tell you what it was about?"

"Nah. She seemed a little nervous, though. I think it may have something to do with this thing on George. Probably wants to say, *I told you so*. I'm worried about her getting too close to it. You know how stubborn she can be."

David was all too aware of Beth's stubborn streak. "Just like your dad when he looked into Charla's killing."

"Yeah. Beth was plenty annoyed when that little bit of information slipped out. Things must have slipped his memory after the stroke, because he didn't mention what he'd learned. But Beth's determined to

148

pick away at things. I'm afraid she's headed on a direct collision course with Bill Harper. You think you could talk to her?"

"I'll see what I can do," David said, suddenly feeling exhausted.

"By the way, I want to run something by you." Carl paused and glanced in the back seat before going on. "You remember when you left...on the Fourth?"

David's grip on the steering wheel tightened as guilt washed over him anew. How could he forget? He had made a complete mess of things for himself, as well as for his son. "What about it?"

David checked on Bree in the rearview mirror. He was fighting sleep.

"I was wondering if you two argued. I heard her crying...way into the night. It sort of scared me."

David's breath quickened. "No, we didn't argue. What's going on, Carl?"

"I understand she had already talked to you about something that happened with Mike at school."

David was relieved Beth had finally confided in her brother. "I'm glad she told you. I tried to get her to talk to you sooner, but you know Beth."

Carl shook his head from side to side. "I'm thankful she had you to talk to. If Mike weren't missing..."

David nodded, understanding Carl's rage. "I know. She's been carrying that load for years."

"I've talked to her a couple of times since then, but she's been rather quiet. She said she felt a little better. I can't imagine what she must've been going through all this time with that memory. And the child." Carl shook his head sadly. "She's always wanted children."

David felt the knot in his stomach tighten. "What do you mean?"

"Well, it's not like God didn't know these things would happen. You and I are so caught up in what Beth can and can't bear that we haven't factored in His grace. As I said before, my sister is an amazingly strong woman."

"Yeah. But it's so hard to stay on track when tragedy hits home."

"And did it hit big!"

David was tempted to ask about Beth and Taylor, but decided against it. He hadn't been able to get the image of their cozy embrace out of his head. He simply couldn't bear to see any man other than himself holding her.

"How does Beth feel about you and Lena getting married?"

"I think she's happy for us, but she's been too busy obsessing about the lack of action from the sheriff's office."

There was a lot more going on than David had realized. He wondered where Manny was in all this. As his concerns forced their way to the forefront of his mind, David glanced back at his sleeping son. "Carl, where does Manny play into all this? I mean, the shooting...Mike's disappearance..."

Carl glanced at David. "You thinking he makes a good suspect for what's been going on?"

"I hate to, but yeah. The funny thing is that the possibility doesn't even seem to occur to Beth."

"I started to mention it to you several times since she told me about Mike," Carl said. "But I didn't want her to overhear me. You know, you're welcome to bunk with me while you're here."

David smiled at his friend. He looked tired and worried. "Nah, I have a lot to take care of tomorrow in Dallas."

"How long will you be here?"

"Just a couple of days." When David pulled the car into the pebbled drive, he noted the new black SUV parked next to Lena's car.

"That's what she got with the insurance money from the accident," Carl said, gesturing with his head.

David opened the door and stepped toward the vehicle. "Nice. She's a real trucker now, huh?"

"I'll take sleepyhead in and put him down," Carl said, pulling open the back door. "Go ahead and take a look if you like. It drives great."

David watched Carl go through the front door with Bree before he opened the door to Beth's car. The interior had that new leather smell, but he could also detect a hint of her flowery cologne. He slid into the driver's seat, leaned his head back against the headrest and closed his eyes. He hadn't realized how exhausted he was.

"Hey, what are you doing, mister?"

David opened his eyes just in time to see Beth's deep-dimpled features coming around the front of the vehicle. All the bruises on her face were gone. Her creamy brown skin shone with life. The sun was just softening in the sky touching her face with a hazy orange glow. For an instant, he wasn't sure he was fully awake, as there was a surreal quality to the scene.

He promptly climbed down from the seat, intending to give her a quick glad-to-see-you hug. But his arms seemed to lock her in as he possessively tightened his embrace. Forcing himself to back off, David stepped back and searched her face. "How's it going, Beth?"

"I'm good," she said, smiling up at him. "Like my new buggy?"

"Very much. When can I take it for a spin?"

"How 'bout after dinner? But I have to go with you," she added, giving him a mischievous grin and playful squeeze.

"Just like horning in on our dates again, huh?"

"Well, deep down, I guess I'm still your shadow."

"I wouldn't have it any other way," he said, pulling her toward the front door.

EIGHTEEN

Beth relaxed to the sound of the soothing jazz David had tuned to on the radio. Though she was nervous about the things she had to tell him and Carl, she was grateful they could spend a little time alone. She was surprised how much she had wanted David to kiss her back at Lena's house. The moment he put his arms around her, it was as if the last four and a half weeks never happened. She had felt his eyes on her all evening.

Bree had been so tuckered out he went back to sleep after he'd eaten. Nevertheless, it had been good to hold him close again. The physical contact seemed to magically erase years of loneliness in her—for a little while, anyway. For David's part, he was attentive toward her, but the detached look in his hazel eyes remained. That puzzled her. Could it be he and Deidre might be getting back together? If so, she certainly wouldn't, couldn't, interfere. She wished she were bold enough to ask him outright, but she was afraid of his answer.

She peered through the darkness at his strong, sculptured profile. The meager illumination from the dashboard exposed muscle-rippled forearms and a tense posture. He looked good. The casual burgundy shirt and denims clung to his athletic build too perfectly. His presence seemed to fill the cab of the vehicle as she inhaled the clean brawny scent of his cologne. It was intoxicating. Beth had stolen several side glances since they had pulled out of the driveway. "Penny for your thoughts."

He looked at her briefly. "I was just wondering what you would think about coming to Seattle."

"Actually, I've given it quite a bit of thought. I would like to get away from Texas and start over. What's it like?"

"You'd like it. And I know Bree would be crazy about the idea of having you so close."

Bree, he says. What about you, David? God help me. My emotions are so wound up, I'm actually longing for this man to want me.

She toyed with her seat belt, trying to regain control of her emotions. "How is the job market?"

"I don't think you would have any problem finding employment. There's a great school out there, as well. Carl alluded to the idea of him and Lena considering the move. It would be like old times."

Though he spoke warmly, his words stung like the unexpected strike of an angry wasp. Her disappointment was stifling. He was lobbying for everyone, not just her.

After a moment, she mentally shelved any sense of rejection and cleared her throat. "My initial plan was to move into Dallas since my job is there. I had assumed Carl and Lena were planning to move there, too. They've been looking for a house."

"Beth, I'd love to have y'all think seriously about relocating to Seattle. There's nothing really holding you here now. And you said yourself you wanted to get out of Texas."

She couldn't deny the truth in his remarks, but the motivation for his campaign was suspect and disappointing. "I don't know right now, David. I'm doing pretty good, working with Taylor. I'll have to think about it."

He pulled the SUV onto the road leading to Tatum's pond. The headlights hit the old house where Shannon used to live. It was no more than an old abandoned hovel now, only walking distance from the ranch. She reckoned George Tubbs had planned on destroying it now that he owned the property. What would happen now that he had disappeared?

Spasms of grief and nostalgia stoked the disillusionment she had been trying to suppress. David pulled the vehicle beneath a couple of large trees that formed a huge archway overlooking the pond. When he turned off the engine, he sat motionless for several long moments, looking straight ahead.

Instantly, Beth's heart began to pound as images of a passionate kiss blossomed in her mind. When he finally opened the door and got out, she sighed in frustration. *Lord, what is wrong with me? Is this really what love feels like?*

She watched as David took long strides around the front and to her door. He helped her from the vehicle and led her toward the pond, which was surrounded by drying grass and hardened soil.

"Beth, do you mind if I ask you a personal question?"

"Yeah, if you have to preface it with that one."

He stood quietly, his hands jammed into the pockets of his denims. The moon cast a ghostly hue over the night. She looked back at the house and wondered where George Tubbs might be hiding. Though it was extremely warm, she shivered a little and pushed her arm through David's to ease her discomfort.

"The pond doesn't bring back bad memories, does it?"

"You mean Shannon?"

"Yeah."

"Not really," Beth said, shaking her head emphatically. "I just can't see her doing that to herself."

"I'm sorry I brought that up," he said, squeezing her arm against him. "Hey, aren't you afraid we might disturb a snake or two?"

Alarmed, she abruptly withdrew her arm from his. The sound of a distant yowl heightened her unease. In the dimness, she could see David smiling wickedly, laughing he scooped her up into his arms and carried her back to the SUV. His laughter, echoing in the darkness, seemed to soothe her edgy senses.

The warmth of his arms around her made her heart soar, and she clung to him like a child. Just before settling her into the passenger seat, David leaned down and lightly kissed her lips. Her pulse pounded madly and hunger for him ignited her heart. Her breath caught in her throat as he placed her on the seat, his arms still around her. After a moment, he released her, pulled back and closed the door.

She tried, but couldn't make sense of his behavior. It was puzzling. If he wasn't exactly courting her, why was he acting as if they were a couple? She didn't want to jump to conclusions as she had after coming home from the hospital. It was too demeaning. But she did love him.

Beth sat wordless as David got behind the wheel. He's probably just lonely, she reasoned, trying to rein in her mounting anticipation. Then she remembered that he wanted to ask her something. As if reading her mind, David turned to her after starting the engine and placed his arm over the back of the seat. "May I ask you that question now?"

She could see his penetrating stare in the dimness. His eyes held her captive. Suddenly, a feeling that bad news was imminent came over her. "Of course."

"How serious is it between you and Taylor?"

Beth's mouth dropped open in disbelief, her face burned with outrage. How wrong, how silly she had been. She thought he had wanted to ask about her feelings—or his. But that wasn't it. Why would he want to ask anything of an inexperienced woman who, only months earlier, he had assumed was so distraught she was about to fling herself off a ridge?

"What?" Beth struggled to suppress her anger, puzzled as to how he had gotten such a ludicrous idea about her and Taylor. Maybe he wanted to lecture her on dating outside her race. Maybe he was just humoring his son's playmate by spending a little time with her.

Her body was rigid with indignation. How dare he make assumptions and try to tell her how to run her life? He obviously still thought of her as a child. Her embarrassment at her own hopeful notions only intensified her anger. It drove her thoughts past reason.

As if shocked by an electric current, Beth's mind raced back to the Fourth of July. Why was she thinking about that, she wondered. A clear image of Mr. Baker walking away flashed into her mind. She recalled Taylor's consoling embrace after she had discovered the note. Then remembered Lena saying it was about then that David had gone looking for her. Apparently, David had seen the scene and mistakenly assumed he had stumbled upon a cozy tryst.

Jolting Beth from her musing, David pressed for answers. "Has he asked you to marry him?"

"I really don't need to hear a lecture about my choice in men."

"I'm sorry," he said, putting the SUV in gear. "I didn't mean to pry."

As soon as they pulled into Lena's driveway, Beth jumped from the vehicle and rushed up the walkway ahead of David. He caught up with her just before she reached the door and gently spun her around to face him.

"Will you please stop this?" he demanded. "I wouldn't dream of trying to counsel you in matters of love. I simply wanted to know where the two of you stood. Can't I ask you a simple question anymore without getting my head snapped off?"

She stared up into his face, noting his troubled expression, and instantly lowered her head. Her thoughts were a muddle of humiliation, fears and disappointments. She just couldn't think with him so close, so in her face. Slowly, she calmed her breathing and allowed her emotions to settle before speaking.

"I'm sorry. I guess I overreacted. I-I just…"

David took her arms and drew her closer to him. "What is it, Beth?"

"Oh, David. Why can't things be simple?" Emboldened by their closeness, she wrapped her arms around his neck and drew his head downward. A current of some kind passed between them, and they were both quivering when their lips met. Neither seemed anxious to pull away. Beth felt as if she had landed in a haven of warmth and safety. "David, I've wanted to tell you for weeks how much I love you."

"Oh, *honey*," he whispered. "I wish you had."

Beth loved the sweet sound of the endearment as David drew her back into his arms and kissed her again. After a while, she rested her head on his chest, afraid to think too hard or too soon about what this new development would mean for them. She pulled away and moved to sit in the swing on the porch.

David joined her and she offered her hand, lacing her fingers with his. "I don't want to be afraid to love, David. But I want to be in God's perfect will."

"What else do you want, Beth? What are those dreams you've held back?"

She lowered her eyes. "I want you, David. You've been a part of my dreams for a long time. I want a family. And I guess I just want...I want God to love me, use me."

"What do you mean?" David sounded perplexed.

Beth raised her eyes. Laughter from inside the house drifted through the window. "I don't know. And there's absolutely nothing between Taylor and me. He's simply a friend and my boss."

David stared at her for a long moment, apparently trying to determine which of her thoughts he wanted to explore. "But I saw...I thought..."

"You're talking about the Fourth of July, aren't you?"

David lifted her fingers to his lips and kissed them. Laughing lightly, he said, "You're beginning to dance between subjects like Miss Virgie. I saw the two of you."

"It was a friendly offer of comfort, David," Beth said. "I was upset about finding the note I told you about in the stack of letters Mr. Baker brought me. Taylor just happened to walk up. It didn't mean anything."

Moments passed before either of them spoke again. But she was grateful that the tension was finally gone. "I'm in love with you, too, you know. I just didn't want to hurt you by interfering in something you might've wanted."

Beth laid her head on his shoulder and let him press several quick kisses on her lips. "I guess now is as good a time as any to talk to you and Carl."

"I'm glad you finally told him what happened in Austin. He told me the sheriff is looking for George. Does that have anything to do with what you want to talk to us about?"

She took a deep breath. "I'm trying to trust God more, one step at a time. I've decided that this thing, this feeling of needing to dig for the truth must come from Him, David. That's why Carl's and your opposition gets in the way."

David lowered his head. "I just want to keep you safe, Beth. Now that we've finally connected, I don't want anything happening to you."

The light from the living room shone through the window. David tenderly brushed his hand along her face. It seemed to energize her. She closed her eyes, savoring the tantalizing touch of his fingertips on her cheeks and lips.

"Do you know how beautiful you are?" he asked, once again capturing her lips with his.

David looked up when the front door opened. Beth, apparently still jumpy from everything going on around them, practically bolted from the swing in panic. Carl and Lena casually strolled out of the house and moved to the top step.

"Kinda jumpy, aren't you, Sis?" Carl asked, looking at them curiously. "You 'bout ready for that talk?"

Not until the two were sitting did David sense that Beth had relaxed. His brow furrowed with concern as he caught Carl eyes.

"Beth," Lena began. "Do you need a little more privacy for this?"

"No. Please stay." Beth turned back to David. "You all are aware that Daddy was getting pretty close to something in regard to Charla's death, right? He even talked to Manny about it."

"That's what I gather, but I don't know if it had any real significance, since he dropped the whole thing. He never said much to Carl or me about it." David looked at her with a raised brow, silently urging her to continue.

"I gave Tricia Peters—she's Taylor's friend and assistant to the DA—Mom's diaries and a box of Daddy's notes a while back. The police lab in Dallas has conducted analyses of samples of his prescription drugs, too."

"Hold on, Beth," Carl said, struggling to his feet. "What have you done?"

"Carl, let her finish," Lena said, pulling him back down beside her.

"The final entries in Mom's last diary are strange. They don't sound quite like her." Beth stared defiantly at Carl. "I had to make someone hear me. Nobody was doing anything."

David saw that she was trembling. He squeezed her hand, hoping it would help. "What's going on?"

She stared at him, her eyes frantic and haunted. David could see that she was indeed keyed up about something.

"Were y'all aware that Sheriff Harper's deputies mistreat people out here? I just wonder why nobody has ever done anything about it."

"I'd heard talk here and there. But, Beth, you can't get all caught up in that," Carl said. "Are you saying this has something to do with Dad's death?"

She looked down at her lap. "Not directly." Very deliberately, Beth looked back at her brother, holding his gaze. "Carl, the lab found something terrible."

Beth now had Carl's full attention. "What did you say?"

"Daddy's medication was laced with other chemicals," she said, her pulse quickening. "The warrant for Mr. Tubbs is for Daddy's murder."

Carl was on his feet again, now glaring at his sister incredulously. David anxiously held up his hands. "Beth, wait a minute. Did you initiate this investigation through the DA's office?"

"Y-yes, I did."

Shocked into stunned silence, their eyes were now glued to Beth's face. David's mind skipped back to the time she, at age seven, had warned her father that something bad was going to happen. Two hours later, the trailer had disconnected from the truck on the interstate. Tragically, one of the horses was killed. She had felt so guilty and had been so devastated that she vowed to never speak of her premonitions again.

"I guess you're right," Carl said. "You've already come up with some hard evidence." Noting Lena's firm hand on Carl's shoulder, David could tell his friend was struggling to control his emotions. "Why didn't Taylor call me? He promised me—"

"Be quiet, big brother. He didn't tell you because I convinced him to let me do it. There's more than meets the eye going on out here, and I believe George Tubbs and Sheriff Harper are involved. So naturally I couldn't go to the sheriff."

"Beth, please," Carl warned. "I've been hearing about your poking around up at the courthouse. I'm sure everyone else involved has heard the same thing."

Her eyes, intense and determined, slowly moved past them. "I'm already in the middle of this," she said, trying to keep her hands still. "And you both know Mr. Tubbs has always treated me like I had a second head."

"You've never been hospitable to George. How did you expect him to treat you?" Carl asked pitifully. "And he apologized for his rudeness on the phone."

"An apology doesn't change the fact that he poisoned our father to get hold of the property, Carl. Don't you forget, an hour after that phone call, you had a broken leg and Midnight was dead." Her eyes shone with the power of truth. "It's strange, though, how quickly he calmed down when you told him the property was already sold. I guess his appearance at the hospital the morning Daddy died was the thing that set me off."

Carl was obviously stunned by Beth's bombshell. But David was more than a little relieved that Carl was finally listening to her.

"Carl, I think Beth has uncovered some solid leads—so solid the law is taking action. Maybe we should all sit down and have a talk with Taylor and Miss Peters. Beth, you can mention it, but I'll set it up when I meet with him tomorrow."

In her quiet way, Beth turned to face David. "There's something else," she said reluctantly. "Carl would probably say I'm being paranoid. But I think someone's watching me all the time. I've been giving that note a lot of thought. And the phone calls are coming more frequently now."

"What phone calls?" David bellowed. "What are you talking about?"

His outburst startled her. Apparently, she thought she had mentioned this already. "Forget it! Maybe this one *is* all in my head."

"Beth, please don't clam up on us, now," Carl pleaded, moving to the chair next to them. He paused, trying to steady his own emotions. "I'm so sorry I didn't believe you."

"Let's just drop it," Beth said calmly.

"No!" Carl snapped. "You brought it up, and—"

"Please!"

Carl looked at his sister long and hard. "All right, Beth. But promise me we'll get around to discussing this *soon*. Clearly, this is nothing to play around with."

After a long silence, Beth began to speak again. At first, it seemed as if she was talking to herself. David and Carl kept looking at each other, concern etched on both their faces. "I've been thinking a lot about Terry and Felix. What if—"

David looked at Beth again, taking her hand in his. He could sense the anxiety surging through her body—her mind. His own pulse was racing and there was a roaring in his ears.

"Honey, nobody's coming after you," he said, trying to reduce the intensity of her fear. "You've been right here in plain sight for years."

She turned to him and smiled, her voice low and controlled. "How did you know what I was thinking?"

"Just a lucky guess," he said, trying to keep himself together. "Why are you worried about Terry and Felix?"

"But what if they're the ones who grabbed Michael?"

David looked at Carl again. "That's very unlikely."

"I know it doesn't make much sense," Beth said, looking down. "But I'm certain that this four-year-old note was an actual threat, and that all this is somehow connected to Mr. Tubbs and the sheriff's office."

The implications of it all horrified Lena. "Why are you so certain?"

Beth shrugged stiffly. "I can't answer that precisely, but I'm thinking one of them might've run down Charla. I know that Shannon and I were indirectly connected to all of them. She's gone, the three of them are gone. I'm the only one left."

David gently squeezed the hand that had tightened around his. "All this *is* rather strange. But I still don't believe you have anything to worry about."

Shaken and wide-eyed, Lena said, "Beth, you're scaring me. I still don't understand how George Tubbs would be connected to the Three Musketeers."

Beth shifted in her seat, a frown creasing her brow. "I don't know. There's a lot that still doesn't add up for me either, Lena."

"Do you think the phone calls are from George Tubbs?" David asked, anxious to keep her talking.

"Can you please tell me why I'm just now hearing about phone calls and somebody being after you?" Carl asked. David cringed, certain his friend had thwarted Beth's willingness to talk.

"Because you've been treating me like a paranoid invalid," Beth said. "Now be quiet and let me think."

At Beth's final rebuke, Lena could hold back the laughter no longer. Her amusement was welcome, because it took the edge off the tense moment. Soon, they were all chuckling without a clue as to why. Then Beth's mood turned dark again.

"Daddy's first stroke was just after finding out something during his investigation, right? After talking with Manny, I came to the conclusion that folks out here are afraid for us more than they are for themselves. Carl, you often comment on how superstitious this community is. I know that mixing superstitions with one's faith can generate some pretty eerie notions."

Carl noticeably stiffened and glanced toward David. David smiled, impressed by the clarity that seemed to flow from Beth. She was talking to them now, free of inhibitions and without all the pandemonium.

Lena drew closer and kneeled down on the floor in front of them. Carl stood. "Take my place, Lena."

"No, I'm fine right here. Sit down," she said. "Beth, what made you keeping digging at George Tubbs?"

"Because even though we were struggling to keep afloat, Daddy was against him buying the property." Beth glanced around at all of them then, a smile on her face and her eyes misting. "It may not mean anything other than I have an overactive imagination, but it started me thinking."

Carl looked at David then back at his sister as if it were the first time he had seen her in months. "I'm so sorry for being so overprotective and less than supportive, Sis. I hadn't looked at things in quite this light, even though you tried to tell me."

Beth and Lena retired for the evening.

While David drove Carl back to his apartment in town, they began to discuss the whole situation in its new light.

"I think I'll take you up on that offer to stay at your place tonight. It's a little late and I'm beat," David said. "Beth's wound up pretty tight about this thing, isn't she?"

"With good reason. She's on to something. She's really making me stand up and take notice of my own slothfulness."

"She desperately needs our support, Carl."

Carl nodded his agreement. "I know this is serious, but my main concern is Beth. I don't want her hurt. Maybe now that she doesn't have to keep her part in this a secret, she'll let the professionals do their job."

"I'm still worried that she wouldn't elaborate on those phone calls she's been getting."

"Yeah, I know. Obviously, my little sister is still keeping some things from us." Carl put his head back, sighing. "I suppose she really *does* have an ear for God's whispers. That night in the hospital…she told me she heard Him right before the accident. I haven't studied that sort of thing much. So I don't really know how to counsel her."

David smiled. "What do you think about it? This ear she has?"

"I can see it now. Even going back to her childhood, I can really see it. I think I'll go over when all this is over and talk with Bishop Orville about it."

David nodded. "I've been thinking about some of the things she did as a child. It's a little disconcerting," David said. "Not just that, but the whole thing. She said it tonight, and I agree. We've got to believe God is leading her. And if He is, He's big enough to keep her safe."

The two men drove on in silence, each pondering his own theories. David broke the silence with another startling thought.

"Did you happen to take a good look at Beth's car after her accident?"

"Yeah, it must have flipped several times. It was banged up pretty good."

"Didn't you tell me she was scared out of her mind when she regained consciousness? I think you said she thought someone was after her. She was like that tonight, too."

"Yeah, I noticed. She still can't remember everything that happened just before she went off the road. That's common with a concussion, but I just can't believe swerving to miss a deer could do as much damage as I saw on the rear bumper. You think it's all related?"

"Beth is frightened. I watched her closely tonight—I sensed it more intently than I ever have in another person. I think her subconscious is blocking that afternoon for some reason."

NINETEEN

The next evening the two long-time friends stood at Taylor's front door. David was trying to pull himself together. Beth's recitation the night before had been revealing—and chilling. Yet in the midst of ugliness, something good and true had emerged: She had declared her love for him. To his relief, it had freed him to do the same.

In spite of a clearer perspective on the situation at hand, David's stomach was churning just as much as it had last night during Beth's disclosures. He had tossed and turned all night, his mind preoccupied with the events she'd described and the terror they had ignited in her. He was thankful that she was too occupied with Bree to come with them today. He wanted to hear what Taylor and Tricia had found out without the distraction of her presence. He would love to simply take her away from Texas. But for now, he had to concentrate on protecting her. He was still thinking of this when the door was suddenly pulled opened.

"Hey, guys. Come on in."

They stepped into Taylor's stylish living room, immediately thankful for the cool temperature inside. "Taylor, I'm real anxious to hear your perspective on what's going on," Carl began.

Taylor smiled. "I know you are. Can I get you something cold to drink? Tricia should be along any minute now."

David sat in the corner of the leather couch and cleared his throat. "I'll take a glass of water."

"Nothing for me," Carl said.

A few minutes into small talk about the heat, the doorbell rang again and Taylor went to admit Tricia Peters. She was an attractive woman, who obviously had eyes for Taylor. Guilt jabbed David's gut as he recalled the off-base assumptions he'd made about Taylor and Beth.

After introductions, Carl straightaway briefed the two on the details garnered from their discussion with Beth the night before. Then Miss Peters spoke.

"Clearly, we have enough evidence to charge Tubbs with the murder of your father, Carl." Carl visibly tensed up. Hearing this from Beth was one thing, but David could only imagine how powerful the impact was coming directly from the assistant district attorney.

David straightened and addressed Miss Peters. "Beth told us you had tests run on Ray's medications. Was the lab able to identify the foreign elements?"

"The chemical analysis revealed that Reverend McDade's hypertension medication was laced with high dosages of nitrates. This is probably what brought on his first stroke four years ago." She paused. "It's really hard to say, because the initial symptoms could have been false, causing the doctor to prescribe incorrectly. I've also been looking into the sheriff's department. Up until now, it's been a covert operation."

"So this really is official?" David asked, looking from one to the other. "I was hoping Beth was overstating things, Miss Peters. She's really worked up."

"Unfortunately, it's very real, David. And please call me *Tricia*. I've already contacted a friend in the state attorney general's office. They're running leads on the sheriff's department. Beth was understandably upset, and naturally wasn't shocked by our findings concerning Mr. Tubbs."

Carl was apparently still mulling over what Tricia had said about Ray's death. He lifted his head then. "To tell the truth, Beth never has been very fond of George, not even as a child."

Taylor chuckled knowingly. "I remember her on the phone with you just after your father's passing. I don't think I've ever seen her so livid."

"For someone who's been through as much as she has...and not be nuts...she's an amazing young woman," Tricia said, shaking her head.

"She's probably a little suspicious of everyone right now. Has she remembered anything more about the accident?"

David shook his head. "No. H-how did you…Carl and I were talking about that last night. We…sort of…we think she may have been run off the road."

"I agree," Taylor interjected. "I've actually had Tricia looking into things ever since the shooting at the ranch. I didn't tell you and Beth, Carl, because I didn't want to worry you or make you think I was ungrateful."

David's stomach muscles tightened. "Are you saying you've suspected something all along? I thought…"

Taylor held up his hand to halt David's objections. "Being fired on is not as small a matter as the sheriff has treated it. I felt obligated to dig a little."

David was dumbfounded. It troubled him that Taylor had recognized danger before the rest of them—except maybe Beth. Why hadn't he and Carl been more receptive to Beth's suspicions? They had been so willing to believe she was distraught and irrational that they had overlooked the obvious. Despite sensing that something was off, even going as far as phoning the sheriff, he had done nothing.

"I'm glad you did," David said, feeling confused. "But this really gives me reason for concern. After talking with Beth last night, Carl and I believe she needs protection."

Carl finally cleared his throat. "We were wondering if we could get her into some kind of protective custody—something she didn't have to be aware of. Oh, I don't know," he said, frustrated. "Is there anything?"

Taylor cleared his throat. "Based on the damage to her car, I'm certain the smashup wasn't an accident. It was an attempt at…"

David's head jerked up. He felt undeniable dread as Taylor's words sank in. "Murder?"

"Possibly," Tricia said. "Maybe just a scare tactic. Either way, Beth saw something. I've talked to a profiler friend in Washington about this. He thinks her mind is blocking something she doesn't want to admit."

Carl stood up and paced around nervously. Moments later, he returned to his seat. The tension began to settle into David's shoulders as Manny's face appeared before him. He worked his neck to ease the stiffness. "Taylor, we really don't want to upset Beth anymore than she already is. But apparently she's been getting some kind of phone calls, too."

"Knowing Beth, if she backs out of this thing as we all want, she'll fall apart," Taylor said, rubbing his chin. "Fear and persistence are keeping her afloat right now. But she's raising a lot of eyebrows with her openly defiant examination of county records. Anything Tricia or her office does out there is under heavy scrutiny, because they expect it. And they rightly assume Beth McDade initiated the whole thing."

"David, what did you mean when you mentioned phone calls?" Tricia interrupted, a skeptical expression on her face.

"Last night, she mentioned getting calls and felt as if someone was watching her."

Both Tricia and Taylor looked startled. "What kind of calls?" Tricia asked.

"I'm assuming threats. She wouldn't elaborate. In fact, she flat out refused to talk about it."

Taylor frowned. "Now that you mention it, I've noticed lately that she's gotten very quiet—almost terror-stricken—after answering a call. She now hesitates before answering the phone when it rings."

"Beth doesn't impress me as someone easily frightened," Tricia said. "Something's obviously going on that she doesn't want to tell."

"Getting Beth under protective surveillance is a good idea. I'm sorry we hadn't thought of it earlier. I know the accident happened a while back, but with these calls...I don't know. We can't be too careful," Taylor said. "It may simply be somebody with a harmless fixation."

Tricia opened her briefcase and pulled out a small pad. "Carl, does the family know anyone by the name of Joab or Silas?"

"No," Carl said. "Not that I can think of. Why?"

"I found those names listed, along with Charla Welch's, among your father's notes. The handwriting was different than his norm—ragged—as if he was struggling, or even angry. It was dated just after his first stroke."

David's brows drew together as he tried hard to remember. "Ray was a little confused at first."

"Actually," Carl interjected. "Joab is an Old Testament military leader, and Silas was a leader in the New Testament church."

"Hmm," Taylor murmured under his breath. "Perhaps he was mixing reflection with writing a sermon." Suddenly, he narrowed his eyes and turned to Tricia. "I think I know just the man to keep an eye on Beth. You remember Todd Levescy, don't you?"

"Yeah, he would love something like this," Tricia agreed. "Carl, Todd is into body-building now, but he used to be a great detective here in Dallas. He took an early retirement because of a little legal problem."

—m—

Bree was napping, so Beth took a few moments to tidy up the place. She had taken the morning off work to see David and Bree off.

She knew with certainty that it would be more difficult this time to let them go. She thought of Bree's smile, and how it always made her heart light up like fireworks. Her eyes began to swim in an overwhelming rush of emotion as she thought lovingly of her little big man, who had brought so much joy into her life. She loved his laughter, the affectionate way he clung to her, and even his sweet way of trying to be gallant. She wanted to keep him with her forever.

Her thoughts jumped back to what she had been struggling with for the last couple of days. She had no idea what she and David would do about their newly declared love for one another.

When she saw the silver-gray Taurus turn into the pebbled drive, her heart leapt and sank in the same moment. Her elation at seeing

David was dampened by sadness at once again having to say good-bye. He looked tired as he walked up to the door.

"Hey, you," she said, managing a smile. "Are you *that* anxious to get out of here?"

"Well, I didn't have anything else to do," he said, drawing her into his arms. "Did my son wear you out?"

She warmed in his embrace. "No, I thoroughly enjoyed him. I'll miss him terribly."

"I know. He has this way of growing on a person." David's eyes shone with pride and the tremendous love he had for his son. But she also saw a hint of sadness.

"You're doing a great job with him," she said, as a couple of rebel tears escaped the thick boundary of her lashes. She pulled away and dabbed at her cheeks. "I'm sorry. I didn't mean to do that." She had to find something to do with her hands. She moved toward the kitchen. "I have a fresh pot of coffee going. Want a cup?"

"Yeah, that would be great. I have a little while before we need to fly out. I was hoping I could talk you into coming with us."

"I wish I could. But I've got to see things through."

They sat silently at the kitchen table, David sipping his coffee and Beth fidgeting with a glass of water.

"Is there anything I can do to change your mind?" he said. "I don't want to leave you here like this. I've already talked to my secretary about your staying with her a while."

She smiled. "You know I can't do that right now, David. I need to be here. Just until this is over."

"No you don't, baby. All you need to do is be safe and happy— with me."

"I love you, too," she said. "I'll be fine. I'm sure this will all clear up after Mr. Tubbs is found. It won't be long."

David leaned forward and drew his fingers along her cheek. "Beth, I want you with me. I need you with me."

Beth's heart leapt with joy and astonishment. She was caught completely off guard by the intensity of his words. She felt strangely disembodied, almost as if she were floating around, bumping into lost elements of her life. "David."

"I need you. Bree needs you," he repeated.

Beth's breath caught in her throat as she hoped against hope that he meant what she thought he did. Elation so filled her she could barely hear his words.

"I've never been good at telling a woman how I feel. I'm sorry to spring it on you at a time like this, but whenever I'm with you, I swell up as big as an ocean inside. I want you to be my wife."

"I didn't expect—I mean…"

Beth struggled to organize her thoughts and words in a way she could make sense of it all. Had she heard him right? Had he said what she thought he had? Her mind was still trying to sort through his last statement when he began to speak again. His voice was thick and gripped her heart like a vise. She willed her emotions back into stillness.

"Beth, please tell me you'll marry me."

She wasn't sure why, but at that precise instant she was certain she was face to face with God's direction. She could literally feel herself turning inside out as she considered His faithfulness. She saw the path she had to take. Carl had been right. It felt wonderful. By now, her mind was reeling with unfettered joy, but suddenly she froze. Her throat constricted and she started to tremble. "David, are you sure? I mean, I'm not—"

"Beth, honey, I thought you were going to let go of the past. As far as God and I am concerned, you *are* a virgin. Michael took something from you that you had no power to stop. That's not your fault. God wouldn't hinder your future for something you had no control over."

David had hit on her hesitation precisely. It was strange how he was able to do that. But she didn't want him to jump into something that he would someday regret. "But—"

He lowered his head and kissed her face. "No buts. I've prayed about this. I'm sure I love you. I'm sure you're the best thing possible for my son and me. Say you'll marry me, Beth."

"Daddy!" Bree said, staggering sleepily into the kitchen.

"Hey, Son," David said, withdrawing from Beth. "Are you about ready to go?"

"No," Bree whined. "I don't wanna."

"Bryson, I believe we agreed that when it was time to go, you wouldn't get like this. You make it real hard on Daddy."

Beth smiled, noticing how David reverted to calling Bree by his given name when he needed to impress upon him the seriousness of a matter. She watched as the child stood perfectly still, his eyes on his father's face. He had a little pout on his lips and tears pooled in his eyes.

"I'm sorry, Daddy."

She wanted to reach out and hug him, but she knew it would only make matters worse. When David excused himself to take Bree's luggage out, she stretched open her arms and he ran into them. She held him tight to her in an attempt to stabilize her own emotional mayhem.

The child sobbed quietly into her neck as he clung to her. "It'll be all right, my little big man. We'll have fun the next time we see each other. Okay?"

"When next time?"

"Soon."

"Okay," he whimpered. "I luvoo."

"I love you, too," Beth said, swaying a little from side to side in an attempt to comfort them both. "Would you do me a big favor?" He nodded, pulling away to look directly into her eyes. "Would you take good care of Daddy for me?"

"I will," he said, giving his head a jerky nod. His smile gradually surfaced and brightened.

"Why don't you go check the bedroom and make sure you got everything, Bree." Beth flushed, realizing that David had returned unnoticed.

"Okay," Bree said, seeming to take pleasure in anything that would prolong his stay.

Beth moved into David arms as if she belonged there. The warmth of his embrace was delightfully intoxicating. "I'll miss you," he whispered. "Are you sure you can't come with us?"

"I would very much like to be your wife when I leave with you," she said, looking up. David brought his lips gently down on hers. The kiss was passionate and tender, and her knees grew wobbly. Her heart thumped wildly against her chest as she allowed herself the freedom of feeling. She was sure she would explode.

As if on cue, David pulled back and touched her face, releasing her just before Bree walked back into the room. Her face felt warm where he had touched her.

Giving them a few moments to get into the car, she walked out onto the porch and waved good-bye. As she watched them drive away, she touched her lips with her fingers. She could still feel the pressure of his skin against them.

TWENTY

The day started much like any other Saturday, except Beth had gotten very little sleep during the night. After dragging herself out of bed, she groped her way into the kitchen. She found herself reliving over and over again her last moments with David. She had restrained herself for hours before giving up and phoning him. His answering machine was on. She did not leave a message.

Beth turned into the kitchen, her slippers making a dragging sound across the floor. She was brought up short to find Lena already up drinking coffee. "What are you doing up so early, Lena?"

"Hey, girl. Waiting on Carl. We're going house hunting this morning. How you feeling about *your* upcoming nuptials?"

Beth giggled and danced a little jig. "I'm so excited, I can hardly stand it. I can't get my stomach to stop jumping around. I wish Manny was around so I could tell him."

Lena scrunched her brow in wonder. "That's right! Where *is* Manny? I haven't seen him in several days. I drove by Miss Virgie's the other day and noticed his dogs over there."

"He said something about a little vacation last week." Beth poured herself a cup of coffee and joined Lena at the table. "Did you know David had already asked Carl for my hand? I was so surprised when Carl told me, I just about choked. I can't believe I'm actually going to marry my prince charming."

When Carl arrived, Lena and Beth were happily chattering about weddings. Carl joined them in the kitchen and gave his sister a hearty squeeze. "I'm happy for you both," he said. "There's not another man alive I'd feel better about handing my sister over to."

She glanced up at him, needing his unqualified approval. "You really think it's okay then? I'm not jumping the gun?"

"I not only think it's okay, I think it's about time. I'm pretty slow sometimes, but Lena has been bringing me up to speed."

Carl kissed the top of his sister's head, but not before she saw the worried expression on his face. "What is it?"

"Nothing, really. You want to go with us to look at houses?"

"Nah. I think I'm just going to stay around today and relax. I didn't get much sleep last night."

"You can sleep on the way," Carl said. "I don't feel right about leaving you here alone."

"Stop worrying so much," Beth said, gesturing dismissively.

"I talked to Taylor just a few minutes ago. He and Tricia were going by the ranch to look around. You want me to call him on his mobile and get him to stop back by?"

"I don't need a babysitter," Beth said, agitated. "Now will you two go on and do what you have to do? Besides, I'm going to try to get some sleep."

Beth dozed off the instant her head hit the pillow. She dreamed of walking down an aisle in a beautiful wedding gown. The train was so long it stretched the length of the church. The dress resembled the one that had belonged to her mother.

She floated toward a groom she at first didn't recognize. Just as she reached the altar, he turned to face her. The face was that of Sheriff Harper holding a rifle in his hands. A small boy stood beside him.

"You only see a reflection now, Beth," he said, with an uncommonly pleasant smile. "But you will know the whole truth soon. Real soon." Then he threw back his head loosed a menacing laugh.

When she turned to run, Beth found herself frozen in place.

She bolted upright in bed. Her throat was constricted, and cool perspiration streamed down her face. Then she heard Lena's phone ringing, and without thinking, rushed to the living room to answer it.

"This is your last warning, little Miss Bethie," the hushed, raspy voice said. Her fingers went cold on the receiver; her body trembled uncontrollably. She wasn't sure if it was caused by the disturbing dream or by the stranger on the other end of the line. Or both.

She peered over at the caller ID. Private. As always, the caller had blocked his number from being displayed. "Who is this?" she managed. She knew it couldn't possibly be Mr. Tubbs.

"Your worst nightmare," he said. Her whole body shaking, Beth stumbled toward the couch. Her fear was so paralyzing, she seemed powerless to simply hang up the phone. "If you don't get that deed back from your boyfriend, you'll be mighty sorry. In just a few short minutes, you'll know I mean business."

The dial tone droned in her ear like an insistent siren. Beth finally hung up the phone and sat as though in a trance. The man had once again referred to Taylor as her boyfriend. Had he seen Taylor embracing her and assumed, as David had, they were a couple? Could the caller be Michael? Nothing was making sense.

Forcibly rousing herself, Beth reached for the phone and dialed Carl's cell number. "Lord, please keep us alert and moving in your wisdom," she whispered, as she waited for her brother to answer. After hearing about the threatening call, he and Lena started back to the house.

Feeling an icy chill, Beth was rubbing her arms for warmth when the phone rang a second time. At first, she ignored it, but then checked the caller ID and saw that it was one of the church members. She almost cried with relief as she picked up the receiver. The respite, however, was brief.

"Beth, the church is on fire!"

Carl, Beth and Lena sat in stunned silence as they watched the commentator on the Sunday morning news. The television screen showed the burned, skeletal remains of the church. A few firemen were shown searching for clues.

"The pastor of Plover Creek Community Church cancelled services today for the first time in its thirty-three year history. The church was a total loss after burning to the ground yesterday afternoon. Based on recent threats to Reverend Carl McDade and his sister, Beth, the fire has been declared the work of an arsonist. Sheriff Bill Harper is investigating this tragic fire."

Carl pushed the off button on the remote and sat back in shock. Lena and Beth moved quietly to the kitchen. Nervous tension moved in waves through the women. They tiptoed around the distraught Carl as if he was a caged cougar.

Beth watched helplessly as tears rolled down Lena's cheeks. There was nothing to say. The events of the previous day cluttered her mind, leaving her numb, fearful and melancholic. Arrangements had already been made for the church to meet at the high school the following week, but this day was a day of mourning for the entire community.

A loud knock at the door yanked each of them back to the present. Carl reluctantly admitted Bill Harper into the living room and remained standing, his hands in his pockets. When Taylor pulled into the drive several minutes later, Beth thought she saw relief in her brother's face.

She had prayed fervently all night that the community would come together and stand united against an insidious enemy in their midst. Perhaps someone had seen or heard something, she thought. Maybe they would do something they had never done in the past: shake the fear, step up to the plate and talk.

She had tried several times during the night to reach David, but was still greeted by his aggravating answering machine. Beth needed desperately to simply hear his voice. She had also tried to phone Manny. She wished he had a cell phone, but he didn't like them. None of them had seen or heard from him in several days. That wasn't like him, especially after such a monstrous tragedy. Doubts once again stumbled into her mind, but she quickly pushed them aside. Manny could never do these terrible things.

Early that morning, several members of the congregation had gathered in Lena's front yard. Seeing them there, Beth had thought they looked like lost and bewildered sheep. She had immediately called Carl at his apartment and he came right over. When he had asked her to help bolster their spirits, she had declined, having never spoken to a large group before. But he insisted.

"Beth, everyone knows you're the one who spearheaded a welcome change out here. They're hurting. They need something from you they can hold on to."

The words had hit home, and she agreed to speak if he stood with her. They had both sat on the front porch then, exhorting and quoting passages of comfort from scripture.

"We've all had doubts at times, but I've never known God to allow a door to be closed without opening another," Beth said, after Carl had prayed. She was amazed at the strength and confidence in her tone despite her nervousness. Her brother had smiled proudly and nodded for her to continue.

"We have to remember that He is with us and He's on our side no matter how things may look." She had opened her Bible then to Psalm 27:3 and read, "Though an army besiege me, my heart will not fear; though war break out against me, even then will I be confident."

The words poured from the deepest part of her being with such force that she realized God was speaking not only through her but also to her. With this realization sustaining her, Beth had boldly moved to the top step to lead the people in the prayer of faith she had recently fashioned as part of her daily devotion.

"I will see light as long as I remain in His light. I will hold firmly to my profession of faith. Though the earth give way and the mountains fall into the heart of the sea, though its waters roar and foam and the mountains quake with their surging. God is our refuge and strength, an ever present help in trouble."

The sheriff's strong brogue tugged Beth back into the present. "How you folks doing this morning? Carl, I'm mighty sorry about the church. I know how much it meant to this community."

"Words come easy, Bill," Carl said without hesitation. "What are you going to do about this deliberate attack? What have you done about anything that's happened out here?"

Beth could see her brother's anger rising. He was on the verge of saying things she knew he would regret. She exhaled the breath she hadn't realized she'd been holding when Taylor came through the front door.

"Sheriff, as you can well understand, my clients are under a tremendous amount of stress. Do you think there's any chance of finding a suspect? I imagine he's the same one who fired on the surveyors at the ranch yesterday."

Beth stared at Taylor in disbelief. "W-what do you mean?"

"I didn't want to tell you, Beth. But Tricia and I were out at the ranch yesterday when the surveyors were fired on."

"Quite a bit going on around here," Bill admitted. "And I can certainly understand why everybody's upset. But I can't figure why Carl here found it necessary to withhold information when these threats first started. I found out last night from the fire chief." His squeaky whine reminded Beth of air escaping from a tightly compressed balloon.

"How dare you question my reluctance to come to you for help," Carl exploded, making a threatening move toward the sheriff. "For years you've shown little regard for this community's welfare. You want to do something? Go find that murdering George Tubbs."

Taylor shot Carl a warning glance. "Carl!"

Bill Harper's expression hardened. "Are you accusing me of willfully neglecting my duties to you folks?"

Carl nodded emphatically. "Yes, Bill, I am."

The sheriff's face turned a deep crimson as he plopped down into the chair next to the television. Beth silently wondered whether it would hold him.

Taylor gripped Carl's shoulder. "Why don't you take a walk?"

Without another word, Carl strolled across the living room floor and out the door. A few moments later, Lena followed. Beth had never seen her brother so incensed. For an instant, she'd been afraid that he would swing at the sheriff. It certainly wouldn't do for the pastor of the community church to be locked up overnight.

The sheriff removed his hat and let it fall to the floor. He mopped his sweaty brow with a handkerchief, then pushed stubby fingers through his thinning hair. His eyes abruptly fell on Beth leaning in the kitchen entrance.

"I know you were digging around for a while, Beth. You under the notion I ain't done right by you folks, too?"

Beth cleared her throat, her hands trembling. She looked to Taylor for a bit of encouragement then straightened, bringing herself up to her full five foot five inch stature.

"You have to admit, Sheriff, quite a few things have happened out here without resolution. Yes, I have to agree with Carl."

Harper, visibly jarred by Beth's quiet reply, put down his clipboard. He again wiped his forehead and the back of his neck. Glancing up at Taylor, he shrugged.

"I don't know what good I can do if folks don't trust me, Mr. Steele." Turning to Beth with what appeared to be a sincere look of anguish, he continued, "Beth, I'm sorry. Things ain't been right out here since I had to lighten my duties on account of my wife. She was diagnosed five years ago with cancer and died two years later. By the time I got my head back in gear, it seems I had lost the respect of most of the folks out here."

Standing tall, Taylor cleared his throat and jangled the loose change in his pocket. "I haven't met anyone out here who doesn't understand family obligation, Sheriff. I'm sorry about your wife, but based on reports I've heard, your office has brutalized the African-American portion of this community. If you're aware of any of this, you've obviously disregarded an oath."

The sheriff leaned back in the chair, his arms resting on the shelf of his belly. "I let an ol' boy go last year for roughing folks up. I wasn't aware it was still going on."

Beth's stomach was still in knots and she longed to sit down. But she couldn't take her eyes off the sheriff's gun hanging awkwardly at his side. She recoiled from the thoughts that popped into her head. Had he encouraged his deputies to mistreat blacks?

"I can't imagine what it will take to regain the respect of this community," Taylor said, finally taking a seat on the sofa.

"Mr. Steele, I've been working out here for nearly twenty years. The last five have been the most difficult. Folks have just clammed up. There's very little any investigating officer can do without leads or evidence."

Beth could hear the distress in the sheriff's voice, and at that moment, she was certain he was being truthful. But where did that leave her suspicion? Sheriff Harper was a heavy-set man, so he had to swing forward in the chair to get himself into a standing position.

Taylor's eyebrows shot up in surprise. "Are you telling me that you just now realized something was wrong out here?"

"Nah. I have a drawer full of unsolved cases I can't do anything about 'cause folks won't cooperate."

"Why not hand the cases over to the state?"

"The DA sent a fellow to make a report because of things Beth has been saying. I hope he has better luck than I did."

Beth evaded the sheriff's gaze and looked instead at her boss. Taylor's expression said he had no intention of showing his hand.

Carl and Lena returned after the sheriff's car pulled away, and the four sat down to discuss the recent occurrences. At one point, Taylor hesitantly turned to Beth. "I hate to say this, but as far as all the shooting goes, Manny is a pretty likely suspect."

Beth felt a rush of heat to her face as she reeled in astonishment. "What!"

"You told me the two of you were best friends. I've been thinking. Since you and Michael Baker weren't very friendly after the breakup, I'm suspecting Manny of involvement in his disappearance as well."

Beth glanced over at her brother, but both he and Lena averted their eyes. She turned an icy glare on Taylor. "What are you doing, Taylor?"

"Hear me out," he said. "Do you realize your car was forced off the road back in June by someone driving a white vehicle?" Taylor's gaze was unwavering, his tone almost hostile. "Manny has a white wrecker.

And wasn't he engaged to marry…" He took a moment to check his notes. "Charla Welch?"

"Manny wouldn't do this," she said, bolting from her chair. "He's always been protective of me. He wouldn't harm anyone."

"I can vouch for his protectiveness," Lena timidly chimed in. "It is odd, though, that we haven't seen him around lately."

Taylor cleared his throat, looking at Carl then back at Beth. "Have you ever known Manny to get violent?"

Beth felt panic stirring in her belly. Manny *had* gotten violent with Michael, but she wasn't about to disclose that. "What does that have to do with anything?"

"I understand he's a first-class marksman with a rifle," Taylor said. "If he was under the impression he would be protecting you by forcing you to keep the land, could he become irrational or aggressive?"

Beth, her brow knotted, peered around incredulously. Her pulse was galloping. "Are y'all out of your minds? First you try to convince me Manny has done something to Michael, he had tried to kill me, and now he's trying to protect me by keeping us from selling the land? Daddy would turn over in his grave if he knew you were pointing your finger at Manny, Carl. Why didn't you place George Tubbs under this much scrutiny?"

Carl stood and moved closer to his sister. "Sis, all we're trying to do is get you to consider the possibility that Manny has gone off the deep end. We believe George had an accomplice."

Her stomach was churning. She wrapped her arms around her midsection, trying to keep it still. She knew they were just being practical. After all, she'd had her own doubts. None of it—not one thing—was making sense to her, either. Her frustration and anger had come to a boil. Before she could stop herself, Beth slapped Carl's cheek and immediately gasped as remorse overcame her. Tears blurring her vision, she cupped his face between her palms. "I'm sorry. I didn't mean to do that."

"I know, honey," he said, placing his hands over hers. "But I need you to think about this. You have to admit Manny was acting strange about us selling. This whispering caller doesn't want us to sell. You said he never asks us to give it or sell it to him; he wants *us* to keep it. Doesn't that seem strange to you?"

"But Manny has known the land was sold from the day Taylor decided on it," she said, slowly pulling away. "When the whisperer called yesterday, I could tell he was quite unclear about some things. He even thinks Taylor and I are a couple."

Everyone grew silent as they looked around at each other. "Beth, think about it," Taylor said. "If Manny only wanted to frighten us, he would have made sure the shots he fired went over our heads. That's exactly what happened. No one has been seriously hurt yet."

"You mean *killed*, don't you?" Beth countered, facing Taylor. "Manny loved Midnight almost as much as I did. He wouldn't have done anything that would force us to put him down. People get uncomfortable around Manny because he keeps to himself. But he's just as normal as you or I. He's not on some rampage here. There's no motive."

Carl cleared his throat. "If you think about it, Terry and Felix disappeared right after Charla was killed. And as Lena mentioned, we haven't seen Manny around in a few days."

"Just shut up!" Beth turned to leave the room, but Taylor reached out and grabbed her arm.

"Beth, wait."

She pulled away and stormed down the hall, overcome with feelings of betrayal. Slamming the door to her bedroom, Beth picked up a stuffed animal and hurled it as hard as she could against it. She flung herself onto her bed and tried to sort through the anger.

Getting nowhere, she impulsively dialed the number at the garage, letting it ring over ten times before hanging up. She had to warn him somehow. She tried Manny's home number. No answer. Where could he be, she wondered. She thought about the times when Manny wanted to be alone that he would go to the woods or even hang around the bunkhouse at the ranch. Her nerves were shot, her sense of dread growing stronger. What could she do?

Beth sifted through all the allegations she had heard, clutching a pillow tightly to her flip-flopping stomach. She had already thought about the fact that Manny was a remarkable marksman, that he had lost his temper with Michael. And she had to admit it seemed strange that he wasn't with the family right now. *Please, Lord, let them be wrong.*

Beth picked up the phone and dialed another number. "David, where are you?" she asked aloud, anguished. Just as she was about to hang up, she heard his voice. But by this time, she was in such a frenzy she could barely get her words out in a way that made sense to him.

"Beth, calm down. I had to go out of town as soon as I got back from Texas. What do you mean the church burned?"

Her stomach was in knots, and the insistent tremors forced her to hold the phone with both hands. Emotions tangled with fear and frustration made her feel like bursting into a screaming fit. "Manny has been a part of our family ever since I can remember…"

"Beth, sweetheart," he entreated with open emotion. "You can't worry about Manny right now. They have to consider every possibility. I need you to calm down and think."

The intense concern in his voice was moving, but Manny needed her help. Yet after several minutes, Beth became calmer and was able to promise David that she would back off and get some much-needed rest.

TWENTY-ONE

David's heart was thumping around in his chest like a jackhammer. He had to close his eyes and try to get fifteen minutes. He turned over on his side, hearing Beth's frantic words over and over in his mind. His heart pounded as he thought of how desperately he loved her.

It was at that instant that he made up his mind to fly back to Texas tonight. He had to go back and convince her to come back with him. She would come back even if he had to hogtie her to get her on the plane.

He sympathized. Her best friend was being accused of some terrible thing, and he didn't know how much longer she could hold up. Newly energized, David picked up the phone and called Ted.

"Ted, something's come up. I've got to get back down to Texas. I hate to impose on you and Patsy anymore, but could you keep Bree for an extra couple of days?"

As soon as he had hung up, the phone rang. He quickly answered it.

"Dave, I need you," Carl blurted out. "George Tubbs was found a half hour ago. He's been murdered. We need to get the women out of here. The next flight leaves Dallas at 9:30. Can you meet them?"

David's facial muscles began to twitch. "I was just on my way to the airport. With us not knowing who the culprit is, it may be dangerous to put them on a commercial flight. Besides, Beth has never flown. I'll be there by 11:30 tonight. Have them at Garrison Airfield."

Beth was still troubled by Manny's absence. Something was just not right. Maybe she could get away and go look around the bunkhouse at the ranch. She would make Carl think she needed to say good-bye before she left with David. She shook herself, feeling heavy.

Although, worried, she was nonetheless elated to be seeing David sooner than expected. She wandered into the living room, where she found Carl staring into space. "Carl, I can't make myself believe Manny is running around terrorizing everyone."

Carl looked as if something was eating away at him. "Is it possible you could be wrong?"

She hesitated before answering. "I've been thinking about that. I, too, have wrestled with a few things in regard to Manny. But I know he couldn't do these awful things."

"If he's innocent, I'll do everything I can to help him. But if I find out Manny had anything to do with this, I'll break his neck myself."

Beth shrank back, staring at her brother's unyielding jaw. Hearing his words was bad enough, but seeing the intense anger in his eyes frightened her. He was one of the kindest men she knew, but Carl could be ferocious when provoked. And she knew he meant every word.

"Carl, promise me you won't hurt him. Please. And don't let anyone else hurt him. No matter what." Beth locked eyes with her brother.

"I'll do what I can if he's innocent. That's all I can promise, Beth."

She lowered her eyes. "I guess that's all I can ask. Where did Taylor go?"

"He left to join Tricia at the Tubbs crime scene," Lena said, coming up behind them. Beth moved toward Lena, feeling as excited as a child, and impulsively gave her a hug before heading to her room.

"I'll go throw a few things together and go out to the ranch to look around one last time. After all, I may not be coming back for a while."

"No," Carl said abruptly. "Absolutely not."

Beth stopped in her tracks and turned back to face Carl, her eyes pleading. She had to find Manny. "Can't I at least go and take one last look around? It won't take long. I'll leave just before we have to go to the airport. Taylor won't mind me leaving the SUV there. You can pick it up later."

"I don't think that's a good idea, Sis. We can leave a little early and go together."

Beth turned pleading eyes on Lena, hoping for help in convincing Carl to stop being so bullheaded.

"Give her just a couple of minutes," Lena said, moving to Carl's side. "Beth probably needs to say her good-byes to the only place she's known as home, honey. She was born there. It's unlikely this nut would be hanging around an empty ranch house, anyway. And we'll be right behind her."

"Well, all right," Carl said reluctantly. "But don't leave until we're all ready to go."

—m—

It was after 10:30 when Beth pulled her SUV through the open gates of what was once the McDade Horse Ranch. The heavy machinery standing idle in the front yard roused a somber ache in her chest.

It had been her home for a long time, and though she was happy her future finally had direction, she sensed a slight sadness at the disconnection from her past. Even the dreadful events of late could not deny, for her, the truth of the old saying, "There's no place like home."

She pulled around to the back gate. Another dark country night, she thought, smiling. She recalled the night she had come home late and thought she'd heard a mouse, but it turned out to be Carl and Lena smooching in the dark. Beth remembered how amused she'd been as she fished around the glove compartment for her flashlight. She looked around carefully for any sign of someone lurking about.

Manny would be most likely in the bunkhouse if he were here. He would also know she was about and come out. She would much rather find him before anyone else did. Maybe she would sit for just a moment, but she didn't have a lot of time and couldn't just start honking her horn.

Still, she knew Lena was right. This person who was threatening them had no real reason to be out here now. She surveyed her surrounding again. The motionless darkness unnerved her. But if Manny was hiding because he knew the sheriff was looking for him, he needed to know it was her in the SUV and not someone else.

Beth pulled the SUV closer to the barn and turned off the engine. She thought of Midnight and how he would run up to nuzzle her arm for a treat. She could almost hear his snorting and felt a sudden surge of emotion. David had teasingly told her she had taken a perfectly good horse and turned it into a kitten. She would miss quite a few things about this place—Midnight, Manny and the smooth sycamore out on the southern ridge. But the entire flavor of the ranch had changed since the trouble started. She was excited to be moving on with her life, especially with the man of her dreams. But what would become of her friend, Manny?

Beth flicked the flashlight on and off. No power. Perhaps the batteries were dead. Tossing the useless lantern into the back seat, she turned on her bright-beam headlights and climbed out of the vehicle. She started down the pathway created by the shaft of light, nervously looking from side to side.

A sense of disappointment filled her as she realized Manny wasn't on the grounds. She felt a rush of apprehension as she moved through the barn door, but quickly ascribed her uneasiness to anxiety about the flight. Anyway, Carl and Lena would be driving up any moment.

She could hardly believe she had agreed to fly out tonight. She imagined Bree's face when David told him she would be his new mother. But joyful anticipation barely compensated for the premonition that had been tapping at her insides.

Beth stooped to pick up a hoof pick that had fallen to the ground. She paused midway down as a shadow fell across the beam of light and moved toward her. Carl had been true to his word, she thought.

Turning her face slightly, Beth realized that the silhouetted figure was too lean to be her brother's and too tall to be Manny's. The sound of thunder rumbled in the distance, and she shuddered involuntarily. Suddenly, the words of a passage from Isaiah flashed into her mind. *When you pass through the waters, I will be with you; and when you pass through the rivers, they will not sweep over you. When you walk through the fire, you will not be burned.*

Beth was now certain she was in danger. The last time she had heard thunder, she had been certain then, too, that God had spoken. It was the day of the accident. "Tricia, is that you?" she called out in a shaky voice. "Taylor?"

She got no answer. The figure continued to move forward.

Ice-cold fear seized her, holding her in a stooped position near the ground. Her next thought was to run, but by the time she rose to do so, the stranger was upon her. She had no time to do anything but strike out with the only thing she had available.

The intruder's outcry pierced the darkness, followed by a stream of profanity. Although the hoof pick had dug a conspicuous trench into his arm, it had failed to facilitate her escape. She could see the dark blood pooling on the ground near her feet and drew back in fear.

Before she could move, the man grabbed her arm and flung her to the ground. When the back of her head hit the hardened dirt floor, she lay stunned for several long seconds.

With renewed fervor she screamed and began to struggle with the shadowy figure. "Let me go!"

He covered Beth's mouth and nose with a damp cloth that had a peculiar odor. She gagged. It was a revoltingly sweet smell—a smell of terror, of demise.

TWENTY-TWO

Weary from the long flight and no rest, David entered the small lobby at Garrison Airfield, anxiously looking around for Carl and the women.

Spying Taylor in the far corner talking into his cell phone, David headed toward him. His pace abruptly slowed when he noticed Taylor's agitated movements. Panic moved through him like a dry brush fire. Taylor was impatiently gesturing with his hands as he yelled into the phone. Something was terribly wrong. Where were Beth, Carl and Lena? As he neared Taylor, an eerie fear gripped him. His anxiety reached new heights; he was ready to explode.

Taylor turned then and spotted David, who stood with his hands at his waist and his brow furrowed, looking ready to pounce on something. His eyes were burning with fatigue and responding painfully to the fluorescent lighting inside the lobby. He watched Taylor struggle for words.

"Let's get out of here. I'll tell you what's going on."

David's heart plunged. He grabbed Taylor by his sleeve. "Tell me now," he said, his nostrils flaring with apprehension. "Is Beth all right?"

Taylor's face turned ashen. "I'm sorry, David. She's been abducted."

David stood speechless, unable to budge from the spot. Fury and pain swirled in a haze around him. He didn't know quite what to say or do. His eyes filled with tears of disbelief and horror. He turned, struggling to keep a semblance of composure in the middle of a nightmare he could never have imagined.

"Oh, God," he whispered, stumbling toward a chair. "Don't take her from me, please."

Taylor sat down in a chair beside him. "Let's go, David. There's a lot you need to know."

David sat numbly in the passenger seat of Taylor's car, without remembering how he had gotten there. Taylor's face was grim, his eyes directly on the road ahead of him. After what seemed like hours of struggling with flashing thoughts and fear, he finally spoke. "I thought Levescy was on her, Taylor. What happened?"

"Beth left the house a few minutes before Carl and Lena to go to the ranch. Wanted to get a last look around the ranch." Taylor's voice cracked. "Probably hoping to run into Manny, too, knowing Beth. She was real upset about the allegations against him."

"Why in the name of good sense would Carl let her do such a reckless thing? My God!"

"David, you know how stubborn Beth can be," Taylor reminded him. "She's headstrong and obviously wasn't thinking very clearly. Without concern for herself, she's worried over a friend she's certain is innocent. After Carl gave in, he phoned Levescy on his cell. He was already out here, so there was no real problem."

"So Carl just let her go?" David asked incredulously. "Did Levescy tell him he was on her?"

"Carl is kicking himself pretty hard right now. If you have any intention of blaming him, *now* is not the time. Levescy *did* follow Beth to the ranch. But Carl and Lena found his body slumped over his steering wheel on the road just past the entrance."

David's stomach began to lurch. He couldn't believe their worst nightmare had come to pass. He shook his head mournfully. "Oh, God. This is not happening. Tell me this is not happening."

"It's obvious there was a struggle. Beth's vehicle was parked with its lights beaming into the barn."

"What do you mean? Is she still alive?"

"We believe so," Taylor said. "When I arrived, the sheriff was already there. Carl was so beside himself he took a swing at him. Someone probably followed Beth to the ranch, killed Levescy and snatched her."

David kept shaking his head in unbelief as he continued to question Taylor. "What do you mean *obviously* a struggle?"

Taylor fell silent as he turned into Lena's drive. "David, I'm so sorry. There was a puddle of blood on the floor of the barn."

—⟶ɱ⟵—

By Monday morning, the atmosphere in the community was charged with fear and fury. Taylor, Carl and David had searched around the ranch and came back to Lena's to try to come up with some kind of strategy, but their minds were too filled with grief and fear to think straight. Taylor had left a few hours ago, promising to return by light.

News of Beth's disappearance had spread quickly. A growing crowd stood in Lena's front yard. Some prayed, while others simply waited to hear word. Carl voiced concern about the temperament of the community when he had to turn away a couple of neighbors who showed up with rifles.

It was apparent to everyone in the house that Manny was absent. While Lena kept making and serving coffee, they continued to throw out ideas about whether to continue searching for Beth on the ranch, wait for a call from the whisperer, or insist that Bill Harper call in the FBI.

"I don't know about calling in the feds," Carl said, a worried look on his face. "Hostages were killed over in Hill County last year when they were called in. I don't want this maniac opening fire on my sister just because a green federal agent needs a new office."

Lena nervously fixed a large breakfast that no one had the appetite to eat, and then she busied herself putting away the food and washing the dishes. David kept as silent as possible, trying to keep his fury under wraps. He knew confronting Carl wouldn't help matters. They were all little more than robots, hanging around in the living room until the sheriff returned.

None of them had gotten any sleep, and David felt as if he was about to suffocate. His stomach was in knots as he walked through the rooms like a skulking stranger. He couldn't believe such an atrocity had happened to them. Not now. He should have insisted that Beth leave with him. He wrung his hands, feeling like a man on the verge of madness.

Could Manny, Beth's best friend, be the culprit after all? Would he stand by and watch the church burn and Beth be abducted without so much as a call?

"Y'all need to clear out and give these folks some breathing space," Sheriff Harper said from the porch. "We're doing all we can."

One of the neighbors yelled out. "And what is that, Bill Harper? Sitting on your fanny and letting your deputies run all over people? We don't intend taking this abuse anymore. It's time…"

Carl quickly moved to the door and let the sheriff inside, then stepped out onto the porch, holding up his hands to quiet the people, mostly members of his congregation.

"I appreciate all of your concern for Beth, and I know you want to help. The best thing you can do is give us any information you might have concerning the other disappearances. Anything. Even if it doesn't seem very significant. Beth is the only blood kin I have left, and I want her back safe. Y'all go on home and think about this. Give us a call right here at Lena's if you think of anything."

The crowd slowly began to melt away, and Carl went back inside the house.

"Are we just going to sit here?" David asked, almost beside himself with anguish. "I need to *do* something."

"Well, now, don't go off half-cocked, David," Harper said with an air of authority. "I need to talk to y'all. Carl, I appreciate what you said out there, but you've got to remember that this is a matter for the law."

"It's been a matter for the law for years, Bill. This is my sister we're talking about now, and I'm not going to just sit here and watch you file her case away as you have the others. Now you get used to that, or go ahead and arrest me now."

"Carl, you calm down!" Lena said sternly, standing with her hands at her waist. "Now we all gotta quit this blamin' and start putting our heads together."

Carl's body uncoiled as the tension in the room began to ease. He backed away and casually moved to the sofa. Carl's reaction had taken David back to when they were boys, and Carl had fought with an incorrigible bully who had teased him mercilessly.

"Lena's right, Carl," David said. "I guess we both should try to give our emotions a rest." Though unrelenting terror continued to flow through him, David tried to ease the tension by assuming a degree of responsibility. He had to push himself to move and focus clearly. He turned to the sheriff. "Bill, would you like to join me in a cup of coffee?"

"Yeah, I'll take a cup if you don't mind," he replied, looking sideways at Carl. "I sent some boys over to pick up Manny after taking your statements last night. They didn't find *him* or the dogs."

"I'll get it, David," Lena said, pushing past him. "You go back and sit down. How do you take it, Sheriff?"

"Black is fine, Lena. Thank you."

Harper placed his clipboard on the floor and took the mug of hot coffee from Lena. Lena then went back into the kitchen, frequently glancing out into the living room toward Carl. Just as she was returning with refills for Carl and David, Taylor knocked on the door and entered without invitation.

David looked up at the lawyer, swallowed hard and tried to marshal his scattered thoughts. "Tricia was called out of town on an emergency late last night," Taylor said. "She asked me to offer her regrets." Taylor stood absently in the doorway, looking as lost and haunted as the rest of them.

"Go on over there and sit down, Taylor," Lena said, tugging at his shirt. "Have you eaten anything this morning?"

"No, thanks, Lena. I don't think I can eat." Lena poured him a cup of coffee, which he gratefully accepted.

"Mr. Steele, a warrant has been issued for Mansfield Jefferson's arrest. I was just telling the others here that we couldn't find him last night. I understand from some of the boys down at the jail that his garage has been closed up for a week."

David looked at Carl, his eyes showing the doubts he was feeling. "Do you really think Manny could hurt Beth?"

"He's the only peg that seems to fit into all the holes right now," Carl said guardedly, pulling his fingers over his hair. "Tubbs is dead."

The phone rang, and all the men jumped up. Lena motioned for them to sit down. "Y'all are too trigger-happy. Let me."

They all watched as she held the phone for several endless moments, her features showing rising distress as she listened. When she hung up, her voice came out in a lifeless monotone, inflected only by its quavering.

"It was him…the whisperer. She's still alive. He wants ten thousand dollars placed in a brown paper sack. He said to leave it in the southwest corner of the rubble at the church by four tomorrow afternoon." Lena closed her eyes and spoke hurriedly, her voice cracking. "If it's not there…well, he's gonna take her apart, limb by limb, until it is."

After she finished repeating the caller's demand, Lena walked back to her bedroom, sobbing. Carl sat transfixed by the horror of it all. David wandered over to the phone and purposely checked the caller ID.

The words 'private call' flashed up on the display, dissolving the slim hope David had of finding out who this animal was, or at least the location from which he had called. He began pacing, straining for a clear thought. "Manny wouldn't do this to Beth. It couldn't be him. He certainly wouldn't ask for money at a time like this. This is different. I can't believe it's him," David said, hoarsely. His mind fast-forwarded over faces he knew in the community. Nothing clicked. "Who in the world could it be?"

Taylor moved around the room aimlessly, jangling the loose change in his pocket. He looked angry and determined. "Sheriff, we can have the cash out here in a couple of hours. But isn't ten thousand dollars a small amount to ask for in a situation like this? David is right. This *is* different. Before now, this hasn't been a money or hostage situation."

A deadening gloom fell over the room. For a moment, no one spoke a word. Finally, Bill rocked himself into a standing position to take his mug to the kitchen.

"That *does* sound like a small amount of cash. Makes you wonder about the state of our kidnapper's mind."

Carl slammed his fist down on the coffee table, looking wild-eyed from one to the other. "I can't stand this. I have to do something."

"I think I'll go on back out to the ranch and take another look around," the sheriff said. "Carl, you're welcome to come with me."

Carl jumped up. "I think I will."

David's head shot up. "Sheriff, you mind if I come along, too?"

"Not at all, David," he said, turning back. "I'll check with the hospital in a bit about the lab results on that blood sample. The hospital's been a little behind lately. Somebody needs to get those funds together…just in case."

Taylor immediately picked up the phone and began to dial. "Y'all go ahead. I'll work on this."

Some time later, the sheriff dropped Carl and David back at Lena's and left. They had walked the grounds of the ranch for two hours, and like the night before, found nothing. After making himself a fresh cup of coffee, David wandered helplessly through the door, feeling as if a tank was driving through his insides. Still, he was relieved they'd finally heard *something*. Nauseating spurts of energy raced through him, splintering his thoughts in several directions. He took leaden steps across the front yard, avoiding a couple of lingering people. *Beth, where are you?*

One of the neighbors approached him. "Do you know anything more, David? Have you heard anything?"

"No. We don't know anything," he said, continuing to walk. He paused only a moment under the large oak beside the road. He needed to get away and clear his head. He thought about Bree. He had called Ted and learned that Bree was adjusting well to his father's extended absence. He'd asked Ted not to disclose his whereabouts because it might cause the child to be less agreeable. Bree had been so excited when he had told him that Beth would be his new mother. What would he tell his little boy now?

He strode down the road, feeling as if he was breathing out steam. The rarely used path was empty of traffic. Only the sound of his feet on the gravel was distinct in the midst of a chorus of chirping birds and buzzing cicadas. The trees all leaned to the north as if bowing in worship.

Beads of perspiration formed on his forehead as his mind went back to the night Beth had described her suspicions. She had been so animated. He recalled the moment he held her hand and had himself sensed her contemplation—her fear. For the first time in his life, he had connected with another human in a way he had never thought possible. He was sure then that she was meant for him. He had been allowed to peek into her soul. "Where is she, Lord?"

All at once, a tingling sensation spread through David, and one of his favorite passages entered his thoughts. *When you pass through the waters, I will be with you; and when you pass through the rivers, they will not sweep over you. When you walk through the fire, you will not be burned.*

He breathed in the dry, dusty air and gazed up into the faded sky. David thought of the whisperer's demands and tried to suppress the doubts assaulting his mind. He had to hold on to God's word. God was indeed with Beth, and He was with him, too.

Though he had been grateful to hear she was still alive, he questioned the wisdom of trusting a man who was clearly unbalanced. He would trust the Lord.

David suddenly thought he caught a faint whiff of Beth's cologne. She always wore the scent of fresh-cut flowers. He smiled, recalling her profession of love. It had been music to his ears. He hadn't felt that free in a long time. But now it was gone, whisked away in a moment when no one was looking.

His arms felt heavy and empty. He wasn't sure how he could possibly go on without her. She had to be okay. She just had to. David pulled a handkerchief from his pocket and wiped his face. "Lord, you *are* where she is. Please keep her safe. I know I can't love her as much as you do, but I want her to be a part of me for the rest of my life. I want her to be the mother of my children. Please, please keep her safe."

"David Lee Spencer!"

David swung around to see Miss Virgie Patterson standing behind him, leaning on the same old cut-off tree limb he remembered from his childhood. It was a wicked looking thing that she had used as a cane for years. Her sudden appearance startled him.

Miss Virgie looked much the same—short with a round face and a small mouth that had always reminded him of a duck's bill. She was stout and wore a long print dress with a striped apron over it. She had to be in her eighties, but her eyes sparkled like that of a young girl.

He warmed at the fond memories of her addressing the young people in her Sunday school class by their full given names. She had once said it kept her brain functioning.

"Miss Virgie," he said, moving to embrace her. He almost felt like a little boy again, feeling her heavy hand patting against his back. "You surprised me."

"I s'pect I *did* surprise ya," she said with a humored grunt. "You 'bout jumped clean out of your skin. Didn't mean to walk up on your visit with the Lord."

"That's all right," he murmured. "It sure is good to see you. I'm hoping you brought some news."

She shook her head and casually spewed tobacco juice toward the side of the road. "I don't know nothing, honey. How y'all holding up down here?"

"Just praying and waiting," he replied soberly. "We don't know what else to do."

"Well, I 'magine your mind is dancing. Try to keep calm," she said. "So...you and Elizabeth gettin hitched, are ya?"

"Yes, ma'am," he answered with a stab of empty anticipation. His voice broke then. "I love her, Miss Virgie. And she's agreed to be my wife. But...this....I'm hurting fiercely."

"Don't fret so," she said knowingly. "Keep the faith. It's times like this the devil tries to slide in and take hold. You two make a right smart match. Come on, walk me back up here to Lena Mae's. I need to talk to y'all."

David slowly accompanied the woman back down the road toward the house. She waddled a lot more now, and had gotten a little heavier with the years, but her keen sense of command was well intact. He smiled, visualizing her chasing them around the Sunday school room with a yellow flyswatter and falling heavily into a chair when she exhausted herself. Her high-pitched laughter had been known to fill the entire church on more than one occasion.

"Did you walk through the bush alone, Miss Virgie?"

"Not exactly. The good Lord was wit' me." David could see that the situation at hand was affecting the woman, though her innate vim did much to conceal it.

"You're not afraid of snakes or tarantulas?" he asked, recalling Beth's fear of snakes and such.

She chuckled softly, leaning heavily on his arm. "I'm a tough ol' bird, David Lee. Vermin don't wanna tangle with me."

When they arrived at the house, Taylor and Carl were sitting on the front porch. Several others in the community had reassembled under the big oak in the yard. Miss Virgie stopped beneath the tree and gazed hard at the small group. Everyone stopped talking and turned toward her, the men removing their hats and the women offering to help her.

"Y'all know anything about what's going on here?" she asked quietly. Several gathered around her, mumbling one thing and another. David stood back and watched in surprise as they one by one stepped away shaking their heads. "Go on home then. Search your property and the nearby woods. If you think of anything odd call us right here. But try not to hang around worrying the family like this."

Carl jumped to his feet as she turned away from the group, and rushed forward to help her up the steps. "Miss Virgie! Come on inside where the air conditioner is going."

"Nah. Ain't never liked 'em. Too cold." She scrunched up her face to emphasize her aversion. "I wanna sit right here with y'all."

Taylor had stood to help. She sat in the metal swing near the edge of the porch and Taylor sat back down next to her. David quickly moved to sit in the chair Carl had vacated. He noticed that the old woman had already begun to look over the top of her ancient eyeglasses at Taylor. Taylor in turn looked helplessly at Carl, apparently telegraphing a plea for rescue.

"Who is this pretty white boy?" she asked. An embarrassed smile spread across Taylor's face as he turned his head.

"This is Taylor Steele. He's the attorney Beth works for. He's helping us…"

Carl's voice trailed off when Miss Virgie lifted her stick. Taylor sat back quietly, seemingly intimidated as well as amused. David could tell he was intrigued, but perhaps unsure what to make of her.

"Hmph," she grunted as she leaned away to spit off the side of the porch.

"Miss Virgie, you still chewing tobacco?" David asked, hoping to draw her attention away from Taylor. But she totally ignored David's question and returned her intense gaze to Taylor, who was literally squirming under her scrutiny.

"Ain't I seen you out here with that woman DA?" she asked, her eyes still giving him the once-over.

"Yes, ma'am," Taylor answered, noticeably surprised.

Then she casually reached across him and used her cane to thump on the storm door. "Lena Mae Hall?"

Drying her hands on a dishtowel, Lena came the door. "Miss Virgie, how you doing?" she asked, peeking around the edge of the door. Though she kept herself busy, David could tell Lena was at the breaking point. "I'll bring you a nice cool glass of water."

The old woman took the water from Lena, who sat down on the steps next to Carl. Miss Virgie drank from the glass without removing her tobacco.

"Where's Bill Harper gotten off to?" she asked, wrapping her agile fingers around the half-empty glass.

"He said something about checking on lab results," Lena replied. "What d'ya want with the sheriff?"

"He didn't even leave a deputy with y'all?" Shielding her eyes from the sun, Miss Virgie spewed another load of tobacco juice into the yard. "Looks to be 'bout one o'clock. Just as well he ain't here."

Taylor looked at his watch. "One five," he confirmed.

"We all love Elizabeth, and Lord knows we didn't want this to happen," she said, taking another swallow of water. "Carl Avery, you ain't doin right by Mansfield, you hear?"

Lena lowered her head, not saying a word. "Where did you hear about Manny?" Taylor interrupted, putting aside his discomfiture.

"You know he'd cut off his arm before he'd harm a hair on her head," she continued, ignoring Taylor's query. "I knowed something was 'bout to happen. The Lord always stirs me when things ain't right. Elizabeth got that sensitivity, too…just ain't learned to listen."

She pointed her cane at Carl. "You better start list'ning to what you preach on Sunday, boy. I know God been talkin' to you. You goin' 'round here blaming cause ya hurting. That ain't pleasing to Him. Mansfield been part of your family just as much as David Lee, and you know it."

Carl stood up abruptly and limped toward the tree where others had stood earlier, remorse written on his face. He shoved his hands into his pockets and leaned against one of the larger branches as he glanced across the road toward the west.

Nobody moved. All eyes were on the old woman, as if expecting pearls of wisdom to roll off her tongue. David hoped beyond reason that she could tell them something—anything that would give them some kind of direction in which to move. He was thankful that members of Carl's congregation had all left. It wouldn't do for them to hear Miss Virgie's chastising their pastor. Was that why she'd sent them away, he wondered.

"David, I know y'all are hurting, especially you, seeing as how Elizabeth is your intended. But you need to keep your focus on God in the midst of the worry and frettin'." She gazed at Lena. "You been sleeping these men folk?"

The question didn't surprise Lena. "Yes, ma'am. Nobody got much sleep last night. But Carl and David stayed in the living room."

"I know you and Carl hitchin' up soon, but it don't look nice. You boys wasn't raised to disrespect a lady like you doing."

Taylor cleared his throat. "Ma'am, Lena shouldn't be out here alone with all that's going on. We've all been waiting by the phone to hear word of Beth."

"Son, you don't much know our ways out here. I'm tellin 'em right. It don't much matter how thangs is. Carl Avery is pastor, and he's gotta take care of how thangs look. And so I aim to stay right here 'til thangs are all right again."

Taylor knew when to back off. Still, he tried another question. "Do you know anything about the others who have come up missing in the last few years?"

"I knowed them, and I know they come up missin'," she answered, closing her arms across her midsection. "You courting that woman DA?"

"I'm not sure yet," Taylor said warily. "Can you tell us anything that can help us find Beth, Miss Virgie? Anything at all?"

David listened, hopeful. He couldn't stop thinking about the night he had reassured Beth that no one was after her. But he had been wrong. She had sensed it all along. Had she been careless because of his rash words?

David looked back at Taylor, who was obviously skilled in taking the reins without the other person knowing it. But he had to learn that very little got past Miss Virgie. He had never known her to say more than she intended. She leaned back, pulling the makeshift cane alongside her.

"Everybody been talking 'bout y'all. Say you been trying to help folks 'round here. That so?"

"Yes, ma'am. Don't seem to be getting very far, though. Lena mentioned Manny's dogs were at your place. You know where I can find him?"

"Mansfield is in Oklahoma City at one of them shooting contests. S'pose to been gone for two whole weeks, but I told 'im Beth needed him back here fast. I didn't have the heart to tell him everythang. He should be back here directly."

Her news stunned everyone. "Why didn't you tell the sheriff about this?" Taylor asked. "I know they came to see you."

"Didn't ask me," she said, shrugging. "They marched in like a bunch of heathens and told us they were looking for him in connection with this, so we let 'em look. Besides, I don't think I could stand to see them hurt Mansfield like I know they of a mind."

"Do you know where Beth might be, Miss Virgie?"

The old woman's eyes suddenly filled with tears. Using the edge of her apron, she wiped them away and shook her head. "Wish I did. That there's my gal. Mansfield coming. He'll help."

"I sure hope he can," Taylor said. "We need all the help we can get...fast."

Quiet sobs shook the old woman's body. "Mansfield knows these woods bett'n anybody round these parts. Had to make sure y'all wasn't aiming to hurt 'im." Her shoulders slumped a little then. "Folks thinking she's still out here. I think so, too. If she is, he'll find her."

TWENTY-THREE

Beth awakened with a dull headache—her thoughts fuzzy, her limbs like lead. Harsh daylight pierced her squinting eyes, provoking a low groan as she tried to shift her bruised body.

Struggling to ease her discomfort, she soon realized she was strung up on something. Vague pieces of memory aroused partial awareness. Someone had taken her from the ranch. She had put up a fight, but hadn't been able to make out her attacker. Now she was gagged, and her wrists and ankles bound. She was going to die.

It was then that terror—real icy terror—seized her. Her stomach cramped up and her chest heaved as she fought to breathe. As she lay feverishly trying to calm herself, the memory of the night before returned in a rush. She remembered the sickening smell of the cloth that had been thrust over her nose and mouth.

Beth was lying on a small cot, her prison a one-room shanty with a dirt floor. Her aching joints resisted as she strained for a better look around. She could tell now that her wrists were tied with the same rope used to bind her ankles, forcing her to curl backwards, and causing her entire body to throb.

Beth's empty stomach was noisily protesting its neglect. She wondered what time it was. As her eyes became more adjusted to the meager illumination, she continued to mentally note her surroundings. She could see trees on the outside through a piece of ragged burlap hanging at the opening to the shanty.

She heard movement nearby and drew back in fear, casting a nervous glance in the direction of the sound. But her view was restricted because of the way in which she had been bound. Anger began to stir in her gut as she recalled David's words the night she had told them all about the investigation she'd initiated.

"Honey, nobody's coming after you. You've been right here in plain sight for years."

He hadn't taken her seriously. Beth began to cry. Just when she was certain God had answered her prayers and shown her the way she was to go everything had gone horribly wrong.

Lord, have I trusted in you to come to such an end?

Though an army besiege me, my heart will not fear; though war break out against me, even then will I be confident. Stunned by the sudden emergence of the passage she had taken to quoting, Beth realized the Lord was reminding her to stay focused on His promises.

"So, you're awake," he snarled, stepping into her view. With great effort, Beth looked up and gasped in surprise. Leonard Ware slowly moved closer until he was standing directly over her. She held her breath and stared up into his icy blue eyes—the same blue as his sister Shannon's.

Hoping he wouldn't hurt her, she quickly lowered her eyes. She couldn't believe Leonard could hate her this much. He dropped down onto the cot. Spotting a knife in his hand, Beth inched back toward the wall against which the cot had been pushed. She felt it give a little, and made a mental note that it may be a way to escape later.

"I'll untie you if you promise to stay put and keep your mouth shut," he said in a gruff tone. "You hungry?"

She nodded and closed her eyes, while he removed the gag and rope. Once released, she coughed until she could get a clear breath, whereupon she nearly gagged from the heavy stench of filth and dankness in the shanty.

"I made some sandwiches, and there's fruit and water," he said. "I ain't hauling a bunch of water, so you'd better make do."

Beth stood and her legs immediately buckled. Leonard grabbed her by the arms and hauled her back to her feet. She moved woodenly toward the crate that was to serve as a table for the scanty rations he had supplied. She was confounded. Why would Leonard be doing this to her? Was he acting on rage ignited by the murder of George Tubbs?

Could he possibly think her initiating the investigation had somehow caused the druggist's death?

Questions kept popping up in her mind, even though her frightful circumstances compelled her to suppress them. What was he going to do with her? Where in the world were they? How long did he intend to keep her here?

Once she had eaten, he replaced the strip of duct tape over her mouth. After handcuffing her to a metal ring on the side of the wall, he stood back and looked down at her. The tall and lean deputy looked much like a confused lion who had caught its prey but was uncertain what he should do with it.

She watched with agitation as he gathered up a few scattered items, apparently preparing to leave. "I'll be back later," he said, without looking at her. "I'm going to see if your boyfriend left me a package."

Muted shock filtered through Beth's disjointed awareness, rendering her limp with terror. Leonard had seen Taylor holding her. *He* was the whisperer. She remembered now. He had been at the ranch after the shooting. Taylor had been comforting her when he and the sheriff had returned from checking out the meadow.

After she was certain Leonard was gone, Beth tried to yank away from the flimsy wall. Her attempts were met with unyielding resistance. The wall was a lot sturdier than she had thought. For the remainder of the afternoon, Beth drifted in and out of consciousness.

She was reawakened by the sound of Leonard stumbling through the shanty. Heavy beads of sweat trickled down his face and neck, and his arm was bleeding profusely. He was obviously in pain. Noticing that she was awake, he swore loudly and hurled a bottle against the wall, barely missing her head.

"They're watching the place," he shrieked, pacing back and forth. "They must think I'm stupid. My own buddies."

Leonard sat down on the stump in the middle of the room, taking a hearty swig from a bottle of liquor he'd pulled from his pocket. Clearly, he had already had enough. She watched in wary silence.

"I don't wanna kill you, Beth, but I will. In a jack rabbit heartbeat, I'll kill you dead as you got to die."

He was tottering as if about to keel over at any moment. She finally caught his attention. It was difficult to watch him suffer and not offer to help. She looked from his arm to his eyes, hoping he would understand her meaning.

He shrugged and moved to release her restraints and the tape from her mouth. Then she made her first mistake.

"Why, Leonard?"

"I let you loose so you could tend my arm, not yak my ear off."

"I'm sorry," she said quietly.

"This is for my sister," he spat out, taking another swig from the bottle. Beth moved cautiously to the bucket of water, pouring a portion into a beat-up metal pan she found on the dirt floor.

"I need something clean to dress it," she said, keeping her eyes away from his face. "Do you have anything?"

"Just the shirt on my back," he said, sitting in a contented stupor. All at once, he grabbed her by the collar and pulled her close to his unshaven face. "You know, Bethie, you ain't a bad looking woman. I could proba—"

"It'll have to do," she interrupted, gently pulling away from him. "Take it off."

"What?" he asked, confused.

"Your shirt," she said, her hands trembling. "Take it off."

Her heart was pumping wildly, but she had to keep her head and avoid letting him know how scared she really was. She moved about, careful to keep her eyes down to avoid conveying even a hint of confrontation. In his state, he'd probably imagine just about anything. She thought of her brother's words the night of the Fourth of July. *"You are a strong lady and God is with you. You can't forget that."*

Leonard obediently removed his shirt. He was thinner than she had thought, and his skin was as white as chalk. He sat back down on the stump, smiling like a mischievous schoolboy. But just as suddenly as it had first flashed across his face, the smile grew cruel.

"I could've killed you last night for this. It's only right you should tend it."

She tore one of the sleeves away, dipped it into the water, and began washing the wicked gouge in his left forearm. It was infected. She could tell by the oozing pus and inflammation. Scared and wild-eyed, Beth gently cleaned the wound as best she could.

"I'll need that liquor," she said guardedly. When he handed her the bottle, she hesitated before making a move.

"I can take it," he said, as if reading her thoughts. "But make sure you save me a nip. I'm still a mite thirsty."

Deliberately defying his command, Beth emptied the bottle onto his wound and threw it aside. Responding to the expected burning, Leonard stamped his feet, and his face turned as deep a red as she had ever seen.

"I told you I wanted another swallow of that," he said through clenched teeth.

She finished ripping the shirt into strips, astonished by her boldness in the face of danger. After bandaging the wound, she carefully stepped back toward the cot. The wound probably needed about thirty stitches, she guessed. But she wasn't about to tell him that.

"Thanks," he said, closing his eyes and looking faint. She realized right away that this might be a perfect opportunity to escape. But he opened his eyes, got up and rebound her. But he didn't replace the duct tape.

Leonard began noisily searching the small shelter for what Beth suspected was another bottle. He didn't find one. Thankful, she began to pray under her breath. Though her faith was intact, her relationship with the Lord had been less than strong the last few years. She frowned as memory of the night before infused her thoughts. She had heard Him again. She was certain of it. Right before Leonard had attacked her. The scripture He had put into her thoughts had been comforting. He was with her. Though she couldn't feel Him, she had to believe that He wouldn't abandon her. She started to mutter her daily affirmation.

"I will see light as long as I remain in His light. I will hold firmly to my profession of faith. Though the earth give way and the mountains fall into the heart of the sea, though its waters roar and foam and the mountains quake with their surging. God is my refuge and strength, and ever present help in trouble."

"Shut that noise up!" he shouted, flinging the metal pan toward her. Terrified, she shrank to the corner of the cot and curled up into the fetal position. She fought hard to restrain her tears, but they kept coming. Leonard's little-boy persona morphed before her eyes into that of a wild animal.

"I was only praying," she said, hoping it wouldn't incite another outburst. He started to laugh—a hollow, eerie sound that caused her to shudder.

"I know what you were doing. All you Bible thumpers are gonna be real surprised when you come to the end and find you was wrong. And *you*—you're Miss Do-Gooder—making friends with the poor white girl," he mocked. "You had Shannon mumbling all that prayer stuff. Where did it get her, huh? Where did it get you? You was always bad news for my sister. George *told* me you could curse folk."

The hurtful words he flung at her had hit home. Beth knew it would do no good to plead her innocence when, at that moment, she wasn't sure of it herself. Where *had* prayer gotten her?

It was drizzling when David awakened the next morning. It was the first time he had slept in over forty hours. He sat at the kitchen table staring out the window, while Lena kept busy expending nervous energy. Every inch of his body felt as if it had turned on him. Life was strange, he mused. Here he was, stressing about the woman he would marry, when just last week he was obsessed with not having a woman in his life. God was too faithful for things to go so wrong. *Have faith in God.*

David jumped and peered around at Lena, who was busy scrubbing the sink. He knew those words were found in the eleventh chapter of Mark, where Jesus told his disciples that they could tell a mountain to move. And if they had the faith of a mustard seed, it would obey.

"Whisperer," he said boldly. "You must let her go. You will not kill Beth McDade."

Lena swung around and stared at him. "What are you doing?"

He smiled. "I'm speaking to the mountain."

She nodded knowingly. "You want a refill on that coffee?"

"No, I've had enough. Carl is still knocked out. We stayed up pretty late last night."

Staring into his empty cup, David was rambling on about his dreams when he became aware that Lena's face was bathed in tears.

"What is it?" David asked, pulling her into the chair beside him. "Lena, what is it?"

"It's all my fault, David," she managed between sobs. "I'll never forgive myself if…"

David shook his head. "What are you talking about? What's your fault?"

"What's going on?" Carl asked from the kitchen entrance, scowling. In two steps, he was at her side, leaning over her. "Lena, honey, what is it?"

"I'm fine," she said almost angrily. "I'm fine and dandy. It's Beth that's not. She should be here."

"What did you mean?" David quietly pressed. "Why do you think it's your fault?"

She looked at him, not answering. He was afraid she had forgotten what she had said, but she wiped her eyes with her apron and, with trembling lips, began to explain.

"I know you've wanted to ask Carl why he let her go out to the ranch alone. Anybody else would've, but you love him too much. You know he already feels responsible. But it was me. I helped Beth talk Carl into letting her go out there. I don't know why I did. We were only a couple of minutes behind her." It was obvious that she could no longer hide her sense of guilt from the others. It was too painful.

"It's not your fault, Lena," David said, squeezing her hand. "We're in a bad place right now. And I have to admit I'm scared out of my mind. But God just reminded me that we've got to have faith, and we've got to speak it. None of this is a surprise to God."

"I know that, David," Lena said. "But God *had* been warning Beth. We all heard her, and still we stood back and behaved just like we didn't have a mind. We knew the danger and let her go out there alone."

"She's right, David," Carl said. "God expects us to use the sense he's given us. We didn't." He lowered his eyes. "Neither did Beth. I can't believe she didn't heed her own weird warnings and just hang out here at the house until it was time to go."

David suppressed the angry words stirring in him. "It's done. We're not going to get anywhere…we won't get her back by beating ourselves up about the mistakes we've made. We all know Beth can be one tough cookie. If she wanted to go, she would have found a way to go. God will keep her safe. We've all got to believe that."

Carl stood and placed his hands on both their shoulders, closed his eyes and voiced a prayer.

TWENTY-FOUR

Leonard dropped food onto the crate in the middle of the hovel. Beth kept quiet and did exactly as she was told, determined to stay in his good graces. Her eyes brimmed with tears she was determined to hold back. Having slept on the filthy cot for two nights and being allowed to refresh herself only twice a day, her optimism was diminishing. After she had eaten, Leonard moved to bind her wrist again.

"I have to...I haven't gone at all today, Leonard. I've been here all night, and I—"

Staggering slightly, he swore loudly and removed the handcuffs. He took her roughly by the arm, pulling her outside the dilapidated structure.

"Five minutes," he said, pointing to the stand of low-growing bushes she had used the day before. "No more."

Although it had drizzled, the moisture hadn't penetrated the thick canopy of trees. Leonard was still leaning against a tree as Beth headed back. As far as she could tell, he wasn't watching her. She ducked back behind the brush, hoping he hadn't been timing her. She had heard the sounds of the creek during the night and had begun to recognize the trees. She had to be somewhere near her southern ridge, but on the other side of the creek.

Hoping against hope, she quietly moved westward, keeping low. Could it be possible that she was being held on property that had once belonged to her family? How ironic. Believing she was out of Leonard's direct view, she ran fast and low to the ground. She remembered how she and Manny used to race through the woods as children. Soon she was out of sight of the shanty and took a deep breath, trying hard to beat back the waves of fear. She kept telling herself that she had to stay in control of her mind. Her life depended on it. At the same time, she intuitively knew that escape wouldn't be this easy.

When Beth guessed she was far enough out of range, she began to sprint, refusing to look back. She thought randomly of Carl, her friends and future family. They would all put this awful time behind them and move on with their lives.

Almost afraid to breathe, Beth's thoughts turned to the scripture that had comforted her the last couple days. *When you pass through the waters, I will be with you.* But she was soon wondering if she had brought all this on herself. Carl had often taught that unforgiveness opened a door to the enemy. Had she opened that door? She couldn't deny it. He had even warned her that late night in July.

She hadn't listened to her own inner warnings. And she had held on to grudges against Michael and Mr. Tubbs. She inwardly shook herself, wondering if this was finally eating away at her mind. Mr. Tubbs was dead and Michael was nowhere to be found.

Beth reached a narrow path leading down into the creek and figured she had curved northward. The sound of distant thunder heightened her urgency to run. She wondered if she would have to swim across. If she could just get across the creek, she would know her way. But the trees were dense, and she was constantly dodging stumps and rock formations. She realized with some despair that she could have easily changed directions again without knowing.

Imagining snakes crawling near the water's edge, she hesitated. Without thinking, she looked back. A terrified scream tore from her throat. Leonard's angry blue eyes were leveled at her just steps away.

In two long steps, he was upon her. He backhanded her across the face, knocking her backwards. She stumbled and slid several yards down the slope before scrambling to her feet again. Wiping her bloodied nose, she went down again and continued on a downward slide. Leonard rushed after her, shouting a string of vulgarities. He grabbed her just as she slid into the water.

"I ought to drown you right here," he sputtered, locking his hands around her throat. His overlapped thumbs, pressed against her windpipe. Beth knew she was no match for his rage. Her only way out was to dig her nails into his injured arm.

Beth managed to loosen his hands by twisting over, but he was still astride her and flipped her back over. In that moment, she drew her knees up and seated her feet against Leonard's torso. She slammed against him with all her meager strength, and he fell back. In the next instant, he was back and slapped her hard across the mouth. The force sent her back into the creek.

When Beth sprang up from the water, Leonard was sitting on the water's edge loosening his bandages. His cold, threatening glare had a maniacal glint to it. The hatred was unmistakable.

"You'd better sit there and cool off while you can. I see now I won't be able to trust you."

Distraught, Beth wondered if she would live to see her wedding day. She didn't know how far she had gotten, but it clearly wasn't far enough. She had lost all sense of direction. Her nose bled onto the front of her blouse and her head pounded mercilessly. She closed her eyes, hoping for relief.

"I'll have to think of a way to punish you," he said, laughing aloud.

She could see relief on his face as he immersed his arm into the cool creek water. "Leonard, please let me go. I don't understand why you're so mad at me."

His eyes raked her drenched, trembling form then he turned to look up toward the ridge. Though it was muggy and gray, the heat was sweltering. They would probably get a heavier rain before nightfall. Leonard's arm needed further attention, but this time she had no inclination to help. "I told you."

"How can you say you're doing this for *her*?" she asked. "Shannon and I were friends, and you know it."

"You was no real friend to my sister. If you were, she would still be alive."

Beth was astounded. What was he talking about? He was obviously deluded. Baffled, she combed her memory for clues, but her mind was coming up empty. How could she have caused her friend's death?

Could she have forced Shannon to tell her what was bothering her? She couldn't believe Shannon, who shrank at the sight of blood, would actually slit her own wrists. And she was certain she couldn't have forced her to talk when she was in one of her moods.

Beth steeled herself to look directly at Leonard. "Shannon left school without telling me why. She didn't say a word. A couple of weeks later, she was…gone."

"She shouldn't have died," Leonard insisted. "I told her to stop that praying 'cause it wouldn't do nothin' but make things worse. But she wouldn't listen. She made me so mad when she wouldn't listen."

"Leonard, can you tell me what she might've been upset about?"

Like an angry boy, he picked up a rock and tossed it hard into the water. "She was always worried about what Miss Too-Good Beth would think."

"What I would think about *what*? The last time I talked with her was right before the big game."

He stood to his feet then, and glared at her. His eyes seemed to bore a hole straight through her. "Why would you ask her to watch Mike for you? His strange notions weren't *her* problem. They were yours. You're the one who wanted him so much."

"What strange notions? What does Michael have to do with any of this—here and now?"

Leonard went silent. She didn't think his eyes could become any more hateful and angry than they already were. But they could. For a moment, his tall, lean frame resembled that of a crouching wild animal ready for the kill. He started to rant incoherently, moving toward her in a fierce rage. Fear shot through her like an electric current. Had she gone too far?

She scrambled to get up, but slipped back into the creek. And then, he was on her like a rabid hound. He reached down and grabbed her by the collar, pulling her to her feet. "I should have killed you on the road when I had the chance," he screeched. "If it hadn't been for that nosey passer-by I would have."

Beth's eyes widened in terror when it hit her that it was Leonard who had rammed her car from behind. Why hadn't she remembered it earlier? Horrified, she broke away from his grip and ran toward the opposite side of the creek. She realized too late that the water was only shallow a short way in.

Rushing toward the middle, she encountered a sudden drop that pulled her under. She struggled to stay upright, but to no avail. She briefly found herself wondering if Leonard had also abducted and killed Michael? Was this the beginning of the answers to all her questions? She remembered the dream in which Sheriff Harper had told her she would soon know the whole truth.

When you pass through the waters, I will be with you. Beth could almost feel the power of the words that streamed through her mind like a river. Leonard lunged at her, grabbing her by her shirt just before she went under again. She coughed convulsively as he pulled her back toward the bank. Her panic-stricken mind hadn't a single clear thought. Why didn't he just let her die?

No, she couldn't think like that. God had promised to be with her. She had to keep focused on His word. She realized with some guilt that her mind was vacillating. But God was always the same; she had to trust Him to hold her steady.

Beth's body hit the bank with a thud. She heard a snapping sound in her shoulder and cried out as blinding pain shot through her body. The ground was littered with rocks, clods and broken branches. "Now we're even," he said, smiling. "One arm each."

Leonard plopped down on top of her, brutally pinning her to the ground. When she opened her mouth to scream, he covered it with his own. She pushed away and clawed at his eyes with her working hand. Unexpectedly, he banged his head against hers and she went limp. She felt as if she had run into a concrete wall.

Moments later, she realized that Leonard was ripping buttons from her blouse. She scuffled again, despite her injured shoulder. Then he ripped open her jeans and began to peel them down. The scream that tore from her throat sounded foreign, and she was instantly transported back to a wooded slope on campus just south of her dorm room.

Suffocating fear raced through her as she frantically tried to push him away. "Michael, please don't do this," she begged, gasping for air. Her heart thrashed violently against her chest as she screamed again and again. She hoped someone would hear her.

Suddenly, Leonard was yelling and shaking her. "Beth, get a hold of yourself!"

He abruptly rolled off her and stared. Feeling shaken by her subconscious reliving of that awful Valentine's night, Beth pulled at her clothes to cover herself. In the next instant, she was rushing up the steep incline. Her sudden burst of energy surprised her. But she had to get away from this monster.

As she neared the top, her sneakers lost traction on the scattered debris. She slid back down on her belly, clawing desperately at the ground. The rocks tearing her skin caused her once again to cry out in pain. Just as she was about to scramble up again, Beth felt her hair being jerked back. She turned and kicked out, causing them both to tumble. When she got to her feet again, she felt the full force of Leonard's wrath as he slapped her hard across the face. She collapsed— battered, drained, and now bereft of hope.

He dragged her up the slope and half carried her back through the woods. Though she was still conscious, she had no more energy to fight him. When they drew near the shanty, he stopped beneath a tree at the edge of a small clearing. After dropping her to the ground, Leonard took the knife from his belt and put it at her throat. A coil of rope and a roll of duct tape lay near his feet.

"I got my revenge on the others—even George," he gloated. "He doubled-crossed me. He's the one who shot your horse, ya know." He laughed fiendishly. "Been giving your daddy mixed medicines for years. Didn't want him to go as quick as your ma did. You're my ticket out of here. I'll only keep you alive as long as I need to."

Beth wept softly. Had he actually said Mr. Tubbs had killed *both* her parents? Her befuddled mind tried to snatch elusive pieces of the last ten years, some of which were beginning to add up.

Her mother had often been ill, and would go to Mr. Tubbs for a tonic he had created for migraines. That must have been how he poisoned her. It was clear she was drugged when she made the final entries in her diary. She had gotten so close, she thought wryly.

Leonard picked up the rope and cut it. Thoroughly confused, and fully convulsed with sobs now, Beth fell against the tree. Once again he put the knife at her throat, pulling the razor-sharp blade across her neck until she could feel trickles of blood dripping on her skin.

"Stand up and hug the tree," he ordered. Extreme exhaustion rendered her less than cognizant, and the trembling was so fierce she became nauseated.

Leonard pulled her arms around the tree and clamped the handcuffs on her wrists. She winced when the bark scraped savagely against her cheek. When he began binding her ankles with the rope, she stood as still as she could. Stay calm, she told herself, as she fought to breathe. Hold on…hold on.

"I'm almost sorry for you, Bethie. You got mixed up back there at the creek. I didn't know Mike had hurt you like that. But it's too late now." Although the words sounded sympathetic, they stung as intensely as the torn flesh on her body. She stared at him as best she could in the position in which she was bound.

After he left, Beth struggled against all odds to free herself. She was still soaking wet, and with each movement, the rope at her ankles became tighter. She whimpered quietly as her frustration grew. Every place on her body ached and burned, and she was certain her shoulder was dislocated.

After a long time of being bound to a tree in the unforgiving heat, Beth could no longer stand straight up. The heat, plus her injuries, had brought her close to delirium. She didn't know if she even had the strength to call out if the gag somehow came loose. She sagged limply against the rough bark, her lids slowly closing.

Then a picture flashed in her mind—a picture of the cross on which Jesus had hung. Her eyes flew open, and she struggled to stand up straight. But the cuffs had moved below a notch in the tree and she was forced to remain crouched. Feeling beaten and defeated, she struggled to whisper a prayer, leaning her head against the tree.

"Lord, I forgive them. I forgive Michael and Mr. Tubbs. I forgive Leonard."

As the breeze hastened in the trees, words seemed to permeate every cell of her body and mind. *You will not die but live, and proclaim what the Lord has done.*

TWENTY-FIVE

Wednesday morning tiptoed into Plover Creek, with an eerie hush in its wake. The sky was steel gray; the air was muggy. The small group gathered in Lena's home jumped almost in unison each time the house phone or one of their cells rang. But it was usually a neighbor checking to see if there was any word of Beth.

Although lifted by the overall concern and trickling reports about old unsolved cases, David was becoming more and more unglued that there was nothing that could help him find Beth. The requested cash had been placed at the church, but no one had yet claimed it. And they were all suffering from anxiety overload. He didn't like, or understand, the whisperer's delay in getting the money and releasing Beth.

Lena answered the phone and handed it to Taylor. After he hung up, he stood, his keys jangling, and started toward the door. "That was the sheriff. It appears somebody has broken into the crime scene at Tubbs' drugstore. I need to meet Tricia at my office in about thirty minutes."

"Who would cross a taped-off scene to break into the drugstore?" Lena asked.

"Anybody wanting drugs," Taylor answered, opening the door. "Sheriff said several pharmaceuticals and some first-aid supplies were taken."

David followed him outside, feeling idle and dysfunctional. "I need to get out, Taylor. Do you mind if I ride along? "

"Not at all. Be good to have the company."

On the drive to Taylor's office, David started free-floating possibilities, hoping something would stand out. One thing that came to mind was the sheriff's revelation that Beth had made a call to his office. He tensed up as he guardedly turned to Taylor. "Why do you suppose we haven't seen Leonard?"

Instead of responding, Taylor slapped his forehead. "That's it!" he said excitedly. "I knew something was a little off, but I couldn't put my finger on it. I think we'd better find out."

David was acutely disappointed to learn that Tricia Peters had been pulled off the case. She was sure the decision to reassign her had more to do with her going over her boss's head to the state AG's office than with anything else.

"I'm just glad I had already filed a formal complaint," she said. "There's not much they can do to stop that."

"What are you going to do now?" Taylor asked.

"I'll continue to help you as much as I can. I'll just have to stay in the background. We'll need to move fast…while my reassignment is still undisclosed."

"Are you sure?" Taylor asked. "We could sure use the help, but I don't want you jeopardizing your position."

"I'll be fine," Tricia assured him.

"David brought up something on the way over here," Taylor said. "I don't know how I could've missed it."

After mulling over the fact that none of them had seen Leonard since before the church burned down, Taylor and Tricia began making phone calls. David was left anxiously prowling the office, wondering what he could be doing to find Beth. Their one-sided conversations kept fading in an out as he paced from Taylor's office to Beth's, where Tricia sat. From what he could hear, the two were calling in favors from friends, associates and acquaintances to get things moving faster. He even heard Tricia mention the Rangers.

David felt frazzled and helpless. Where was Manny? Taylor had advised them against telling the sheriff what Miss Virgie had told them about the tournament in Oklahoma City. But by the time they located the hotel where Manny had stayed, he had already checked out. Miss Virgie thought he was headed back home.

David wandered into the copy room and bowed his head. "Oh, God," he breathed. "I'm trying to hold on. Please don't let her die. If I've opened the door to misfortune by not forgiving Deidre, forgive me. I choose to forgive her now. Help Beth see that she needs to forgive those who have offended her. I declare Psalms 118:17 over Beth. She will not die, but live."

He lifted his eyes, feeling a shade more at peace. Still, he wanted to get back to Plover Creek. But he also wanted Taylor and Tricia to do what they could to get Beth back safely.

After Tricia and Taylor finished their calls, the three sat down at the conference table. Tricia pulled out a floppy disk from her briefcase and fanned it around a little. "I didn't need the warrant to obtain the Tubbs' pharmacy log after all," she said with an impish smile. "Which, by the way, looked perfectly fine. When they found his body, a friend of mine took the time to look around. Apparently, Tubbs kept a journal on his computer." She shook her head ruefully. "He was completely obsessed with getting all his alleged ancestral property back."

"Obsessed enough to kill for it?" Taylor interjected.

"Yeah. Just like we thought. And that includes coming after you." She waved the floppy again. "He still had plans."

David's eyes narrowed as a new wave of panic surfaced. "How can this nightmare be so all-encompassing? I just don't understand. If Tubbs was a murderer, who murdered *him*? And who has Beth out there doing God knows what to her?"

Despite his earlier calm, David became more undone with each word. He wanted something done. He wanted to do something. It was all going too slow. Rubbing the back of his neck, he stood and walked to the window. He couldn't abide the way little bits of information kept creeping in from the shadows signifying nothing of value. They needed to find Beth. And they needed to find her now.

"David, I have obtained the lab analysis of the blood taken from the scene."

He hurriedly returned to the table. "I thought the sheriff was supposed to get back with us on that."

"The results were not available until late last night. He may not have them, yet." She paused, looking at David. "It's not Beth's."

Relief flowed through David like a cool breeze. "Thank you, God. Thank you."

———— ♏ ————

As evening drew near, the long wait continued in Lena's living room. Despite her show of boundless energy, it was obvious that the emotional strain was taking its toll on her. Signs of exhaustion in Lena's face and manner impelled Miss Virgie to insist that she go to bed and rest.

Soon after, a deputy arrived on the scene with Manny in handcuffs. Surprise and relief triggered a glimmer of hope in David as he and Carl sat at the kitchen table, staring into the living room. Manny stumbled through the door ahead of the deputy. His left eye and lip were cut and bloodied. Taylor, who stood leaning against the wall closest to the kitchen, was aghast.

"Looks like another example of your cleaned-up department, Sheriff. Do you rough up everyone you bring in for questioning?"

"There's no need to jump to conclusions, Mr. Steele. The captive must have resisted arrest."

"Is that so, Deputy?" Taylor asked, his eyes cutting through the man. "And I'd be careful how I answered. My client may decide to press charges."

"Wouldn't that be a conflict of interest, Mr. Steele?" the sheriff asked. "Manny can't be your client, too."

"No, it's not, Sheriff. I'm convinced that Manny isn't guilty of anything. And yes, if he'll have me, I intend to represent him."

Manny simply nodded his consent. The deputy thought better of the words he was about to utter, looking nervously at the sheriff. Appearing uneasy and baffled, Manny looked around the living room.

He seemed to relax when he saw Carl and David through the kitchen doorway.

Taylor cleared his throat. "Are those irons really necessary?"

"Nah, I guess not." Harper gestured to his deputy to remove the cuffs.

Miss Virgie waddled out of the back bedroom and did a double take when she saw Manny's bruises. Shaking her head in disapproval, she pressed her lips together into a tight line. "God don't like ugly, Bill Harper." She continued into the kitchen and dampened a paper towel, her mouth clamped shut.

Sheriff Harper wiped the sweat from his brow with a handkerchief and looked accusingly at Manny, who was sitting on the couch. "We've got an officer keeping watch on that money at the church. I'm surprised you haven't picked it up yet."

Manny looked at Taylor, confused.

His impatience rising, David glared at the sheriff, openly annoyed. "Manny doesn't know anything about what you're implying, Sheriff. And just what makes you think the culprit will show when you have a deputy out there in plain sight?"

"Don't worry none about that, David. My deputies know how to handle themselves in situations like this." Harper returned to Manny. "You are a hard man to find, Manny."

"I didn't know anybody was looking. Your deputy told me I was in some kind of trouble about Beth." He looked around the room again. "If y'all bring her out here, I'm sure she'll clear this up."

"Now, Manny, you know Beth ain't here, don't you?" Harper asked, his voice a mixture of skepticism and sarcasm.

Manny's expression darkened as he opened his mouth to reply. Miss Virgie waddled over to the couch with the dampened towel and placed it on Manny eye and lip.

"Bill Harper, don't you go bothering this boy in my hearing. You know Mansfield ain't done nothing wrong. And what could he have done to aggravate this nincompoop you call a deputy?"

"Miss Virgie, I'm trying to conduct an official investigation here. Now please—"

"Then why ain't you doin it down at the jailhouse?" she asked, turning to face him.

Carl and David got up from the kitchen table and moved to the living room with the others and sat on the floor near the deputy.

"I do aim to take Manny here down to the jail. My deputy brought him over here under my orders."

"On what charge?" Taylor asked, his smile changing into a ruthless straight line. At that instant, David was certain he wouldn't want to be on the other side of a courtroom from Taylor Steele. "I don't see that my client could possibly be a suspect. He's just gotten back into town."

"What do you mean?" Sheriff Harper asked. "Where has he been?"

Taylor casually moved toward Manny, placing himself between the couch and the chair the sheriff occupied. "Manny, I realize you don't know what's been going on here. But the church burned Saturday afternoon and Beth went missing Sunday night. Miss Virgie told us where you were."

He nodded. "She said Beth needed me to come home."

"Well, she didn't have the heart to tell you that Beth has been abducted. Can you answer a few questions for the sheriff's satisfaction?"

Clearly shaken by the news, Manny nodded. "How long were you in Oklahoma City?"

"I didn't know he was in Oklahoma City," Harper growled, attempting to peer around Taylor. "Miss Virgie, why didn't— Oh, never mind."

He fell back into the chair, shaking his head in frustration. David had watched Manny closely from the moment Taylor mentioned Beth's abduction. This man hadn't hurt Beth. He would bet his life on it.

In the meantime, Manny's eyes had become as hard as black marbles. He stood and pressed past Taylor, glaring in turn at Bill Harper and his deputy.

"You think I'd hurt Beth like that?"

Before Taylor could stop him, Manny drew back his fist and slammed the deputy in his jaw. Carl jumped to his feet to help Taylor restrain him as Sheriff Harper rocked himself into a standing position. He held out his hand to hold back the deputy, who had fallen against the storm door. "Mr. Steele, I think your client has given me just cause to take him on down to the jail."

"Not when your deputy has obviously used unnecessary force and brought him into the home of a private citizen for questioning," Taylor said. The sheriff threw up his hands and returned to his chair. Miss Virgie raised her cane and tapped Manny lightly on the shoulder.

"Come sit back down, Mansfield. No need of getting' yourself in any more trouble."

Turning to the old woman, Manny began weeping. "I shoulda been here," he said between sobs. "I knew she was scared half out of her mind before I left. I promised I'd watch over her. Oh, Lord, Lord. I shoulda been here."

Manny wrapped his arms around himself, his tears continuing to fall like great drops of rain. Miss Virgie gently placed an arm around the man's shoulder, her own tears beginning to flow. Both Carl and David stood to their feet, moved by Manny's emotional outburst. David sat on the other side of Mann. "To who, Manny? Who did you make that promise to?"

"Rev'n Ray," he said, his eyes still swimming. "I promised a long time ago I'd watch after Beth for him."

"When was that?"

"The first time was just after you and Carl went off to college. We were 'bout nine or ten then. But Beth depended on both y'all more than you probably know about. She went through a spell of grief. Felt left behind. Rev'n Ray and Miss Clara was real worried there for a while."

Carl nodded. "I think I remember them mentioning that to me."

"One evening when I came by to help with chores, Rev'n Ray talked to me 'bout it," he continued. "Probably 'cause he didn't wanna worry Miss Clara too much. She was having those bad headaches."

David leaned forward in his chair. "Did Beth ever know you had made this promise?"

"Nah. Rev'n Ray said it was between him and me. He didn't much like telling her some things on account she's so high-strung. She's strong, but she takes things real hard. That's why she didn't know a lot about what was going on out here. Rev'n Ray reminded me of my promise when we was in high school. Him and Beth had been at odds for so long then."

David smiled and looked away, feeling guilty for his earlier suspicions. In all honesty, he had always admired the deep devotion the two had for one another. It was genuine and gentle, and yet had the strength of iron.

"How long were you in Oklahoma City?" Taylor asked a second time. "And why were you there?"

"About a week. Went for the shooting competition. It was a tournament. I been savin' for a whole year to go."

"Did anyone else know you were going?"

"Kia Paine, Miss Virgie and her niece, and I think Beth knew," Manny said. He frowned, shaking his head slowly. "Come to think of it, I don't believe I got a chance to tell her. She was real upset about some things. I got my hotel receipt and meal vouchers right here."

"Do you mind if we take a look?" Taylor asked.

Manny pulled out a worn black wallet from his pocket and began searching for the documentation. They could all see by his trembling hands that he was terribly upset. Taylor gently pulled the wallet from Manny's hands and retrieved the papers. He noted the signature on each voucher, and then handed the papers to the sheriff.

Harper leafed through the receipts and vouchers and turned to the deputy. "You can go now, son."

"Sheriff, I've been wondering about something," Taylor said. "Where's Leonard been lately?"

"Leonard took a leave of absence about a week ago. Said he had to go take care of an ailing relative down in Austin. Why?"

"Do you mind if we go off the record here?" Taylor asked.

"Mr. Steele," Harper said, lightly chuckling, "we've been off the record ever since I met you. This is a most unusual way of handling a case, but I s'pect I owe it to these folks."

"What type of personal vehicle does Leonard drive?"

"He drives the patrol car so much…let me see," he said, scratching his head. "It's an old white Ford pickup, '78 or '79 model."

"Beth's already been out there for two nights with an obviously demented person," David said. "We need to find her."

Harper's eyes bulged. "Are you saying Leonard has something to do with this?"

"I won't know for sure until I check with his family. But his name kept coming up when I checked into Tubbs' background."

"Well, George was a sort of guardian to Leonard when his parents up and moved to San Antonio."

"Why should a grown man need a guardian?" Taylor asked, puzzled.

Harper glanced down and fidgeted with the brim of his hat. "Leonard sometimes has these spells. George always knew what to do in the way of doctoring and medicines."

"What type of spells?" Taylor asked.

"Epileptic," Harper said. "For a while, he was seeing a head doctor over in Dallas, too. But George told him he didn't need to go back and started mixing him some medicine to keep him hinged. Seemed to be working pretty good."

"Maybe not," Taylor said. "I'm in the process of contacting colleagues to get some help on this case."

"Help?" Harper cut in, indignant. "I'm the sher—"

Miss Virgie leaned her plump frame forward and gazed hard over the top of her glasses. "Bill Harper, we ain't in no mood for you to all of a sudden start feeling your toes. We got to get that chile' back here alive. Now you can help us, or we gonna do it without cha'?"

No one batted an eye at the old woman's stout words. People in the community had voluntarily started reporting different things to the DA's office since she had moved into Lena's house.

"Mr. Steele, we're doing everything possible, but you're the only one who has been able to get a word out of folks. You're farther along than I've been able to get. I'll open my files to anyone you send to look them over."

"I appreciate that, Sheriff. If you don't mind, I first need to know everything you have on Leonard Ware and his family."

Just then, the phone rang and David grabbed it. The voice on the other end was raspy and low. "I've got the money," he whispered.

"Where's Beth?" David blurted out. "Is she all right?"

"Hold on, hold on. Since y'all tried to trick me by putting a guard on that money, I might just have to break Miss Bethie up a little. *Then* I'll decide if she's fit to live." The line went dead.

The whisperer's final words triggered the dread that had consumed David, even in his dreams.

TWENTY-SIX

After searching most of the night with Manny, David awakened in a haze of fury the next morning. Beth had been missing for three nights, but it felt more like years. He thought about the voice he'd heard on the phone the night before and wondered if Leonard was really the culprit. The cleverly disguised voice could be just about anybody's.

They had all agreed to get a fresh start by first light. He walked restlessly around the living room, afraid to even imagine what Beth might be going through out there. He prayed ceaselessly for her safety and peace of mind.

Many in the community had brought food, but more importantly the congregation was holding a prayer vigil. He glanced up just as Carl dragged himself into the living room. "There's a fresh pot of coffee in the kitchen."

"Thanks," Carl said, pausing to look at Manny, who was sprawled in the corner of the living room floor. "I owe you a huge apology, Manny. I've been going a little crazy around here, but that doesn't excuse me for thinking the worst of you in this whole mess. I guess I just needed somebody to blame. I'm glad I was wrong."

"That's all right, Carl," Manny said. "I understand. I might've done the same thing in the right situation."

Carl shook his head. "No. You would have done just what Beth did—gone to bat for those you knew and trusted. She was ready to box my ears. In fact, she did give me a good pop."

"That's Beth, all right," Manny said, smiling knowingly. "She gave me a good talking to for slugging Mike."

David shot him a curious glance. "When did you do that?"

"After Rev'n Ray passed. Heard he was gonna stop by and offer condolences, and I convinced him not to bother."

Carl's face flushed with indignation. "You're a good friend, Manny."

David felt a now-familiar flash of panic. "Do you have any idea where someone would keep Beth hidden?"

"You thinking 'bout Leonard again?"

"Yeah."

He scratched his head and shook it, puzzled. "I been thinking about him all night. I saw a few tracks last night when we looked, but I lost them. I didn't think much about those push marks on Beth's car until the sheriff described Leonard's truck. I knew he was the one helped her out of the car. When he called me, he said he'd tried to get it out of the ditch, but only managed to make matters worse."

"He was probably covering himself," David said. "Where would he take her, Manny?"

Manny eyed David soberly, and then he bolted upright as if suddenly remembering something. "Let's go look around Beth's sycamore."

It was about eight in the morning when David raced toward Beth's ridge ahead of Carl and Manny. They had ridden most of the way in Manny's wrecker, but had come the remainder on foot. He hoped he would see something, hear something. The clouds were gathering thicker. He ran toward the smooth sycamore—the big old split miracle that lay high enough off the ground for Beth to use as a couch. He seemed to sense her presence.

Memory of the last time he and Beth had sat on the sycamore seized David. He swallowed dryly, desperate to find her. "Oh, God. Please help us."

How could he have been so close to happiness and lose it just like that? He felt Carl's hand on his shoulder. "Speak to the mountain. We've gotta hold it together until we find her. And we *will* find her."

"I don't know what I'd do if I lost her now, Carl. We need some outside help."

"Yeah. I've already mentioned it to Taylor. He said something about the state police or Rangers, since I had a problem with the feds. We'll find her."

Manny stood back, quietly watching, as was his way. After a moment, he moved closer. "Right there," he pointed. "Under the sycamore is where I saw Leonard digging one time. The tree was whole back then. It was later the lightning struck it like this."

Carl frowned. "Digging? What was he even doing on McDade property? And out here where Beth spent quite a bit of time?"

"I figured he was burying a dead animal or something. Beth had already left for college by then, so I didn't see any reason to stir up nothing."

David and Carl looked at each other, both apparently thinking the unthinkable. Using his fingers, David raked away the thick covering of leaves and pine needles beneath the sycamore. The dirt looked as if it had been freshly packed into place.

"We need something to dig with," Carl said.

David noticed the black plastic bag further to the right of the sycamore. "Take a look in that bag, Carl. See if there's a shovel and hoe."

Carl found a shovel, hoe, rake and several hand tools. Manny and David took turns digging, but the going was slow. Because the tree was growing horizontally, it blocked the site and they had to dig at an angle. Carl retrieved the hoe and began moving the mound of dirt to the side. As the sky grew more ominous, Manny paced about, stress lines forming on his brow.

"Manny, why hadn't you told us about seeing Leonard over here earlier?"

He shrugged, a look of guilt clouding his face. "At the time, it didn't seem important enough. He wasn't really hurting anyone."

"But, you knew—"

Manny turned away abruptly and moved toward another tree. "There's something I ain't told y'all about."

"It has any bearing on this?" David asked.

"Maybe. See, Pa wasn't my daddy. Arthur Patterson was."

David paused for several moments. "That means Miss Virgie's your grandmother. I knew something was different about the way she acted toward you."

"She didn't know until a few years back, just before Ma died. Ma and my real pa was supposed to get married, but he got sick and died before they could. Since she was pregnant with me, Tom Jefferson married her to keep her name out of the mud."

"I don't understand," Carl said. "What does that have to do with this now?"

"Just trying to make you see why I obliged Leonard a little," Manny said, almost apologetically. "He found out about everything one night when Pa got drunk. After I saw him over here, he threatened to tell everybody if I didn't keep my mouth shut. He said if hurting my ma wasn't enough to convince me, he'd find a way to hurt Beth."

For several moments, the men stood in complete silence. No one knew what to say, so David began digging again, remembering a comment Beth had made about this place.

"The thunder would rumble just over the trees and my whole body would shake with the vibrations. I was almost sure it had some mysterious meaning. Sometimes I actually thought I understood it."

A loud rumble of thunder sounded then, followed by a lightning flash. Finally, about two feet down, David hit on something and yelled out in horror.

The rain came sporadically at first, then it began to come down in relentless sheets. Carl immediately took out his cell and dialed the sheriff, and then Taylor.

—m—

By noon the county sheriff's office had been relieved of duty. The state police and Texas Rangers had assumed jurisdiction over the case.

David stood a distance back, his chest tightening with each passing moment.

Although he tried to continue quoting the Bible passages, he became dumbstruck with horror after authorities unearthed the remains of yet another body. Manny sat on one of the fresh stumps and wept openly. Although Bill Harper had been suspended pending an investigation, he was allowed to be present as long as he didn't interfere with the proceedings.

The state police and Texas Rangers came together and assembled a special task force to comb the area. Machinery was brought in to dig up the entire tract. Crushing agony closed in on David as he watched Beth's beautiful flowerbed being devoured by the earth-moving equipment.

The coroner's office was also there. And, apparently, word had been leaked to a news crew about the horrific findings, and there had been rumors that the feds had finally been alerted and were planning to move in to take over the case. David was certain Tricia had been the source of the leak.

Taylor arrived on the scene with several other government officials. He looked grim, but relieved that something was finally being accomplished.

David's eyes stung from intense anxiety. He wanted Beth back safely in his arms. He was pondering what else they could be doing to find her when he saw Manny limping toward him.

"I just thought of something. There's a little shack just across from here," he said, pointing across the creek. "It's a little ways deep, but not far. Leonard used to go out there and sleep. That's when we all thought it was George's land. I tried to stick to McDade property 'cause Rev'n Ray said I could, but sometimes I'd cross the creek."

TWENTY-SEVEN

An hour later, Manny and David were in Manny's wrecker headed north on the old Bayless Road. David prayed under his breath. Gus and Tiger stood at attention in the back. When Manny turned the truck onto a grassy path that was barely visible, David looked around worriedly.

"It's safe," he said. "It's just not used very much. Leonard comes out here a lot. We'll have to get out and cross the creek at a shallow place and come up on the other side. It's a pretty long walk."

"I can handle it," David said, checking to see if Carl and Taylor were behind them. They were, but he wondered how long Taylor would be able to follow them in his sports car.

Manny took a quick turn and pulled into a concealed clearing. Yellow tape had already been strung across the path leading deeper into the woods.

"This is as far as we can go," Manny said, turning to see Taylor and Carl climbing to join them. "Has anybody checked out Leonard's apartment?"

"Yeah," Taylor answered. "The police have it under surveillance."

"Are you sure we can trust the sheriff hanging around?" Carl asked.

"Yes. I think he's just been negligent. He seemed sincerely unaware that his deputies were still running wild," Taylor said. "Beth's voice will be heard a long time in this community. Things will change when all of this is over."

Two state police officers appeared carrying shotguns. "Mr. Steele, I'm Ronnie Campbell and this is Willy Gaines," the taller of the officers said. "I've been instructed by the state attorney general's office to allow you to search the woods, but my partner and I have to stick with you."

"That's fine," Taylor said, as he motioned to Manny to move out.

"Carl, how's your leg?" David asked. "Can you do this?"

"I'll stop when I have to," Carl answered, moving out behind Manny.

Manny walked ahead of them all. Despite his pronounced limp, he moved fast, alert and driven. When he slowed, they all slowed. David was right on Manny's heels, hoping to stumble on some clue to Beth's whereabouts and praying she was still alive.

He forced his mind to see her face—her deep dimples, her luminous smile. This vision of his beloved put to flight thoughts of her body lying beneath a tree. Such thoughts had plagued sporadically.

An animal sound penetrated the tempo of their rushing steps. Perhaps it was a lost dog, or a wolf. David noticed that Gus' wet nose was twitching excitedly. The dog stopped for a moment, listened intently and at Manny's urging continued sniffing the area.

Manny pointed out broken branches and low brush that appeared recently disturbed. David stopped and toyed with a small broken twig. "I could track a whole lot better if it hadn't rained so hard," Manny called back. "We're almost to that ol' shack."

The burning in David's gut intensified as various scenarios crowded his mind. The thought of finally seeing Beth filled his heart with newly aroused apprehension. What would they find? Was she alive?

He glanced at Carl's worried face and whispered, "Beth will live and not die."

He nodded and they started out again. The officers branched out, but kept Manny in their sights. Despite the denseness of the woods, Manny could still point out tracks.

"The rain didn't wash the prints away in this dense area," he said. "The splatter was slowed by the trees."

The creek's water was clear and cool in spots. When they all stopped for a drink where the water moved over the rocks, the dogs began to whine and sniff about, clearly agitated. Manny moved to Gus' side and stroked him softly, whispering to him. When Gus began howling at the edge of the creek bank, they raced over to investigate. They found blood and several low-growing bushes with broken branches. Manny motioned for the officers. They checked the broken branches and bloodied rocks, and Officer Campbell placed several pieces, along with a couple of loose buttons they found on the ground, into an evidence bag.

Seeing the buttons had made David's anguish more acute; he found himself wanting to call out her name. Manny followed the dogs as they abruptly broke into a run, rushing toward a tree standing at the edge of a small clearing. He pulled a shred of cloth off the rough bark and looked at the rope wrapped around the foot of the tree. The sound of the dogs whimpering was almost more than any of them could stand.

David cringed when he saw faint traces of blood staining the bark. Compelled to touch it, he sank to his knees. "Lord."

Carl and Taylor came up just as David was getting to his feet. He forced the image of her smile into his mind. He didn't want to think about what she must've been going through. He just wanted her back.

"We need to keep moving, just in case she's out here," David said.

Manny handed the cloth to the officer, who showed it to Carl. He looked at it numbly, tears filling his eyes. "That's a piece of the blouse she was wearing," Carl said brokenly. "Please, God, help us."

David headed out and Manny caught up with him. They all raced to the rickety structure. David hurried inside and saw the dried blood on the crate that had been apparently used as a table. He saw the rotting fruit and the filthy water in a metal pail, almost gagging on the putrid odor permeating the room.

One of the officers reached under the cot and pulled out the white cloth. It was a man's handkerchief. He smelled it.

"Chloroform," he said. "He knocked her out."

David slammed his fist into the wall, collapsing the entire side of the structure. "Where is she?"

"We should move back outside," one of the officers said.

They did and began to search the area. "Hold up, Manny," Taylor called. They all stopped. "I've got an idea. Did you know Felix and Terry very well?"

"They were Mike's best friends. Hardly ever went anywhere without each other. They didn't have much conscience—would do anything on a dare."

"That's why Dad was so upset about Mike and Beth," Carl said. "She seemed oblivious to the kind of boy he was."

Taylor pulled out his cell phone and dialed a number. "Tricia, what is the date of Shannon Ware's death?" The men looked antsy and perplexed as they listened to Taylor's side of the conversation. "How did she die? Who found her? Was there an autopsy?"

He then turned back to Manny. "When was the last time Beth saw Shannon?"

"I believe it was just before the big basketball game that year. She was plenty upset that night 'cause Rev'n Ray wouldn't let her go."

"Did you go?"

"Yep. Saw Shannon come in with Leonard. I remember thinking how odd it was that she left with Mike. But I figured they were going to visit Beth together. I guess I remember it because, later on when everybody else was leaving, Leonard came looking for her."

"Did you say anything to him?"

"I told him I saw her leave with Mike, and that they might be headed to the McDade ranch."

After looking a while longer for more clues, they all returned to Lena's to await confirmed identification of the victims found. Manny, frustrated at not getting any closer to finding Beth, sat in the kitchen with Miss Virgie while Tricia and Taylor tried to keep David and Carl focused.

"David, how did you figure out that the perpetrator could be Leonard?" Tricia asked.

David placed his mug on the floor. "It was your making such a big deal over the two names you found in Ray's notes. You remember asking us about Joab and Silas?"

Tricia nodded.

"Well, you said their names were listed alongside Charla's. I figured there had to be more to it than the beginnings of a sermon, so I tossed a few ideas around."

"Such as?" Carl pressed.

"Well, both men were seconds to someone, Joab to King David and Silas to Paul. We've all seen Leonard with Bill Harper and thought of him as a sort of second to the sheriff."

"Clever," Carl said. "Dad wrote a code."

"But why didn't he just write Leonard's name?" Manny asked.

"Probably didn't want to accuse him without having all the facts," Taylor guessed. "Maybe he thought he would get back to his findings and encoded them for safekeeping. Based on the notations in Tubbs' journal, Reverend McDade didn't even suspect his medications were being doctored."

"If that's true, why was Dad so opposed to George buying the property?"

"Maybe just had a gut feeling that something was off," Taylor offered.

Taylor took a call on his cell phone, making notes on a pad on the coffee table. After hanging up, he read aloud the names he had written down.

"Michael Baker, Felix Evans, Terry Johnson and Tom Jefferson." He placed the pad back on the table, looked at Manny and said quietly, "I'm sorry."

"I have a list of names readied to read after the victims' identities had been confirmed," Tricia said. "They're in chronological order, by date of occurrence.

Clara McDade died in July 1991
Shannon Ware, April of 1993
Charla Welch was killed May 1993
Tom Jefferson disappeared November 1993
Felix Evans disappeared January 1994
Terry Johnson February same year

Ray McDade had a stroke in December of 1995 and died in May 1999

And Michael Baker disappeared May 1999"

"It's just like Beth said," Manny said dejectedly. "Everybody was connected to Michael in some way—except Charla and Pa."

Taylor placed a hand on Manny's shoulder. "I need you to think hard, Manny. Is there any place else you can think of that Leonard would hide Beth?"

"I think I'll take me a ride," Manny said, springing to his feet. When David leapt up to join him, he shook his head. "I best go by myself. I'll likely be looking all night. Promise to call if I need some help."

David opened his mouth in protest. "But—"

"I do better by myself, David. You gotta trust me."

TWENTY-EIGHT

Beth gradually regained consciousness, and was surprised to discover that she was no longer gagged. She was, however, still bound at her hands, and her eyes were covered now. She thrashed about, uncomfortable in the damp clothing. She strained to remember the last few days.

The memories began to seep into her mind in dribbles. Leonard had tied her to a tree and it had stormed. He must have returned for her. But why were her eyes covered?

She struggled futilely against the restraints. She couldn't recall how long she had been away from her family. Had it been a week? Two? She was almost sure she had a fever. Hunger and congestion were also factors in her discomfort. She trembled as she remembered how frightened she had been when the sky grew dark and lightening flashed around her. She had calmed herself by talking to the Lord as if He were sitting on a stump beside her.

Beth didn't know how or when, but she had renewed confidence that she would live to see David again. Her resolve grew as his declaration of love resonated in her heart. She could almost smell his scent and feel his arms around her, evoking a sense of warmth and of well-being. The sounds of the breeze fanning the trees the low-pitched droning of the cicadas produced a measure of peace in her.

"Everything is fine," they seemed to whisper. Beth braced herself for a sneeze that exploded into three. She began to shift around, pleasantly surprised that her shoulder was no longer in pain. She leaned forward, hitting her forehead against something. She was clearly in a different location. The bed was different—larger. She bounced a little. It squeaked and had a headboard, too.

Sniffing the air, she got a faint whiff of fish, mildew and dust. She could hear movement. The sound was like the soft paws of a kitten. Beth wondered if she had been drugged again. She was extremely groggy and weak. Perhaps she was hallucinating. She sat up listening, trying to determine if anyone else was in the room. She was tempted to call out, but was afraid of the consequences. She had learned firsthand that Leonard wasn't averse to getting violent.

Her head was pounding. She lay back against the headboard and tried to remember her Bible verses. She was perspiring a lot, and feared Leonard may have broken one of her ribs. She became rigid with fear when she heard something stir outside. Was it him? Was he coming back to finish her off?

She soon relaxed, assuming the sound was that of an animal moving about in the underbrush. But then, the hollow sound of foot-steps on a wooden floor shattered the sounds of nature. She felt para-lyzed. Not with trepidation but with anxious frustration. She wanted to go home.

The scream Beth attempted was soundless. Her voice was gone. *Oh, God, please help me!*

She drew back the moment the door opened, not sure what to expect. She heard someone moving toward her and instinctively recoiled against the headboard.

"I brought you some more medicine," Leonard said.

His voice, steps—everything sounded so hollow and loud. He slowly walked over and pulled down a shade, which snapped loose and fell to the floor. He swore and walked back toward her, sliding some-thing across the floor. She could feel little puffs of air as he moved about. She tried to talk, but no words would come. Her agony rose to a level beyond her capacity to contain it. She thrashed about against her restraints, sobbing uncontrollably.

"Beth, hold up here," Leonard said, placing his hand on her fore-head. "You're burning up. I would've gotten you out of these wet clothes, but— well, here, I brought you something to put on. Do you think you can handle it?"

Beth nodded anxiously. He sat on the bed, causing the springs to squeak loudly. Pulling her head forward and away from the headboard, he pulled the blindfold from her eyes.

"I suppose you wanna go to the bathroom," he said smugly. "We have indoor plumbing now." She strained to speak, but again, no words came. "I'm sorry I had to punish you like that, but I didn't know it would rain. You was plumb out of your head, and a real handful to carry." He grinned. "You kept talking to Jesus and calling for David, mumbling something about getting married. I thought you and that Mr. Steele was courting."

Why was Leonard being almost decent to her? He attached the handcuffs to a chain connected to the underside of the bed. She knew this because of the sound it had made when she had bounced.

"I popped your shoulder back in place last night," he said, pulling on the chain to make sure it was secure. "This is long enough for you to go in the next room. I'll be right outside. If you try anything, you'll regret it."

Beth's vision had cleared enough that she could see the menace in his eyes. He was obviously reverting to the monster he truly was. She looked up and saw an object hanging from the ceiling over the bed. That must've been what her head had hit earlier, she thought, as she leaned back to get a better look. Her vision, however, was still too blurry.

Leonard jerked her up from the bed. "Either you wanna go or you don't."

Her chest burned. Her weak legs gave way, causing her to stumble against him. After catching her, he shoved her toward the door and into the next room off the hall, tossing a pair of green scrubs at her.

Beth wondered how she could possibly remove her wet clothes and put on dry ones while in handcuffs. She surely didn't want to ask Leonard for help. His frame of mind had been so erratic she wasn't sure what he'd do.

Beth stood studying at herself in the mirror; her focus had sharpened considerably. Her face was bruised, her lips swollen and cracked, and her eyes were slits. She had no clear recollection of how she had gotten most of her injuries. Her torn and bloodied blouse offered no clues.

Despite her aches, she slid down the wall to the floor to change. A gnawing at the back of her mind confirmed her fears. She wouldn't be able to completely change without Leonard's help. She removed her sneakers and socks then her denims, replacing them with the bottoms of the scrubs. She stood up to work on the blouse, but the chain and handcuffs made it impossible.

God, she didn't want to call for Leonard. Her frustration became so overwhelming that she began to pace about the small bathroom. *I can do this. Just slow down and think. Everything will be okay.*

She washed her hands and splashed water onto her face, then decided to rip away the rest of her soiled top. Perhaps she could tear up the back of the scrubs top. No, no, she thought. She still wouldn't be able to put it on over the manacles.

Without conscious intention, she hit the mirror with her bound hands. Broken glass was flying everywhere. Her aggravation was so intense now that she continued hitting at the mirror, barely noticing that pieces of glass had cut her hands.

Hearing the sound of breaking glass, Leonard burst into the bathroom. The sight of Beth's blood draining over the slivers in the sink shook him intently. She had stopped hitting the mirror, probably because she had used up what little energy she had left.

"This is just like Shannon!" Leonard shouted, rushing toward her wildly. Beth moved away in fear as he grabbed her by the shoulders and began to weep. "I'm sorry. I didn't mean to."

He washed her hands free of the blood and went through the house looking for something to dress them. Unexpectedly recalling that it was Leonard who had found his sister's body, Beth leaned limply against the sink and waited. Then she began to swoon, and darkness slowly closed in around her.

When she came to, Leonard was leaning over her in the bathroom. He had dressed her wounds with strips from his own tee shirt. His eyes were filled with tears as he silently helped her to her feet and back to the bed. She felt sick and longed to simply go back to sleep.

"Beth, I got some more medicine. It might make you feel better," he said, shoving two tablets at her and a plastic cup half filled with water. She swallowed them down quickly and lay back, just wanting to sleep.

The next time she opened her eyes; Leonard was gone. Though grateful to be dry, she was repulsed by the fact that Leonard had finished dressing her. Just the thought made her stomach churn violently.

She forced her thoughts from Leonard, replacing them with images of David and Bree. She couldn't wait to see them again.

Lord, thank you for keeping me alive. Thank you for the hope of seeing David and Bree again. Forgive me for my part in prolonging your plans for my life. I choose to leave everything behind and allow you to rebuild it. I choose to live.

Beth propped herself up a bit and looked more closely at her new prison. It seemed vaguely familiar, she thought. Then she remembered. She had come here many times with Shannon. This was Shannon's old room and her old bed. It hadn't been used in years.

She lay back and set her eyes on the object hanging above the bed. For a moment, she thought it was an old pest strip of some kind. Upon closer inspection, she saw movement and beheld the most ghastly tarantula staring back at her. The sound that tore from her throat was little more than a gravelly moan. When Leonard reentered the room, Beth lay curled in the corner of the bed staring wildly at the creature.

"I see you've met Alice. She's a real looker, ain't she?"

Beth's eyes swung from the creature to Leonard's curious face, and she wasn't at all sure which was the more monstrous. She felt intense horror and tried pleading with him with her eyes. Leonard began to laugh maniacally. "That's right," he said. "Shannon told me you were phobic."

He laughed so hard he collapsed onto the bed. "Oh, Beth, this worked out great. I have a guard. And she's real temperamental, so you'd better behave yourself. I gotta figure out what I'm gonna do with you."

She stared at him silently.

"At first, I just didn't want them digging on your old property. Don't much matter now 'cause they found all the bodies. I saw 'em. Your little hideaway ain't nothing like it used to be, Bethie. Now I just gotta get away from here."

Beth's heart stopped. What bodies could he be talking about? Was he going to kill her? Was he going to leave her here to die?

Oh, God. I'm scared. Help me hold on to my faith. I know this is just a snap for you. And whatever I was supposed to learn from it, I pray I've learned it. Please let them find me—whether or not it be to marry David. I'll continue to trust you.

TWENTY-NINE

Slipping in and out of consciousness, Beth had a recurring dream in which she was on a large ferry surrounded by people she didn't know. David appeared among the crowd dressed in a tuxedo. She was drawn to his overpowering magnetism and moved toward him, but could never get close. She called out to him, but he couldn't hear her.

In the dream, she could tell he was frantically looking for her. "Beth, Beth." Though she waved her arms wildly, he couldn't see her. A large crystal punch bowl separated them, and no matter how she tried, she could never get on the other side of the bowl. The more she navigated the crowd, the farther away he seemed to be. She knew that she would never get to say her vows unless she could get him to notice her.

A sound awakened Beth. She felt extremely warm, and forced herself upright in the bed. Her head hurt, and her thoughts were a tangled mess. She strained to grip a fragment of just one reliable thought and hold it long enough to get her bearings, but objects in the room swirled around in shapeless forms.

In between troubled sleep and semi-consciousness, Beth heard the frantic barks of Gus and Tiger in the distance. She had never heard them so excited. Gus, the more animated of the two, sounded louder and livelier. Perhaps he had finally treed a squirrel. Or maybe he was on the hunt for some fictitious rabbit. She could envision him running and climbing a hill, his ears flapping in the wind like a little girl's pigtails.

He was awfully loud, she thought, lifting up on her elbows. Uncertain whether she was awake or asleep, Beth looked into a grimy mirror and saw her best friend. She frowned. Was it a mirror? Or the window?

Elated, she reached for his hand. She had never been so happy to see anyone in her life. She wanted to ask him where he had been, but she couldn't make her voice work. Seeing him, though, gave her the courage to hope. But the mirror was between them. She limply waved and tried again and again to reach for him, but several tarantulas stood guard around her and she became too frightened to move.

"Close your eyes, Beth," Manny whispered. "Don't cry. Me and David will come back for ya. I promise."

"I wanna come now," she tried to say, pressing her hand hard against the mirror. But he didn't hear her. He had already vanished.

When she awakened, a damp cloth was on her forehead. Leonard sat beside her bed with a rifle across his lap. Thankful that the room was no longer spinning, Beth studied her captor's appearance. He was dressed in camouflage and had on all kinds of belts and buttons, and there was a pistol in his waistband. Her head ached and her chest felt as if an iron stove was on top of it.

"Leonard," she croaked. "Water!"

"You won't need any where you're going," he said cruelly. "As soon as you can walk on your own, we're leaving. With this bad arm, I'll need you going under your own steam. They're gettin' too close. Maybe with you as hostage I can get out of this."

Beth gazed woozily at the deranged man who danced dangerously from one extreme to the other. There was no real point in attempting to coax him back into coherence. She half believed she was having another nightmare, and longed to turn over and go back to sleep.

When Leonard pushed another white tablet down her throat, she swallowed it without resistance. She then turned her head away from him and quietly slipped back into the darkness.

—〰—

Screeching tires and urgent honking brought Lena running to the door. Miss Virgie waddled her way from the back room to the front porch. Carl and David jumped to their feet and ran outside. Manny's wrecker was pulled up behind Lena's car.

"I found her!" he shouted. "Gus, Tiger—get down and stay here." He began pulling away before David and Carl were safely seated in the cab. "I don't want the dogs giving us away. We may have a fight on our hands. He has that house wired to blow."

"Hold up, Manny," Carl said. "I know very little about explosives. Let's leave word for the law to get a bomb squad out here." Manny put the truck in reverse and backed up.

"Lena, call the Rangers or police over at the sheriff's office!" Carl shouted. "Tell them we found Beth, but we may need help from a bomb squad or SWAT team. The house is wired."

"Where is she?" Lena asked, just as Miss Virgie came up behind her. Carl realized he hadn't even asked, signaling Manny to answer.

"She's chained up in that old abandoned house on the Tatum place."

Lena rushed out to the truck and grasped the door handle. Her eyes were red and swollen. "Manny, is she okay?"

"She's alive," he answered. "But she's real sick…been through a lot, from the looks of her."

David swallowed and continued to pray silently. Lena swiped at the tears streaming down her face and pushed herself away from the truck. "Thank God, she's alive!"

"Leonard showed up and I had to get the dogs and go before he saw us."

"Go!" Lena shouted. "Bring her home safe. I'll make the call."

Manny pressed the accelerator and pulled out into the road, sending dust and pebbles flying high into the air.

David didn't know whether to be excited or scared. "Tell me how she looked, Manny?" he asked, almost beside himself.

"Eyes were wild and she couldn't seem to understand me. He's got a tarantula hanging over her head. I think I finally got her to hear me, and she laid back down. She'll be all right now, David."

They drove the few miles down the road, passing the ranch in a blur. When Manny turned into the private road that led to the pond, David remembered the night he had driven Beth's new SUV. She had gotten so mad at him when she thought he was challenging her about Taylor. How things had changed.

THIRTY

David suppressed the urge to suspend good judgment and rush the house. They kept low, following closely behind Manny. When they got within sight of the dwelling, they situated themselves behind fallen limbs. This would give them a clear view of the front door, as well as of the road leading up to it.

Despite the heavy rains, the ground was hard. Lying on their bellies in the tall grass, they waited for what seemed like an eternity for the authorities to arrive. Manny propped himself against a felled log, pulling his rifle up beside him. Then he took out a small pair of binoculars and peered through them.

Pointing, he said, "I know he's in there. See that second window to the right of the door? Beth's in there. He's got her chained to the bed."

David wanted to get his hands around Leonard's narrow throat for this. His breathing was labored, his throat raw. Manny took another look through his glasses. "I see you came prepared," David said, eager to get a look. Manny took the glasses off and handed them to David.

The grimy old structure was little more than a roomy shack. It was but a shadow of what it had once been. The white paint had long changed to a dingy gray. The porch sagged at one end, and grass grew through its boards. The picket fence that had once enclosed the front yard was rotten and broken down. Most of the windows were broken, but the window to the room Manny had said Beth was in was still intact.

The yard was littered with trash and the grass, though sparse, grew high. A scattering of colorful flowers managed to survive, but they didn't do much for the yard's decrepit appearance.

The heartbreak of being only a few hundred feet away from Beth and unable to touch her was maddening. David could feel the thunderous pounding of his heart, his head seeming to amplify the sound as he moved closer to Manny to get a better look.

"We have to stay out of his line of view," Manny reminded them. "We can guide the law in when they get here."

David peered through the binoculars a long time trying to see into the room. But it was so bright outside that the inside was pretty well shielded from view. He wished he could just walk up to the house, knock on the door and ask for her. He offered the glasses to Carl, who took a long look before handing them back to Manny.

Manny lay comfortably on his belly, dressed in coveralls. David wasn't surprised to see that this odd, quiet man was a real master of heroes. Beth had known it all along and had staunchly vouched for his innocence when everyone else, including himself, had doubts. He felt a strong sense of indebtedness to him for his loyalty to a friend.

They heard a car door slam shut. "I'll go guide them up here," Carl said, moving back toward the road. David watched as he inched his way back, careful to stay close to the dense grove of trees.

"Lord, please help us get her out of there," David prayed.

"Amen," Manny said, still gazing through the binoculars. "I think I'll move closer to the house. The law will more n' likely take over and push us out of the way. End up getting her hurt."

"If you don't mind, I'd like to tag along," David said. "Carl won't mind. His leg has been aching a bit."

"Can you climb a tree?"

"I'll keep up with you."

David watched as Manny scouted the area for a place for them. Finally, he pointed to the large, thickly foliaged oak south of the house. When he moved out, careful to stay hidden, David was right behind him.

He looked back and saw Carl looking at them. He gestured for him to stay with the authorities. Manny scurried up a large limb and tested it for strength by jumping up and down.

"It's okay," he whispered. "Come on up."

David hugged tightly to the trunk until he felt comfortable enough to let go. Living in the city had displaced his childhood proficiency at climbing trees. Seeing David's awkwardness, Manny snickered benignly.

They were well hidden but had a good view of Carl, Bill Harper and the state police officers. They now had a view of the side of the house. Manny lifted his binoculars again, grunted, and then handed them to David.

"That first window with the wire going down into it—that's where Beth is. Look into the next one."

David did as he was instructed and saw Leonard bending over the bathroom sink. He looked like a human booby trap, splashing water onto his face. When he left the room, David moved his focus to the room Beth was in. But he couldn't see through the window from this angle. "God, keep her safe."

"Mr. Steele and that woman DA are here. And a truckload of officers in black," Manny whispered, pointing.

The front door was suddenly pushed open, and everyone hit the ground. Leonard was headed down the steps when he abruptly halted and looked around suspiciously. He had evidently heard something because he retraced his steps, carefully backing away from the edge of the porch. When he began connecting wires, David's heart plunged to a new low. He was sure their only chance to seize him had passed.

The sound of another car door closing made them fear they were in danger of being detected. They had come too far, gotten too close to lose their hand now. "I need to try and get his attention," David whispered. "Maybe I can talk him…"

"No. It's way beyond that now, David. Best go slow. We'll get her."

David held his breath as he watched Leonard walk to the edge of the porch again and scan the area. Why didn't they just capture him and go in and get Beth? Then he remembered that the house *and* Leonard were wired. They were looking at a hopeless situation. Beth was so close, yet so very far away.

David looked out past the group that lay flat on the ground and saw a local TV channel's news van. When he heard the helicopter overhead, his heart froze. Leonard instantly began backing toward the door again.

When the door was slammed shut, a sense of doom enveloped David and he hit the trunk of the tree with his open palm. Fear of losing this battle overwhelmed him.

THIRTY-ONE

One of the officers located David and Manny. Manny quickly hid his rifle from sight while the officer radioed his superior for instructions. He was ordered to keep an eye on them.

The officers were scattered like ants over the property. They all froze when Leonard once more opened the front door to the shack. Then some scurried through the woods looking for better positions, while others seemed to scatter further, careful to stay out of sight.

Heart pumping, David was thankful that the one watching them had moved away. They slowly closed in on the house. Several officers moved silently toward the back door and around to the side where Leonard's white pickup was parked. They didn't try to enter, apparently afraid of setting off an explosion.

Leonard reappeared, dragging Beth's half-conscious body onto the porch. David straightened and grabbed the glasses from Manny's hands. She wore green scrubs and no shoes, and appeared too out of it to even walk. She looked as if she had undergone a hellish ordeal.

Using his captive as a shield, Leonard made his way to the edge of the porch, a revolver aimed at her head. The officer who had been standing near Taylor escorted Bill Harper to the front of the house. Approaching the gate, Bill raised his hands above his head and continued into the yard.

"Why don't you put that gun away, son," Harper said. "Everything will be all right."

"Bill, you get back, or I'll kill her," he said, shifting his weight from one leg to the other.

"Leonard, please don't harm Beth. She ain't done nothing to deserve this." Harper moved his large round body ever so carefully toward the front porch with his arms stretched wide and high.

Leonard's movements were becoming jerkier, while Beth's body began to slide. He tried to keep her in an upright position, but he was struggling. He dragged her to the wall, giving himself something to support his own unsteadiness.

"She killed my sister, Bill."

"Son, you're mixed up. You're off your medicine, ain't you?" Harper asked. "Beth looks to be sick. Why don't you let me get her to a hospital?"

He shook his head wildly, resembling a little boy anxious to get to the bathroom. "You tell 'em if they shoot, this whole hill is gonna blow."

"What can I do to help you?" Bill asked.

"I wanna get out of here. Maybe go down to Florida." He laughed then—a loud, unhinged sound that made David's skin crawl.

"What's all that ammo you got there?"

He wore a look of crazed arrogance. "I'm connected," he ranted. Then he began to laugh again. "Get it, Bill? I'm connected."

Looking through the binoculars, David saw Beth slide further down Leonard's camouflaged body. Her bruised face was swollen, her eyes closed, her body limp and battered. Her hands were wrapped in bloodstained bandages, and her wrists were handcuffed. What in God's name had he done to her?

When Leonard let out another demented laugh, the officer returned to the foot of the tree. David handed the binoculars to Manny and slowly climbed down.

"What's wrong with Beth, Leonard?" Harper asked. "Why ain't she standing on her own?"

"She's a frisky little thing. She got away and I had to punish her. I didn't know it was gonna storm. She got sick. I gave her some medicine from George's store, but it just made her sicker, so I mixed it with some of mine."

"What did you give her?"

"Happy pills." For a moment, Leonard looked as though he might turn and run; instead he reached down and grasped Beth's hair to hold her in a sitting position. "Make 'em go away, Bill."

"Leonard, give Beth to me. You know she and Shannon were good friends. She wouldn't have hurt your sister. You know that, don't you, son?"

"Ain't no way out now. I gotta kill us all."

The officer at the tree spoke into his radio, informing his commander that they didn't have a clear shot because one of the detonators might be hit. Both David and Manny overheard this grim assessment.

David had had just about enough and he started moving forward, unsure what he would say or do. He only knew he had to do something before Leonard killed them all. The officer tried to pull him back, but David yanked free, shoving the man hard against the tree.

After he resumed walking toward the house, he considered that it might help to sing. Maybe it would distract Leonard and keep the others at bay until he could get to Beth. He didn't care.

David broke into a rendition of "Swing Low" and marched forward, swinging his arms so Leonard could see that he was unarmed.

Carl couldn't believe his eyes when he saw David walking straight-backed toward the house, singing loudly. "What in God's name is he doing?"

"Exactly what he's supposed to," Taylor said with a determined smile. "Protecting his intended."

"Get him out of there," the officer in charge barked into the radio.

"No," Tricia said, placing her hand on the officer's shoulder. "This just might give us the break we need. Let him try. Please."

When Leonard saw David approaching, he put the gun back to Beth's head. "Stay back, David," he shouted, moving so his view would take in both men.

"Leonard, what will it take for me to get Beth safely out of here?" David asked, his hands in the air.

"I had to kill 'em. I had to. They hurt my little sister."

"I'm sorry about that," David said, a little confused. "But I want to take Beth to the hospital. You don't want to hurt her anymore, do you?"

The unstable man unexpectedly released Beth's hair and she slid to the floor, landing flat on her back. An officer stood and took aim, but Leonard fired his revolver, hitting the officer in the arm and knocking him to the ground. His fellow officers ran to his aid.

"Bill, you get him out of here," Leonard said, tears rolling down his face. "I'm a dead man, and Beth here is going with me."

"David, please go back and leave this to me," Harper pleaded, his hands still lifted.

David's eyes stayed on Leonard's. "No. This has gone on long enough. I want Beth. And she's not going to die out here like this."

"I don't wanna hurt her, but I will. You know I will."

David's heart sagged under the weight of all the emotions flowing from it. He wanted to rip Leonard's head right off of his shoulders, but he had to stay calm and get Beth. He continued to move toward the porch, his eyes on Beth.

"I know, Leonard, but wouldn't it be better to have two hostages?" David asked, his hands still in the air. "I see you're wounded. I can carry her for you. I don't mind."

David was about two feet from the porch when Leonard pointed the gun at him. "Don't come any closer."

"I love her, Leonard. I want to get us out of here. Can I just touch her?"

A sound whizzed past David's right ear, and driven by raw emotion he dived toward Beth, scooping her up into his arms. Feeling as though he was in a fog, he crushed her to him and ran as fast as he could toward the road.

"Stay with me, Beth," he crooned, hope and relief centering his determination.

Carl and Taylor rushed toward them. "Give her to me," Taylor said, his arms outstretched. Manny also hurried over, his rifle strapped to his shoulder. One of the officers stopped him.

"Sir, you'll need to come with us."

"He's with me," Taylor said, moving past the small group gathering. "And if you have questions, you'll have to ask them in my presence at another time."

"This man is guilty of obstructing justice."

"From where I was standing, he took the chance you weren't willing to and saved all our lives," Tricia chimed in. "I agree with Mr. Steele. Now I suggest you let them get this woman to a hospital."

David got into the ambulance with Beth, confused by all the conversation around him.

THIRTY-TWO

Beth opened her eyes, relatively alert but addled as to where she was and how she had gotten there. A crisp white sheet covered her. She peeked beneath the covers and saw the white gown with blue dots. "Hospital."

It took every ounce of strength she could muster to lift her head. She felt stiff, and in an effort to stretch out her arms became entangled in the tubes that were attached to them. While she struggled to get away, Beth saw someone in the recliner next to her bed. Was it Leonard? But he didn't have a gun lying across his lap. She was in enormous pain, but she continued taking stock of her surroundings. She felt drained and disoriented, but she was grateful to be in a clean room filled with beautiful flowers.

As her vision cleared, she saw the IV poles on both sides of her bed. "Thank you, God. Thank you for bringing me back to safety."

Despite her sluggish physical state and aching head, she craned to get a better look at her visitor. It was David!

The pure joy she felt gave her a floating, almost light-headed, sensation. She tried to ease out of bed, but her energy was lacking. She lay back and contented herself with watching him sleep. He was stretched out over the recliner like a big wonderful teddy bear. She resisted giggling as she listened to him snore. It was music to her ears. The nightmare was all over. She was safe.

"Thank you, Lord," she repeated. "Even though I almost turned my back on you, you remained faithful."

She wondered where Leonard was. She thought of how he had switched back and forth from the cruel captor to the contrite, confused man who grieved the death of his sister. Unexpected awareness energized her, and she once again tried to sit up, struggling weakly. She finally gave up and lay back down. She could tell her ribs were snugly wrapped.

She smiled, her eyes again on David. Was she really engaged to this man? She panicked. Was she still in the hospital because of the car accident? "Oh, God." Her memory *was* sketchy, and she could be a bit presumptuous sometimes.

Maybe she had dreamed it all, as in one of those movies in which the entire storyline turns out to be a dream. She strained to remember her last day of reality, praying that her imagination wasn't playing tricks on her. She had been in a car accident, and everything was a little mixed up. If she found out David had never proposed, she would just die.

David opened his eyes and stretched. It was morning, and he could see the pinkish-orange hue the early morning sun had painted the small private room. He didn't think it could get any more beautiful. The room was bursting with fragrant flowers. They had been arriving in bunches for the last few days. People across the nation, including city and state officials, had sent good wishes.

When the doctors insisted that some of them be taken away, he and Carl had given them to other patients. Smiling, he was thinking about how much he wanted to love and take care of Beth the rest of his life. She and Bree were his life, and he intended to build his world around them. *Thank you, Lord. Help me be worthy of being her husband.*

He looked somber as he thought of the previous few days. A nightmare. Beth had been terribly dehydrated when they brought her in. The doctor had been astonished that she wasn't in worse shape, but concluded that her physical stamina had probably been her defense. The barbiturates Leonard had given her in his deluded state had probably kept her calm, which was a benefit considering what she was going through. And the antibiotics kept infection away after being out in the rain all night and being cut up like she was.

She had suffered from two broken ribs that miraculously had not punctured her lungs, heat exhaustion, and some pretty nasty lacerations and scrapes. And she had a cold. Taylor had told them that in addition to having epilepsy, Leonard had been diagnosed several years ago as suffering from paranoid schizophrenia and severe depression. It wasn't clear how long he had been feeding Beth on his medications.

David stretched, making a rubbing sound on the vinyl recliner. It had been four days since the rescue. He turned toward her, desperately needing to see her face. When he saw her gazing back at him, he bolted from the chair. The dimples set in her cheeks called for him like beacons.

"Beth," he whispered. "Sweetheart, you don't know how glad I am to see that beautiful smile." He leaned forward and kissed her forehead, her nose, and each dimple. He stopped when he noticed her frown. "What is it, baby?"

"Did I dream it?" she croaked, barely above a whisper.

"No, I'm afraid not. It was a real nightmare, but it's finally over now. You're safe."

Her smile vanished and tears welled up in her eyes. "Not Leonard. I meant…"

Her eyes held his for a long time, melting his heart. David began going through his pockets, finally pulling out a small black velvet box. He opened it ever so carefully and removed an engagement ring. He held it up to the light briefly, then slid it on her ring finger. When he smiled down into her eyes, tears were spilling down both sides of her face.

"Just in case you can't remember, I'll ask you again. Elizabeth McDade, will you marry me?"

A long moment passed before she could answer. "I will." David leaned closer and touched each eyelid with his lips. Her tears continued to flow as she weakly wrapped her arms around his neck. "It wasn't a dream."

He couldn't resist any longer and gently, very carefully, pulled her into his arms. "I love you so much, Beth." When he started to release her, she resisted.

"Please don't. I want to feel your strength around me." He smiled and gladly reclaimed her in his embrace. "How long have I been here?"

"Four days."

"When can I go home?"

"Don't rush it."

"But—"

"No buts. I'll be right here."

"David?" She paused and gazed up into his eyes. "I-I don't…do you think we can go home to Seattle already married?"

"Are you sure you want to do that? You don't want a big wedding?"

"I just want you and Bree," she said, her voice strained and raspy. Her eyes shone with the intensity of her love and conviction. David grinned with the brightness of the joy filling his heart.

"The next few days aren't going to be easy, Beth. You're going to hear some hard things. I want you to promise me you'll draw strength from your faith."

"What things?"

"Not now. Just promise me."

"I will," she said. As long as you're with me."

David was sitting on the bed still holding her when Carl, Lena and Manny came into the room. He had raised the bed so they both could sit up comfortably.

"Hey," Carl said, hurrying to her side. "Good to have you back with us."

David cleared his throat. "Reverend McDade, if you would agree to perform the ceremony, we'd like to get married as soon as possible."

Lena started to cry and giggle at the same time. When David moved to give them all room to visit Beth, she leapt into his arms. "Congratulations!"

Manny moved in next to Carl and took one of Beth's hands in his. "Congratulations. I'm real happy for ya, Beth." She pulled him closer and wrapped her arms around his neck, giving him a gentle squeeze.

"Thanks for being my friend," she whispered. "I want you to be as happy as I am."

"I will be," he said grinning. "I've asked Kia Paine to marry me. She said yes."

"Kia Paine!" Carl exclaimed, offering Manny a hand. "I heard you mention her the other night. She's real nice, Manny. Congratulations, man."

Manny smiled shyly as everyone added their good wishes. "I think I'd better be going. I've got a date. Just wanted to come by and make sure you were doing okay."

"Wait Manny," David said. "I can't remember much about what happened out there. Why were they trying to arrest you?"

Manny shrugged. "I had a good shot, so I took it."

"You mean, *you're* the one who shot Leonard?"

"Yep," Bill Harper said, walking into the room. "He's pretty good with that rifle. Manny, I appreciate you not killing him."

"He deserved to die," Manny replied, looking somberly at Beth. Turning back to Harper, he added, "But I just needed to stop him."

Again, Manny started to leave the room, but Harper reached out for his arm and continued, "I think you might wanna hear what I came to say."

Harper leaned heavily against the wall. He wore a dark blue suit and rotated his hat nervously in his hands. Lena sat down in the recliner, and Carl moved to its arm and motioned for Manny to get the straight chair next to the window.

"Okay, Bill," Carl said. "What is it?"

"I sure am sorry about all of this. It's a mess. Leonard—well, he was transferred to the hospital in Dallas for security reasons. But I wanted to let y'all know so you won't hear it on the news. You already know George Tubbs had gotten him all tangled up with getting your land." His voice broke. "I think you're also aware he murdered both Reverend and Mrs. McDade."

"My God," Lena said, holding onto Carl's arm. "Did you know this?"

"Yeah," Carl answered, squeezing her hand. "Taylor and Tricia told us."

"Leonard built up a real hatred for blacks when he was attacked and beaten in the school he came from in Dallas. That was before his family came to Plover Creek. He hooked up with George Tubbs, who apparently turned him into a carbon copy of himself. He used those mixed-up drugs he made to control him. When three blacks raped his sister, he went a little ballistic."

Beth began to tremble and David gave her a gentle squeeze and whispered in her ear. "Remember your promise."

"Leonard's medication could control his mood swings, but he had stopped taking it," Harper continued.

"We didn't really know what had happened to make Shannon leave Plover Creek High her senior year until the other day," Carl said, somberly eyeing his sister. "She didn't even tell Beth."

"I take it Mr. Steele told you the girl was raped," Harper said. "Did he tell you by whom?"

"No," Carl said, his brows lifting expectantly.

"It was the Three Musketeers," Beth said, looking numbly at Manny. David held her closer. Harper squirmed a little against the coral-colored wall, crossed his arms and hung them atop his belly.

"That note you found was something Leonard sent Michael after *his* part of the killing got started, Beth. He confessed to not only killing Mike and the four found in the grave on your ranch, but four more. Charla Welch was among them."

The news was a blow too many for Manny. He rushed to the door and pulled it open with an angry jerk. "Manny," Beth croaked, her hands reaching for him. He never turned his head.

"I'll be all right," he said, without looking back. "I just need to get out of here."

When he had gone, Bill straightened and moved to the door as well. "Who else, Bill?" Lena asked. "Charla make's only one more."

"George Tubbs and this feller y'all hired to keep an eye on Beth, Todd something or other."

"Levescy," David said.

"Beth, I'm real glad to see you feeling better," he said. "I really am."

"That's three," Beth said. "Who else?"

"I shouldn't tell you this, but it'll be a matter of public record after a while. Shannon didn't kill herself, Beth. She was Leonard's first victim."

"Oh, dear God," Beth said. "His hatred for blacks was stronger than his love for his sister."

As Beth wept in David's arms, a sad silence pervaded the room. "Hatred is a powerful and dangerous thing, Sis."

"Hate is not stronger than love," Beth said, whimpering into David's chest.

"Hate is stronger only if you *choose* it above love," Carl said after a moment of reflection. "You were not to blame for all of that, Sis. You know that, don't you?"

She nodded quietly.

"Leonard had so let hatred poison his insides that he didn't even know the difference from right and wrong anymore," Lena interjected. "Not to mention the fact that his psychosis probably magnified it, as well as the drugs and alcohol he consumed."

"I'm black," Beth whispered. "Why didn't he kill me?"

"Who knows?" Carl asked with a shrug. "Killing his sister might have pushed him over another ledge. Maybe he regretted it and in his deranged state still associated you with Shannon."

EPILOGUE

Beth sat in the cradle of her husband's arms on the love seat in their Seattle living room. Midnight looked down on them from his picture hanging over the mantle. They were watching a special broadcast video sent by a Dallas television station. It was an expose on pockets of racial tension in the nation. The television journalist narrated scenes from Beth's life in Plover Creek. Shivering, she moved closer to David, who gave her shoulder a gentle squeeze. "It's all over."

"Will it ever really be over?"

"All we can do is pray, teach our children and be who God made us to be. I have to believe that will say something." They turned back to the special and watched to the end of the tape.

Pulling herself up from the leather love seat, Beth strolled out to the patio and leaned on her elbows against the railing. She still missed her southern ridge, but she had found the secret place in her heart—one where she could once again hear the voice of God. She felt safer and more at peace than she ever had.

She almost felt regret at Carl and Lena's decision to stay in the community. But Plover Creek needed them, and they were in the process of rebuilding the church. After taking responsibility for Leonard's actions, the county had contributed to the building project. In an effort to mend the broken trust in the community, officials were doing as much as they could to help.

Manny was planning a visit in a couple of months, after the elections. He was running for sheriff of Plover Creek. Taylor had called earlier just to say hello. He and Tricia were spending a lot of time together.

Beth closed her eyes and savored the sense of tranquility offered by the surrounding evergreens. When David moved up behind her, she laid her head back against his chest and accepted the kiss he planted on her head. The perplexity furrowing her brow did not escape his attention. "What's that?"

"Why do you think I had to go through so much to hear God clearly? I mean, I know He was always with me, but why did I have to go through all that?"

David turned her to face him. "God didn't do those awful things, Beth. But He made good what the Enemy intended as harm. We all have to go through things that will challenge our faith. It's a part of living. You proved faithful through this one."

Beth turned and pushed her face into David's chest. "I almost turned my back on him for good."

"But you didn't."

"But there are still so many questions."

His lips pressed gently against her right temple. "That's normal, sweetheart. Just try to remember that your trust must always be in Him. I love you, but I'm human just like you. I have flaws and am very capable of disappointing you, even when I don't mean to. But God will never fail you."

Beth began to remember all the instances that the words of scripture entered her thoughts and stabilized her. "I know." She wrapped her arms around his neck. "I'm glad He didn't give up on me."

"Daddy!"

They both turned toward the patio door, where Bree stood in his pajamas. "Yes, Son?"

"Can Beth come tell me a story *now*?"

ABOUT THE AUTHOR

Annetta P. Lee grew up on the farm of her grandparents in Starkville, Mississippi. She later moved to Oklahoma City, where she met and married her husband, Kenneth. She works as Editorial Assistant for Lifesprings Resources, the publishing branch of the International Pentecostal Holiness Church.

After graduating from The Institute of Children's Literature in 1997, Annetta obtained her lifelong dream of becoming a published novelist. She also finds great pleasure in serving her community and church as a lay minister.

Mrs. Lee has been a popular guest on numerous radio programs and has lectured at Mississippi State University, as well as to many church groups and conferences.

2007 Publication Schedule

January

Corporate Seduction
A.C. Arthur
ISBN-13: 978-1-58571-238-0
ISBN-10: 1-58571-238-8
$9.95

A Taste of Temptation
Reneé Alexis
ISBN-13: 978-1-58571-207-6
ISBN-10: 1-58571-207-8
$9.95

February

The Perfect Frame
Beverly Clark
ISBN-13: 978-1-58571-240-3
ISBN-10: 1-58571-240-X
$9.95

Ebony Angel
Deatri King-Bey
ISBN-13: 978-1-58571-239-7
ISBN-10: 1-58571-239-6
$9.95

March

Sweet Sensations
Gwendolyn Bolton
ISBN-13: 978-1-58571-206-9
ISBN-10: 1-58571-206-X
$9.95

Crush
Crystal Hubbard
ISBN-13: 978-1-58571-243-4
ISBN-10: 1-58571-243-4
$9.95

April

Secret Thunder
Annetta P. Lee
ISBN-13: 978-1-58571-204-5
ISBN-10: 1-58571-204-3
$9.95

Blood Seduction
J.M. Jeffries
ISBN-13: 978-1-58571-237-3
ISBN-10: 1-58571-237-X
$9.95

May

Lies Too Long
Pamela Ridley
ISBN-13: 978-1-58571-246-5
ISBN-10: 1-58571-246-9
$13.95

Two Sides to Every Story
Dyanne Davis
ISBN-13: 978-1-58571-248-9
ISBN-10: 1-58571-248-5
$9.95

June

One of These Days
Michele Sudler
ISBN-13: 978-1-58571-249-6
ISBN-10: 1-58571-249-3
$9.95

Who's That Lady
Andrea Jackson
ISBN-13: 978-1-58571-190-1
ISBN-10: 1-58571-190-X
$9.95

2007 Publication Schedule (continued)

July

Heart of the Phoenix	Do Over	It's Not Over Yet
A.C. Arthur	Jaci Kenney	J.J. Michael
ISBN-13: 978-1-58571-242-7	ISBN-13: 978-1-58571-241-0	ISBN-13: 978-1-58571-245-8
ISBN-10: 1-58571-242-6	ISBN-10: 1-58571-241-8	ISBN-10: 1-58571-245-0
$9.95	$9.95	$9.95

August

The Fires Within	Stolen Kisses
Beverly Clark	Dominiqua Douglas
ISBN-13: 978-1-58571-244-1	ISBN-13: 978-1-58571-247-2
ISBN-10: 1-58571-244-2	ISBN-10: 1-58571-247-7
$9.95	$9.95

September

Small Whispers	Always You
Annetta P. Lee	Crystal Hubbard
ISBN-13: 978-158571-251-9	ISBN-13: 978-158571-252-6
ISBN-10: 1-58571-251-5	ISBN-10: 1-58571-252-3
$6.99	$6.99

October

Not His Type	Many Shades of Gray
Chamein Canton	Dyanne Davis
ISBN-13: 978-158571-253-3	ISBN-13: 978-158571-254-0
ISBN-10: 1-58571-253-1	ISBN-10: 1-58571-254-X
$6.99	$6.99

November

When I'm With You	The Mission
LaConnie Taylor-Jones	Pamela Leigh Starr
ISBN-13: 978-158571-250-2	ISBN-13: 978-158571-255-7
ISBN-10: 1-58571-250-7	ISBN-10: 1-58571-255-8
$6.99	$6.99

December

One in A Million	The Foursome
Barbara Keaton	Celya Bowers
ISBN-13: 978-158571-257-1	ISBN-13: 978-158571-256-4
ISBN-10: 1-58571-257-4	ISBN-10: 1-58571-256-6
$6.99	$6.99

Other Genesis Press, Inc. Titles

A Dangerous Deception	J.M. Jeffries	$8.95
A Dangerous Love	J.M. Jeffries	$8.95
A Dangerous Obsession	J.M. Jeffries	$8.95
A Dangerous Woman	J.M. Jeffries	$9.95
A Dead Man Speaks	Lisa Jones Johnson	$12.95
A Drummer's Beat to Mend	Kei Swanson	$9.95
A Happy Life	Charlotte Harris	$9.95
A Heart's Awakening	Veronica Parker	$9.95
A Lark on the Wing	Phyliss Hamilton	$9.95
A Love of Her Own	Cheris F. Hodges	$9.95
A Love to Cherish	Beverly Clark	$8.95
A Lover's Legacy	Veronica Parker	$9.95
A Pefect Place to Pray	I.L. Goodwin	$12.95
A Risk of Rain	Dar Tomlinson	$8.95
A Twist of Fate	Beverly Clark	$8.95
A Will to Love	Angie Daniels	$9.95
Acquisitions	Kimberley White	$8.95
Across	Carol Payne	$12.95
After the Vows	Leslie Esdaile	$10.95
(Summer Anthology)	T.T. Henderson	
	Jacqueline Thomas	
Again My Love	Kayla Perrin	$10.95
Against the Wind	Gwynne Forster	$8.95
All I Ask	Barbara Keaton	$8.95
Ambrosia	T.T. Henderson	$8.95
An Unfinished Love Affair	Barbara Keaton	$8.95
And Then Came You	Dorothy Elizabeth Love	$8.95
Angel's Paradise	Janice Angelique	$9.95
At Last	Lisa G. Riley	$8.95
Best of Friends	Natalie Dunbar	$8.95
Between Tears	Pamela Ridley	$12.95
Beyond the Rapture	Beverly Clark	$9.95
Blaze	Barbara Keaton	$9.95

Other Genesis Press, Inc. Titles (continued)

Blood Lust	J. M. Jeffries	$9.95
Bodyguard	Andrea Jackson	$9.95
Boss of Me	Diana Nyad	$8.95
Bound by Love	Beverly Clark	$8.95
Breeze	Robin Hampton Allen	$10.95
Broken	Dar Tomlinson	$24.95
The Business of Love	Cheris Hodges	$9.95
By Design	Barbara Keaton	$8.95
Cajun Heat	Charlene Berry	$8.95
Careless Whispers	Rochelle Alers	$8.95
Cats & Other Tales	Marilyn Wagner	$8.95
Caught in a Trap	Andre Michelle	$8.95
Caught Up In the Rapture	Lisa G. Riley	$9.95
Cautious Heart	Cheris F Hodges	$8.95
Caught Up	Deatri King Bey	$12.95
Chances	Pamela Leigh Starr	$8.95
Cherish the Flame	Beverly Clark	$8.95
Class Reunion	Irma Jenkins/John Brown	$12.95
Code Name: Diva	J.M. Jeffries	$9.95
Conquering Dr. Wexler's Heart	Kimberley White	$9.95
Cricket's Serenade	Carolita Blythe	$12.95
Crossing Paths, Tempting Memories	Dorothy Elizabeth Love	$9.95
Cupid	Barbara Keaton	$9.95
Cypress Whisperings	Phyllis Hamilton	$8.95
Dark Embrace	Crystal Wilson Harris	$8.95
Dark Storm Rising	Chinelu Moore	$10.95
Daughter of the Wind	Joan Xian	$8.95
Deadly Sacrifice	Jack Kean	$22.95
Designer Passion	Dar Tomlinson	$8.95
Dreamtective	Liz Swados	$5.95
Ebony Butterfly II	Delilah Dawson	$14.95
Ebony Eyes	Kei Swanson	$9.95

Other Genesis Press, Inc. Titles (continued)

Echoes of Yesterday	Beverly Clark	$9.95
Eden's Garden	Elizabeth Rose	$8.95
Enchanted Desire	Wanda Y. Thomas	$9.95
Everlastin' Love	Gay G. Gunn	$8.95
Everlasting Moments	Dorothy Elizabeth Love	$8.95
Everything and More	Sinclair Lebeau	$8.95
Everything but Love	Natalie Dunbar	$8.95
Eve's Prescription	Edwina Martin Arnold	$8.95
Falling	Natalie Dunbar	$9.95
Fate	Pamela Leigh Starr	$8.95
Finding Isabella	A.J. Garrotto	$8.95
Forbidden Quest	Dar Tomlinson	$10.95
Forever Love	Wanda Thomas	$8.95
From the Ashes	Kathleen Suzanne	$8.95
	Jeanne Sumerix	
Gentle Yearning	Rochelle Alers	$10.95
Glory of Love	Sinclair LeBeau	$10.95
Go Gentle into that Good Night	Malcom Boyd	$12.95
Goldengroove	Mary Beth Craft	$16.95
Groove, Bang, and Jive	Steve Cannon	$8.99
Hand in Glove	Andrea Jackson	$9.95
Hard to Love	Kimberley White	$9.95
Hart & Soul	Angie Daniels	$8.95
Havana Sunrise	Kymberly Hunt	$9.95
Heartbeat	Stephanie Bedwell-Grime	$8.95
Hearts Remember	M. Loui Quezada	$8.95
Hidden Memories	Robin Allen	$10.95
Higher Ground	Leah Latimer	$19.95
Hitler, the War, and the Pope	Ronald Rychiak	$26.95
How to Write a Romance	Kathryn Falk	$18.95
I Married a Reclining Chair	Lisa M. Fuhs	$8.95
I'm Gonna Make You Love Me	Gwyneth Bolton	$9.95
Indigo After Dark Vol. I	Nia Dixon/Angelique	$10.95

Other Genesis Press, Inc. Titles (continued)

Indigo After Dark Vol. II	Dolores Bundy/Cole Riley	$10.95
Indigo After Dark Vol. III	Montana Blue/Coco Morena	$10.95
Indigo After Dark Vol. IV	Cassandra Colt/	$14.95
	Diana Richeaux	
Indigo After Dark Vol. V	Delilah Dawson	$14.95
Icie	Pamela Leigh Starr	$8.95
I'll Be Your Shelter	Giselle Carmichael	$8.95
I'll Paint a Sun	A.J. Garrotto	$9.95
Illusions	Pamela Leigh Starr	$8.95
Indiscretions	Donna Hill	$8.95
Intentional Mistakes	Michele Sudler	$9.95
Interlude	Donna Hill	$8.95
Intimate Intentions	Angie Daniels	$8.95
Ironic	Pamela Leigh Starr	$9.95
Jolie's Surrender	Edwina Martin-Arnold	$8.95
Kiss or Keep	Debra Phillips	$8.95
Lace	Giselle Carmichael	$9.95
Last Train to Memphis	Elsa Cook	$12.95
Lasting Valor	Ken Olsen	$24.95
Let's Get It On	Dyanne Davis	$9.95
Let Us Prey	Hunter Lundy	$25.95
Life Is Never As It Seems	J.J. Michael	$12.95
Lighter Shade of Brown	Vicki Andrews	$8.95
Love Always	Mildred E. Riley	$10.95
Love Doesn't Come Easy	Charlyne Dickerson	$8.95
Love in High Gear	Charlotte Roy	$9.95
Love Lasts Forever	Dominiqua Douglas	$9.95
Love Me Carefully	A.C. Arthur	$9.95
Love Unveiled	Gloria Greene	$10.95
Love's Deception	Charlene Berry	$10.95
Love's Destiny	M. Loui Quezada	$8.95
Mae's Promise	Melody Walcott	$8.95
Magnolia Sunset	Giselle Carmichael	$8.95

Other Genesis Press, Inc. Titles (continued)

Matters of Life and Death	Lesego Malepe, Ph.D.	$15.95
Meant to Be	Jeanne Sumerix	$8.95
Midnight Clear (Anthology)	Leslie Esdaile	$10.95
	Gwynne Forster	
	Carmen Green	
	Monica Jackson	
Midnight Magic	Gwynne Forster	$8.95
Midnight Peril	Vicki Andrews	$10.95
Misconceptions	Pamela Leigh Starr	$9.95
Misty Blue	Dyanne Davis	$9.95
Montgomery's Children	Richard Perry	$14.95
My Buffalo Soldier	Barbara B. K. Reeves	$8.95
Naked Soul	Gwynne Forster	$8.95
Next to Last Chance	Louisa Dixon	$24.95
Nights Over Egypt	Barbara Keaton	$9.95
No Apologies	Seressia Glass	$8.95
No Commitment Required	Seressia Glass	$8.95
No Ordinary Love	Angela Weaver	$9.95
No Regrets	Mildred E. Riley	$8.95
Notes When Summer Ends	Beverly Lauderdale	$12.95
Nowhere to Run	Gay G. Gunn	$10.95
O Bed! O Breakfast!	Rob Kuehnle	$14.95
Object of His Desire	A. C. Arthur	$8.95
Office Policy	A. C. Arthur	$9.95
Once in a Blue Moon	Dorianne Cole	$9.95
One Day at a Time	Bella McFarland	$8.95
Only You	Crystal Hubbard	$9.95
Outside Chance	Louisa Dixon	$24.95
Passion	T.T. Henderson	$10.95
Passion's Blood	Cherif Fortin	$22.95
Passion's Journey	Wanda Thomas	$8.95
Past Promises	Jahmel West	$8.95
Path of Fire	T.T. Henderson	$8.95

Other Genesis Press, Inc. Titles (continued)

Path of Thorns	Annetta P. Lee	$9.95
Peace Be Still	Colette Haywood	$12.95
Picture Perfect	Reon Carter	$8.95
Playing for Keeps	Stephanie Salinas	$8.95
Pride & Joi	Gay G. Gunn	$8.95
Promises to Keep	Alicia Wiggins	$8.95
Quiet Storm	Donna Hill	$10.95
Reckless Surrender	Rochelle Alers	$6.95
Red Polka Dot in a World of Plaid	Varian Johnson	$12.95
Rehoboth Road	Anita Ballard-Jones	$12.95
Reluctant Captive	Joyce Jackson	$8.95
Rendezvous with Fate	Jeanne Sumerix	$8.95
Revelations	Cheris F. Hodges	$8.95
Rise of the Phoenix	Kenneth Whetstone	$12.95
Rivers of the Soul	Leslie Esdaile	$8.95
Rock Star	Rosyln Hardy Holcomb	$9.95
Rocky Mountain Romance	Kathleen Suzanne	$8.95
Rooms of the Heart	Donna Hill	$8.95
Rough on Rats and Tough on Cats	Chris Parker	$12.95
Scent of Rain	Annetta P. Lee	$9.95
Second Chances at Love	Cheris Hodges	$9.95
Secret Library Vol. 1	Nina Sheridan	$18.95
Secret Library Vol. 2	Cassandra Colt	$8.95
Shades of Brown	Denise Becker	$8.95
Shades of Desire	Monica White	$8.95
Shadows in the Moonlight	Jeanne Sumerix	$8.95
Sin	Crystal Rhodes	$8.95
Sin and Surrender	J.M. Jeffries	$9.95
Sinful Intentions	Crystal Rhodes	$12.95
So Amazing	Sinclair LeBeau	$8.95
Somebody's Someone	Sinclair LeBeau	$8.95

Other Genesis Press, Inc. Titles (continued)

Someone to Love	Alicia Wiggins	$8.95
Song in the Park	Martin Brant	$15.95
Soul Eyes	Wayne L. Wilson	$12.95
Soul to Soul	Donna Hill	$8.95
Southern Comfort	J.M. Jeffries	$8.95
Still the Storm	Sharon Robinson	$8.95
Still Waters Run Deep	Leslie Esdaile	$8.95
Stories to Excite You	Anna Forrest/Divine	$14.95
Subtle Secrets	Wanda Y. Thomas	$8.95
Suddenly You	Crystal Hubbard	$9.95
Sweet Repercussions	Kimberley White	$9.95
Sweet Tomorrows	Kimberly White	$8.95
Taken by You	Dorothy Elizabeth Love	$9.95
Tattooed Tears	T. T. Henderson	$8.95
The Color Line	Lizzette Grayson Carter	$9.95
The Color of Trouble	Dyanne Davis	$8.95
The Disappearance of Allison Jones	Kayla Perrin	$5.95
The Honey Dipper's Legacy	Pannell-Allen	$14.95
The Joker's Love Tune	Sidney Rickman	$15.95
The Little Pretender	Barbara Cartland	$10.95
The Love We Had	Natalie Dunbar	$8.95
The Man Who Could Fly	Bob & Milana Beamon	$18.95
The Missing Link	Charlyne Dickerson	$8.95
The Price of Love	Sinclair LeBeau	$8.95
The Smoking Life	Ilene Barth	$29.95
The Words of the Pitcher	Kei Swanson	$8.95
Three Wishes	Seressia Glass	$8.95
Through the Fire	Seressia Glass	$9.95
Ties That Bind	Kathleen Suzanne	$8.95
Tiger Woods	Libby Hughes	$5.95
Time is of the Essence	Angie Daniels	$9.95
Timeless Devotion	Bella McFarland	$9.95
Tomorrow's Promise	Leslie Esdaile	$8.95

Truly Inseparable	Wanda Y. Thomas	$8.95
Unbreak My Heart	Dar Tomlinson	$8.95
Uncommon Prayer	Kenneth Swanson	$9.95
Unconditional	A.C. Arthur	$9.95
Unconditional Love	Alicia Wiggins	$8.95
Under the Cherry Moon	Christal Jordan-Mims	$12.95
Unearthing Passions	Elaine Sims	$9.95
Until Death Do Us Part	Susan Paul	$8.95
Vows of Passion	Bella McFarland	$9.95
Wedding Gown	Dyanne Davis	$8.95
What's Under Benjamin's Bed	Sandra Schaffer	$8.95
When Dreams Float	Dorothy Elizabeth Love	$8.95
Whispers in the Night	Dorothy Elizabeth Love	$8.95
Whispers in the Sand	LaFlorya Gauthier	$10.95
Wild Ravens	Altonya Washington	$9.95
Yesterday Is Gone	Beverly Clark	$10.95
Yesterday's Dreams, Tomorrow's Promises	Reon Laudat	$8.95
Your Precious Love	Sinclair LeBeau	$8.95

Order Form

Mail to: Genesis Press, Inc.
P.O. Box 101
Columbus, MS 39703

Name _____
Address _____
City/State _____ Zip _____
Telephone _____

Ship to (if different from above)
Name _____
Address _____
City/State _____ Zip _____
Telephone _____

Credit Card Information
Credit Card # _____ ☐ Visa   ☐ Mastercard
Expiration Date (mm/yy) _____ ☐ AmEx   ☐ Discover

Qty.	Author	Title	Price	Total

Use this order

form, or call

1-888-INDIGO-1

Total for books _____
Shipping and handling:
  $5 first two books,
  $1 each additional book _____
Total S & H _____
Total amount enclosed _____

Mississippi residents add 7% sales tax

Visit www.genesis-press.com for latest releases and excerpts.